Introduction

Patterns of Love by Frances Devine
Dragged away from the scene of her magical childhood—including a promising career as an ice skater—and raised in poverty, Carla Daniels is delighted to return to Colorado Springs. But the man who loves her back home fears she may never return. How can he convince her that what they have is magic, too?

Unraveling Love by Cynthia Hickey
Zoe Barnes left Colorado Springs the day after high school graduation, dumping her sweetheart without so much as a phone call on her way out of town. So it's poetic justice that he happens to rescue her when her car breaks down on her way back. Can two wary, wounded souls survive a road trip to Colorado Springs?

Stitched in Love by Winter A. Peck
Pro volleyball player Danni Lindsay runs into her old love in the airport, a man from whom she'd parted when their careers diverged—hers to the beach and his to the Army. Now neither knows the other's career is soon to change. Will pride and an independent streak keep their hearts from changing?

Designed to Love by Marilyn Leach
Career gal Eve Kirkwood looks forward to a much-needed vacation in Colorado Springs to work on her grandmother's quilt, but her stay in a luxury hotel is ruined when her quilt squares are stolen. The hotel detective says he's on the case, but he's not moving fast enough for Eve. Could it be that he intends to steal her heart?

THREADS OF LOVE

FOUR-IN-ONE COLLECTION

FRANCES DEVINE, CYNTHIA HICKEY,
MARILYN LEACH & WINTER A. PECK

Print ISBN 978-1-61626-749-0

eBook Editions:
Adobe Digital Edition (.epub) 978-1-62416-012-7
Kindle and MobiPocket Edition (.prc) 978-1-62416-011-0

Cover design: Kirk DouPonce, DogEared Design

Published by Barbour Publishing, Inc., P.O. Box 719, Uhrichsville, Ohio 44683, www.barbourbooks.com

Our mission is to publish and distribute inspirational products offering exceptional value and biblical encouragement to the masses.

Printed in the United States of America.

PATTERNS OF LOVE

by Frances Devine

Dedication

To all my friends at the Michelle Kwan Forem. Thanks for all the great fun through the years. To all the skaters of the world. And to the most graceful, talented skater who ever put on a pair of skates, Michelle Wing Kwan, thank you for the wonderful adventure.

Commit your works to the Lord
and your plans shall be established.
PROVERBS 16:3

Chapter 1

Anticipation nibbled at Carla Daniels and threatened to explode into full-throttled, unbridled excitement. Rapid breathing accompanied each swish of the bleach-soaked dishcloth across the shiny, red vinyl table.

"Carla, are you trying to rub a hole in that table?" Todd Berry's voice sounded friendly, but a hint of something not so genial underlay his tone.

Carla straightened, tossing her thick blond braid back over her shoulder where it belonged and glanced at her friend and employer. Todd stood at the register filling a large bank bag with the day's proceeds. She threw him an apologetic grin before moving on to the next booth in her station.

She was going home. Would it feel like home? It had been twelve years since her parents had packed their belongings into a U-Haul trailer and changed their lives forever. This was the time of year when Carla grew a little homesick. The air would be crisp in Colorado Springs and the trees ablaze with color. If her memory served her right, snowfall was usual in October, so maybe she'd see some white stuff earlier than here in Cedar Hill, Kansas.

Ten minutes later, the chrome and vinyl booths gleamed with sanitized cleanliness. Carla nodded as she compared them to Hannah's pristine station. The older woman had trained her, and although Carla didn't intend to work as a server in the diner forever, she still took pride in doing her job well. Grabbing the pail of bleach water, she headed across the silent diner to the kitchen.

When she stepped back into the dining room, Todd was sitting at a corner booth, two cups of steaming coffee in front of him.

"We need to talk before you leave." A glossy black curl fell over his forehead as he nodded toward the seat across from him.

Resisting the urge to smooth his hair back into place, Carla tossed her purse on the table and slid onto the seat. "I know this is a bad time for me to be taking off work."

"No, no." He waved his hands. "That's all right. Hannah has a couple of friends eager to earn some Christmas money. They'll come in to help. And after all, except for your grandmother's funeral last year, you've never asked for time off before." But the tapping of the spoon against his cup indicated something was bothering him.

"So you're okay with me leaving?"

He turned his gaze on her and pain flashed in his azure eyes. The next instant it was gone. Maybe she'd imagined it.

"You are coming back, right?"

"Of course. I'll only be gone for three weeks." She'd already told him that. A twinge of guilt nagged her conscience. She didn't really need three weeks to fulfill Grams's request to complete her memory quilt. In fact, the reservation in the magnificent Broadmoor Hotel didn't even begin until the end of the second week of her vacation. She flicked the annoying thought aside. She needed the extra couple of weeks for herself. She had some past to come to terms with and maybe some ghosts that needed to be laid to rest.

Todd nodded and raised the tan vintage coffee cup to his lips.

"Why would you think I might not come back?"

He shrugged. "Isn't Colorado Springs where you trained to be a figure skater?"

"Yes. Years ago." She sighed. "I had big dreams in those days."

"You still have big dreams, Carla."

She nodded and gave him a sideways grin. "But when I was fourteen, I dreamed of skating for gold in the Olympics."

"Whatever happened to that guy you skated with?" He ran his finger around the rim of his cup.

"Leland Swann? He got another partner. They made it to Nationals last year."

She'd wondered from time to time just how far she and Lee could have gone in their career if Mom and Dad hadn't dragged her across the country so suddenly. Another of Dad's wonderful job opportunities that didn't last.

"I should get home and pack, Todd, then get some sleep. I have an eight-hour drive ahead of me in the morning."

He nodded and rose. "I hope everything works out well for you. Maybe the inheritance will make you rich. You might not need to work at a crummy diner after this."

She chuckled. "I don't think my inheritance will make me rich, considering it's divided four ways, although it should still be a pretty nice chunk, I guess." She waggled her finger at him. "And don't call the Berry Patch a crummy diner. I think it's one of the coolest spots in Cedar Hill."

She stood and faced him, looking up into his gorgeous face. "Wish me a safe journey."

Todd's lips curved in a smile, and he reached over and

tipped her chin up. "I'll do better than that. I'll pray for you."

"Good idea. Take care of yourself while I'm gone." She stood on tiptoe to plant a kiss on his cheek, but he pulled her to him, and his lips pressed against hers.

The kiss lasted only a moment, but warmth surged through her, and suddenly she wasn't so sure about leaving, even for three weeks.

Jerking herself back to reality, she said a hasty good-bye and made her escape. But the memory of Todd's lips on hers stayed with her as she drove to her apartment, even while she gave herself a pep talk. They were just friends. Sure, they'd dated a few times, but only friendly dates. She raised her fingers to her lips, still tingling from his kiss.

Thirty minutes later, she stood in front of her closet, staring helplessly at the row of slacks, sweaters, jeans, and skirts. Should she call one of her cousins to find out the proper dress for the swanky Broadmoor Hotel? She bit her bottom lip. Nope. It was bad enough being the youngest of the four. And the least successful. She wouldn't announce she was probably also the poorest. She'd promised God she wouldn't give in to feelings of inferiority anymore.

She walked into the living room and retrieved the attorney's letter from her handbag, skimming it once more, although she practically knew the contents by heart.

Grams had left instructions in her will for her four granddaughters to get together at the Broadmoor Hotel in their hometown of Colorado Springs. They were to bring the quilt squares she'd left them, create their own squares, and put them together to make a memory quilt. If they complied, they would then receive their inheritance.

Carla sighed and picked up the quilt square she'd worked

on the night before. She bit her lip and frowned at the crooked stitches. Two ice skates hung by their laces. Did they even look like ice skates? She sighed. How was she supposed to help make a quilt when she couldn't even sew a stitch straight? Maybe she should call the attorney and tell her she couldn't come. But Grams had made it clear she wanted her family reunited. It was all or none. If even one of the cousins didn't show up, no one received their inheritance. And Carla could certainly use some extra cash. Besides, her cousins would kill her if she didn't show. She wondered if she would feel close to them. Eve was only a year older than she, and they'd been friends before Carla got so involved in skating and no longer had time for anything much except training, practice, and school.

She looked at the square again and slapped her hand to her forehead. Her ice skates. Jumping up, she walked into the hall and retrieved her skate bag from the coat closet. She set it by the front door, giving it a pat. She'd been so busy at the diner lately she hadn't had much time to spend on the ice. At least there would be lots of time to catch up on her skating over the next couple of weeks. Her mind went to the small rink where she used to train, but she pushed the thought away. Why pour salt on the wound of her disappointment? She'd skate at the new arena.

She went back to her chair, picked up the needle and thread, and began again, immediately pricking her finger. She jerked her hand away and grabbed a tissue. She wasn't about to show up at the quilting session with blood on her squares. She dabbed at the wound until the tiny drops stopped forming then picked up the needle and started again.

Todd paced his living room floor. Why hadn't he told Carla how he felt about her? He'd let his foolish pride hold him back. But what did he have to offer her? A crummy diner that was barely bringing in enough to cover expenses. She deserved better. She had big dreams, and they'd never come to pass if she tied up with him.

Maybe he should accept Jacob Harrington's offer to back him. He could open a nice restaurant that would pay its way and more. Something he could be proud of. Of course, even though the man said there'd be no strings attached, Todd wasn't sure. Harrington's daughter, Julie, hadn't exactly been subtle in her flirting when they'd met at a banquet the year before. Besides, he wanted to make it on his own. Not take a handout from someone.

The doorbell rang and he grabbed his wallet from the coffee table and headed for the door.

The pizza delivery guy on his front porch grinned. "Here you go, Mr. Berry. Fresh and hot. That'll be. . ." He peered at the ticket attached to the oil-splattered box. "Fourteen ninety-nine." Todd traded a twenty for the box and told him to keep the change.

After one slice of the meat-and-cheese-loaded special, he shoved the box aside and took his iced tea out on the deck.

The woods at the back of his immense yard were thick with evergreens and oak. Up closer, the lawn was dotted with what he called his Christmas trees. Cedar and pine. Perfectly shaped. Courtesy of his Uncle Jack, who'd left Todd the house when he passed away back in May.

Okay, he needed to get himself out of this crummy mood.

So Carla was going away for three weeks. It wasn't the end of the world. She'd come back. But what if she didn't? What if that Swann guy was still around? She'd talked about how close pairs skaters were. Had to be. And she'd admitted she'd had a crush on her older partner. Todd had a crush on a girl when he was fourteen, but couldn't even remember what she looked like. He'd seen a recent photo of Swann in one of the skating magazines Carla left laying around. He looked like one of those golden boys. Perfect physique, perfect smile, perfect hair.

Suddenly realizing how ridiculous his thoughts were, Todd gave a short laugh.

He breathed in deeply of the crisp autumn air then let it out with a whoosh. You'd think he was a kid the way he was acting. He'd be thirty in a couple of months. Carla wasn't some moonstruck kid either. That girl had a head on her shoulders. He grinned. And besides, she'd kissed him back. Not for long. But she'd kissed him all right. Nearly bowled him over—and she'd looked a little shaken when she left the diner, too.

She'd promised to call when she arrived in Colorado Springs tomorrow. In the meantime, he needed to stop wallowing in self-pity. He had a business to run, even if it wasn't a fancy restaurant. Maybe he needed to concentrate on improving Berry's Diner instead of pining after what he didn't have. Carla always called it the Berry Patch. Said the name gave it character. Maybe she was right. Should he change the name? Nah. Whoever heard of a diner called the Berry Patch?

Chapter 2

The hotel wasn't the Broadmoor, but it was clean and affordable, had a coffeepot in the room, and would provide free breakfast. Carla hummed while she peered in the mirror over the dresser and applied fresh makeup. When she'd arrived at four, it was too early for dinner, so she'd tried to take a nap. When her thoughts kept straying to the skates in her bag, she'd hopped off the bed, made a quick call to the arena, and found out they had public skating at six. Then she'd jumped into the shower.

She finished with her makeup and braided her hair, grabbed her jacket and skates, and headed for her car. Late afternoon traffic was heavy, and she tapped her fingers on the steering wheel while waiting for an opening to turn left. Maybe it wouldn't hurt to drop by and see if any of her former friends still trained at the old rink. She turned the wheel to the right and pulled out. But this was silly. They were almost sure to train at the new arena. Oh, well. She'd like to at least see the place. Maybe take a few turns around the ice.

The outside of the building looked pretty much the same, although it appeared to be freshly painted. The sign above the door still said FROMAN'S ICE PALACE. Carla's stomach tightened. A reflex action from memories of taut nerves when she was a child. Funny, she hadn't remembered how nervous she used to get coming here. Every time she had to learn a new routine. Every time she competed in a competition. Every time her mother—she drew in her breath—her mother scolded her for missing a jump or a spin or even getting a hand movement wrong.

Carla laughed. A short little laugh that almost sounded like a hiccup. She'd built things up in her imagination, just as most children did.

She shoved the memories or impressions or whatever they were back into the recesses of her mind and got out, slamming the car door behind her.

By the time she stepped inside the building, her excitement had returned. She glanced around the lobby. A young man she didn't recognize was crossing the foyer. He nodded and went through the double doors leading to the hallway.

She walked toward the counter with a cash register at one end. Shelves behind the counter held skates and other paraphernalia. Candy lined a glassed-in case beside the register. The tall stool was empty and no one seemed to be in charge. Not very professional. That station was manned at all times in the old days.

When she tapped the button on the bell, it rang out loudly. A teenaged girl scurried around a corner and stood facing her. "Sorry, I was shelving some things in back."

"That's okay. I just want to watch for a while and maybe skate a turn or two." Carla pulled some cash from her wallet. "How much?"

"Will you need skates?" The girl chomped on her gum and blew a bubble that immediately popped on her lips. "Oops." She grinned and licked the gum off.

Carla lifted her skate bag and raised her brows.

"Oh. You have your own skates. Okay. That's five bucks."

Carla's stomach clenched as she pushed through the doors. Nostalgia washed over her as she walked down the short hallway. It was the same. The same photos and posters on the wall, with the addition of a couple of recent medal winners. She came to the changing area and sat on a bench to put her skates on then walked to the ice. She was grateful for the new rubbery material over the floor that made skate guards unnecessary. Other than that, the place seemed just the same. She caught her breath as she rested her hand on the rail. The same dent. You'd think they'd have fixed it by now. She took a deep breath then stepped onto the ice.

A skater whizzed by her, did a quick spin, and skated back. "Carla? Carla Daniels?"

Carla flashed a glance at the movie-star-handsome guy who skidded to a stop and stared down at her. Her breath caught. "Hi, Lee. Yep. In the flesh."

A smile lit up his eyes, and his grin matched hers. "I can't believe it. Little Carla Daniels." His eyes ran over her. "You grew up."

She laughed. "So did you."

He grabbed her hand and spun her around. She couldn't believe how quickly she responded to the movement. He laughed out loud and slipped an arm around her waist. "Come on." They glided around the ice once, and then he started around again.

"Don't do anything fancy, Lee. I haven't skated with anyone in a long time."

"Yeah, you sort of dropped off the face of the earth." He pulled her a little closer. "I was crushed when I got your note."

"Sure you were. It took you a whole three weeks to find another partner." She gave him a sideways glance and smiled.

"That wasn't my doing. It was our dear coach and my parents. What could I say? I was fifteen."

He picked up speed and changed his hand position. "Okay, get ready. Here we go."

"No!" But the next thing she knew she was twisting and sailing through the air, then her skates hit the ice. She stood, trembling, and glared at him. "What are you trying to do, kill me?"

He laughed. "You don't look anywhere near death to me. And you landed it, even if you did two-foot it."

Amazement shot through her. He was right. She grinned. The first throw-jump in years, and her body remembered exactly what to do. "Let's try that again."

The second and third times she was conscious of every move, and she fell, hard. The fourth time she hit the ice, she got up shaking her head. "I'm done. That first landing was a fluke."

He skated her over to the gate. "I don't think it was a fluke, Carla. You've still got it. You just need practice."

"Well, not today." She rubbed her thigh. "I'm going to be black and blue."

"Put ice on it before you go to bed tonight. It'll be fine. Let's get out of here and go somewhere we can talk. I want to hear everything you've been doing."

"Oh." She glanced around. "Where's your partner? Aren't you here for practice?"

"No, I don't train here anymore."

By now he'd guided her to the gate. Carla grabbed her skate bag from under the bench where she'd stowed it and sat to remove her skates. Ten minutes later they sat across from each other at a coffeehouse.

Carla took a sip of her latte and patted her mouth with a napkin. "So tell me, what were you doing at the rink if you don't train there?"

He stirred his coffee. "I like to stop in every now and then. For old times' sake, I guess."

She sighed. "I can understand that. I'd planned to check out the new arena, but the next thing I knew, here I was at the old rink. It sort of pulled me, I guess."

"I've missed you, Carla." A sad expression crossed his face.

"Well, I've missed you, too, Lee." In all honesty, she'd thought of him very little the last few years, but when she did think of him, nostalgia kicked in. And there was no denying her heart sped up every time he looked at her. She'd forgotten his amber-flecked brown eyes that went so well with dark gold hair. Even his skin tone had a touch of gold. Probably from a tanning bed, but who cared? She swallowed. "And I've missed skating with you."

"Who have you been training with? I haven't heard anything since you left."

"I trained for a while, but after a few months we couldn't afford it. Grams was the one who'd always paid for my skating, and suddenly Dad wouldn't let her anymore." Carla set her cup on the table and picked up her napkin. "I think it broke Grams's heart more than it did mine."

"Why didn't you ever stop by when you came to visit?"

"We didn't come very often, Lee. And when we did, we were always busy with the family. Grams would come see us a couple of times a year before she got sick." She took a deep breath. "She passed away last year."

"I'm sorry, honey. I didn't know." He reached for her hand and gave it a quick squeeze.

"It's all right. How could you know?"

"Where did you go when you left here?"

"We went to Tulsa." She frowned at the memory and shuddered. "I hated the dry heat there, but Mom and Dad love it. They're still there."

"They? Not you?" He glanced at her left hand and she grinned.

"No. I went to Wichita to college. But I had to drop out at the end of my junior year due to finances." The old anger and grief came back at the memory and she bit her lip and pushed it back. "I hope to go back and get my degree soon. Maybe very soon."

"Oh, what's causing the change?"

"I'm about to receive an inheritance. I'll keep working, but I don't mind that. I love my job." She shifted and sat up straighter. "Enough about me. Tell me about your partner."

He drew in a breath and blew it out in a loud whoosh. "No partner."

"What happened to her?"

"Blamed me that we didn't make it to the World Championships this year. She found another partner and left me flat."

The phone on the kitchen wall jangled. Todd yanked his hands out of the dishwater and made a grab for it while dripping soapy water all over the floor.

"Berry's Diner." *Please God, let it be Carla.*

"Oh, I'm sorry. I have the wrong number." The voice was polite, but Todd felt like slinging the receiver across the room.

He slammed his hands into the water and resumed

scrubbing the enormous stockpot. She'd promised she'd call when she got to Colorado Springs yesterday. It wasn't like Carla not to keep her word. He'd finally called her cell phone around eight o'clock, but she hadn't answered. She might have turned her phone off and gone to bed early after traveling all day. He'd hardly slept last night, picturing her in a pileup on the highway or in a ditch on the side of a winding mountain road.

He'd tried again this morning and still no answer. He had to restrain himself from calling the highway patrol and checking for accidents. More than likely she and her cousins were catching up and she'd forgotten her promise.

But if she didn't call him within the next hour or two, he was calling the highway patrol. He could kick himself for not finding out where she was staying.

When the kitchen was clean, he removed his apron and headed for the coatrack. He might as well head home.

He groaned as he heard the bell over the door. He'd forgotten to lock up. He went to the front and found Julie Harrington standing inside the door, a radiant smile on her face.

"Hi, Todd. I was afraid I might have missed you. But this was perfect timing." Her eyes danced, and she waltzed over and gave him an uninvited hug.

He stepped back. "What's up, Julie?"

She pouted her lips—very luscious lips, he had to admit. "That didn't sound very welcoming, Todd."

"I'm sorry. I've had a hard day and I'm tired, but I didn't mean to be rude."

"Oh, I understand, and all is forgiven. Actually, I'm having a dinner party next week, and I'd love it if you'd come."

"I don't know, Julie. The diner is really busy. What night?" He had no desire whatsoever to spend an evening with Julie and her friends.

"Wednesday night. Dad will be there, and he asked me to invite you. I think he wants to discuss the business venture the two of you are working out." She closed the gap between them and looked up into his eyes. "I'm sure you'll have a great time, and I do hope you'll say yes."

He felt sweat break out on his forehead at her nearness and stepped back again. "Sorry. I don't think I can make it."

Her chin lifted, and for a moment her eyes stormed, then she lowered them. "At least think about it. Okay?" She flashed him a smile.

"Okay, I'll think about it." Anything to end this. "I really have to go. I'm expecting a phone call any minute." He said a quick prayer for forgiveness, but then again, there was a *very* fine line between expecting and hoping, wasn't there?

Chapter 3

The training session for beginners was in progress. Children, some eager, others with fearful expressions on their faces, stood on the ice staring at the young woman who was teaching the class. Carla's heart did a somersault as a memory flashed through her mind.

She'd stood trembling at her first session, wobbling on her beginner skates. The rest of her group followed their teacher bravely across the ice, but Carla, panicking, took one hesitant step and froze. Suddenly, an angelic creature with a smooth black ponytail and smiling Asian eyes glided up to her and held out her hand.

"Hi. Would you like to skate with me for a while?"

Mesmerized, Carla reached for her angel's hand, and by the time they'd gone slowly around the rink and pulled up next to her group, confidence had risen up inside her.

A beautiful smile flashed in her direction, graceful tapered fingers waved at the teacher, then her angel glided away.

"What is Michelle Kwan doing in Colorado?" one of the parents asked.

"She and her sister are skating with a group of special needs kids next hour." The group trainer grinned. "Guess she came a little early. She's wonderful, the way she loves to help beginners."

Her teacher's words confirmed what Carla's five-year-old

heart had already grasped. Michele Kwan was special.

She smiled at the warm memory. Michelle would always be an angel to her.

A warm breath touched her neck, and she turned to see Lee grinning. "I know it's not those little kids that have you so entranced."

Why did her heart lurch at the sound of his voice? She smiled. "Hi, Lee. No, just lost in memories. What are you doing here today?"

"When you didn't answer your phone, I thought you might be here."

Carla gasped and grabbed her cell phone from her jacket pocket. She'd turned it off during the drive yesterday and, in her excitement and exhaustion, she'd forgotten to turn it back on.

"Oh no." She shook her head. "My phone's been off since yesterday. I need to check my messages. Excuse me for a few minutes?"

"Sure, I'll meet you in the break room when you're finished."

Carla glanced at the time. Todd would be busy at the diner. She couldn't call him now. But she knew he'd be worried sick. There were several missed calls from him, and a number of text messages. How could she have forgotten to contact him and let him know she'd arrived safely?

She sent him a text with an apology and a promise to call that night. Then she took a deep breath and went to meet Lee. Hopefully, she could keep her heart rhythm from speeding up. He'd always been a nice-looking guy, but now, oh brother. His partner must have been an idiot to leave him.

A warning twinge ran through her. She'd only heard

Lee's version of what caused the breakup. She knew he'd had problems at Nationals, falling several times, but that could happen to anyone. She couldn't imagine anyone leaving their skating partner over one failed competition.

She found him leaning against the wall outside the break room.

He pushed away from the wall. "I've got an idea. It's getting close to lunch time. How about we go grab a pizza? I'd like to talk to you about something."

Curious, Carla agreed. A few minutes later, they were seated in a nearby pizzeria with a pepperoni and mushroom on the table between them. Carla served herself a slice then took a sip from her glass of iced tea.

Lee got right to the point. "Carla, have you ever thought of competing again?"

She almost choked on the cheesy bite. She swallowed and grabbed her glass again.

Lee laughed. "Are you okay?"

She nodded. "I'm fine. But to answer your question, of course I've thought of it. Who wouldn't? It was part of my life for years."

"Well? What do you think?" He lifted his brow in a quirky way that sent chills down her arms.

"What do I think? I think it's been way too long since I've trained. I told you we couldn't afford it after we left. I think I was fifteen when I had to stop. No coach would take me now and certainly no partner. I'm twenty-four. Way too old to get started again."

"I disagree. You still have great form. Your edges are good. Your jumps and spins will come back. And what do you mean no partner? How about me?"

Her skin went clammy and she felt numb. Suddenly she couldn't breathe. No, no. Not now. She hadn't had a panic attack in three years.

Suddenly a bag was placed in her hands and she breathed slowly. Slowly. In and out. Breathing in the brown paper bag. Everything was okay. She just had to focus. Finally, she pulled the bag away from her mouth.

A waitress stood over her and Lee was leaning forward with one of her hands in both of his.

"You okay?"

She nodded. "Where did the bag come from so fast?"

He grinned and patted her hand. "I remembered that's what you did when we were kids and you'd have one of those attacks. So I asked the waitress for one."

Carla smiled up at the kind-faced woman. "Thank you so much. I'm fine now."

When the waitress left, Carla glanced at Lee. "Sorry about that. I'm not sure what brought it on. Too much excitement, I guess. Of course you weren't serious. Your coach would never stand for it."

"I'm very serious. And as a matter of fact, I've changed coaches." He grinned again. "Andrei is coaching Laura and Conrad. I decided to save him the anguish of divided loyalties, so I signed with Vladimir."

"Well, still. He's not likely to want you to pair up with someone like me, who hasn't trained professionally in so many years."

"Nonsense. I've already had a talk with Vlad, and he is quite agreeable to coach us on a trial basis." He took her hand again. "What do you say, Carla? We had so much promise."

"We were kids." But the protest was weak, and she could

tell from his triumphant smile that he knew it. "I don't know. I'd need to think about it." What in the world was she saying? She'd have to change her whole life.

"Of course. I don't expect you to make a decision right now. But you can meet Vlad and talk about it, can't you?"

"All right. But make sure he knows that I'm not committing to anything. And even if I agree, it will have to be on that trial basis you mentioned."

Todd clicked on his living room lights and walked through to the kitchen. He put the Styrofoam to-go box on the table. He hadn't eaten since his early lunch and now it was after eight. His stomach rumbled. He'd eat and then take a quick shower. But the sudden awareness of the restaurant smell clinging to his skin and clothes changed his mind. He headed for the bathroom.

Ten minutes later, he was back in the kitchen, his hair dripping down his forehead, wearing sweatpants and a sweatshirt. Nothing quite so comfortable on a cold autumn evening. He slid the chicken and vegetables onto a plate and slipped it into the microwave. The phone rang, and he almost tripped getting to the counter where he'd left it.

The sound of Carla's voice sent waves of relief over him. She'd said in her text she'd call tonight, but he hadn't wanted to get his hopes up again.

"I'm so sorry, Todd. I can't believe I forgot to call you or even turn my phone on. I've had so much going on." Her voice sounded breathless, as though she'd just gotten in from the cold.

"Well, why don't you tell me all about it? What's been

going on? I guess you're having fun with the cousins." He needed to slow down. He must sound like an idiot.

A little pause on her end of the line sent his radar soaring.

"Well, I won't actually see them until the end of next week. Then we'll start our week at the Broadmoor. I'm not sure they're even in town yet."

"Oh? You wanted to do some sightseeing on your own, I guess?" He winced. What right had he to question her?

Her breathless little laugh came through the phone. "Well, that was the original plan. But I ran into Lee Swann. You won't believe this, but he's without a partner and asked me to train with him."

His stomach tightened as though he'd been punched. He took a deep breath.

"Is that right? What did you tell him?"

"At first I laughed. I thought he was joking, but he's serious." She paused. "I don't know, Todd. I told him I'd think about it."

His stomach continued to tighten. He didn't know what to say. It would be easy at this moment to start yelling at her. Tell her to come home before she did something stupid. He took a deep breath. "I'll pray that God will show you what to do. Let me know when you decide. I'll need to find someone to replace you if you aren't coming back." The harsh words were out before he could stop them.

He heard her catch her breath. "I will, Todd. Well, good night."

He pushed END, took his plate from the microwave, scraped the food into the garbage disposal, rinsed the plate, and put it in the dishwasher. His hunger had disappeared.

He poured a mug full of coffee and went out onto the

deck. He stood by the rail looking out over the lawn. Well, he'd always known Carla didn't belong working in a diner. He'd tried to fight off the feelings he had for her, but he just couldn't shake the hope that she might love him, too. That he'd be enough to make up for her dreams. Or that maybe he'd be the one to make her dreams come true.

He laughed. Sure. Him and his diner. He sighed. Maybe if he took Harrington's offer. But he knew this had nothing to do with his business. Carla loved the diner. This was something entirely different she had to figure out on her own. He wouldn't try to manipulate her.

The phone rang again and he grabbed it, hoping she was calling back. But he didn't recognize the caller ID.

"Hello, Todd Berry."

"Hi, Todd." He had to hold back a groan at the sultry voice.

"Hello, Julie. What do you need?" Maybe she'd get the hint and hang up.

"No, what do *you* need?" Her suggestive laugh irritated him.

"Nothing that I can think of at the moment, Julie. Stop kidding around."

"Well, you don't have to be so mean. I just called to invite you again to my dinner party. Have you changed your mind?" How ironic. That's what he wanted to ask Carla. "Don't forget, Todd. Daddy will be there, and he really wants to talk to you about backing your new restaurant."

Once again, the possibility of having more to offer Carla ran through his mind. He knew he'd have his restaurant someday, but would it be too late? There he went again. He couldn't buy Carla's love. If he accepted Harrington's offer, it had to be because it was the right thing to do.

"Thanks. I'll think about it."

A sound of exasperation came through the phone. "Oh all right. But don't wait too long. There are others standing in line for Daddy's financial backing."

She hung up and Todd went inside. This was another thing to think about. If he signed with Julie's father, he was pretty sure he'd have to put up with his daughter.

Chapter 4

"Nervous?" Lee grasped her hand and squeezed.

Carla shook her head as she looked out over the Olympic-sized ice. She'd agreed to come to the arena to meet Vladimir Demetriev, Lee's coach. She couldn't deny the excitement that coursed through her to be in the middle of the skating scene again. But she also had an underlying sense of unease and wasn't sure why.

She sent Lee an anxious look. "Don't forget. I haven't decided yet."

He grinned and gave her braid a little tug. "Okay, I won't forget. Want to take a little spin around the ice while we wait for Vlad?"

"I guess so. I haven't been on ice this good in a long time." She sat and took her skates out of her bag.

A whispered murmur caught her attention, and she turned to see a dark-haired, petite woman about her age. She looked familiar.

"Carla?" The woman stepped forward, her eyes guarded. "Lee told me you were back in town."

The haughty voice and unfriendly look in her eyes revealed her identity, even if she had changed physically. Although, on closer inspection, Carla could see she hadn't changed that much. How could she have forgotten her old rival and sometimes downright enemy, Cassandra Winters?

"Hi, Cassie. Nice to see you again."

"I haven't heard a word about you since you left. I guess you haven't been competing."

Before Carla could stop herself, she said, "That's right. I thought perhaps you had, too, since I've heard nothing about you either."

Annoyance flashed across the face that would have been very pretty if the bad attitude hadn't been written there so plainly. "Well, you'll hear about me this year. I got a new partner last year, and our coach is certain we'll make the top three at Nationals."

"Really?" Carla nodded. "Well, be careful. The ice is slippery."

Cassie tossed her head at the familiar expression and skated out onto the ice.

Lee grinned. "I see some things never change. Cassie always was jealous of you."

"Well, at this point, she has nothing to be jealous of me for." Carla gave a rueful smile as she watched the brunette pick up speed and land a perfect triple-toe loop. "She's really gotten good."

Lee shrugged. "She's fine on the practice ice. So is Carl. But they still haven't won a major competition."

"Don't be mean, Lee. They came in fourth at Nationals one year."

He laughed. "Aha. So you have heard about her." He tweaked her ear.

"Yes, I was being catty. I'll have to watch that." After all, she wasn't fourteen anymore, and she was a Christian now.

"Hey, there's Vlad," Lee said.

Carla looked with interest at the tall fortyish man who

walked toward them, a huge smile on his face. She didn't remember him. He must be new to the area. She stood.

After Lee made the introductions, Vlad asked to see them do a few elements on the ice.

"No throw-jumps, Lee."

"All right, all right." He took her hand and they skated onto the ice.

After warming up for a few minutes they did several spins and ended with a side-by-side single jump.

Vlad was waiting for them. Without saying what he thought of their skating, he suggested they go to the coffee shop and talk.

The coffee shop was very modern. A far cry from the little break room at the old rink. Only a few people were seated around the room. After all, it was midafternoon. They ordered coffee and found a booth in back.

"Carla Daniels. Lee has told me a great deal about his first partner. So you are considering a return to competing?" His heavily accented voice was low and soothing, but his eyes scrutinized her. She had a feeling they didn't miss much.

"I don't know that I'm considering it at this point. I agreed to talk to you, that's all. I haven't trained since I was barely fifteen. And I've been planning to return to college to get my degree in business. I'm not sure I'm willing to give that dream up for one so risky."

He frowned and darted a look at Lee. "I see. So you don't have a true desire to return to skating?"

"I'm not sure." She glanced from Vlad to Lee. "That's why I said I'd think about it. But I do appreciate your willingness to train me."

"Yes, but only if you're willing to put skating first. Ahead of everything else." He pursed his lips. "Your training schedule would by necessity be brutal. There are so many upcoming young skaters. In order to compete with them, you would have to breathe, eat, and sleep skating."

Once more a niggling uneasiness bit at her. Was she willing to do that? Willing to give up everything for the chance that she might make it to Nationals or even the Olympics?

She sighed. The dream had always been there. Deep inside. Ever since she'd left Colorado. Could she pass up the opportunity to try again?

"Don't look so glum, honey." Lee chucked her under the chin. "You know you want to come back."

"Don't push her, Lee," Vlad said.

Carla sighed. "Could I try it for a few days while I think it over?"

"Absolutely." Vlad stood. "I'll expect you both here at six in the morning. Don't be dragging in here at noon." He walked away.

Lee jumped up. "How about another spin around the ice?"

She didn't really feel like skating now, but they might as well get the feel for skating together. See if the moves would come back to her easily. How much of her training had stuck with her after nine years?

"Sure. But just remember, I'm not a child anymore. So don't try bossing me around." She threw him a mock frown.

He laughed and hugged her. "It's going to be so much fun. Just you wait and see."

Carla threw her skate bag on the bed and limped over to the table/counter by the bathroom that held the coffeepot and coffee packets. She was bruised and sore from numerous falls the past few days, and she and Lee had skated for two hours after Vlad left this afternoon, taking a break for a quick supper, then skating an hour more. She wasn't used to skating that much, and the blisters on her feet bore witness to the fact. She hated to think how bad they'd be if she had new skates, which she'd need soon if she decided to continue. Skate boots were stiff even after they were broken in, and new ones were almost unbearable. At least they were to her.

She made herself a cup of coffee, dumped in a packet of dry creamer, and limped back into the bedroom. She eased into the comfy chair.

Her mind whirled with thoughts of the day, especially the incident when Cassie ran into her, knocking her over. Of course, Cassie had been apologetic and horrified. But Carla remembered the same thing had happened several times when they were kids. Apparently Cassie hadn't grown up yet. Several skaters she recognized had come up to her and introduced themselves, but most of the ones she knew were no longer around. Including their old coach, Tom Fordham, who'd retired last year.

She yawned and glanced at the bed. Maybe she'd call it a night. She'd need to be up at five. She slipped her phone from her pocket and glanced at her messages. One from Todd. A sudden wave of homesickness washed over her. She missed him.

The memory of his good-bye kiss sent a shiver running through her. She'd always been attracted to Todd's muscular good looks, and he'd been a wonderful friend to her. But the kiss had suddenly vaulted their friendship into another dimension or something. Was this why she'd subconsciously blocked him out the past couple of days? Even to the extent of forgetting to call him? But that was silly. Todd hadn't changed. And neither had she.

She read his message then punched his speed dial number and hit SEND. The call went straight to his voice mail, which surprised her. He seldom turned his phone off except for church or Bible study. She groaned. Of course. This was his Bible group night at the pastor's house. She left him a message, giving him a short, condensed version of her day, then told him she was going to bed and would call him tomorrow. But an unusually hollow feeling of loneliness clutched at her. What in the world was wrong?

Todd waved good-bye to Pastor Stephens and his wife and walked to his car. He slipped his phone from his jacket pocket and turned it on. Seeing he had a voice mail, he punched in his mailbox number and password.

Carla's voice sounded tired. As she talked about her day, he sensed sadness or depression that didn't match the words she was saying. Of course, blisters on the feet could bring one's spirits down, he supposed. He sighed. He wanted nothing more than to put his arms around her and comfort her.

But who was he to think she needed his comfort? It sounded like she had Lee Swann. Jealousy rose up in him and he berated himself. Hadn't he just given Carla to God? And now here he was, at the sound of her voice, taking her back again. He whispered a quick prayer and before long, peace enveloped him. He knew that whatever happened, he'd be okay. And so would Carla. God loved her more than he did.

Not wanting to go home just yet, where he'd be alone

with his thoughts, he drove to the diner. Inventory was just what he needed to get his mind off the situation.

He threw a burger on the grill. When it was done, he slid it on a bun and piled it high with pickles, onions, lettuce, and tomatoes. The only way to eat a hamburger. He sat at the counter with his back to the booth where he'd sat with Carla before she left. He didn't need any reminders of that kiss. He drank a glass of milk and downed his burger as quickly as possible. He needed to get busy. Halfway through inventory, after moving what seemed like thousands of boxes, he found himself wishing he'd found another way to occupy his mind. How had he ever ended up with so many cans of tomato paste?

Just after midnight, he got into his truck and drove home.

He wasn't feeling much better, but at least he was tired enough he'd probably sleep.

As for Carla, he couldn't very well drag her home by the hair, caveman-style. If she cared for him the way he hoped she did, she'd come home.

Chapter 5

Relax now. You've done this hundreds of times." Lee's voice was soothing as he massaged the tight muscles in Carla's shoulders.

Carla tried to relax her face so her tension wouldn't show. They'd been on the ice with competitive-level skaters again today. Cassie and her partner flew by and sailed into the middle of the ice, where they executed a triple throw. Cassie landed perfectly on one foot without even a teeny wobble.

"I can't do this." Carla turned away.

"Yes, you can." Lee spoke with confidence. "We'll stick with the single we've been doing instead of the double we practiced last night. You'll do fine."

Carla pressed her lips together. Lee was right. She mustn't let fear get under her skin. "Let's do this." She grabbed his hand and flashed a determined smile. After a week, she still wasn't sure she wanted to compete again, but she at least wanted to give herself the chance to find out.

They glided around the ice several times, doing simple lifts and a side-by-side single jump. Carla motioned to Lee not to do the throw. She wasn't up to it today.

"Aw, come on, Carla." The next thing she knew she was sailing through the air again. And two-footed the landing.

Cassie and her partner passed them on their way off the ice. Cassie gave a little laugh as they skated by. "A little rusty, aren't you?" she threw over her shoulder.

Lee laughed. "A little green-eyed jealousy?" he called out. "You always knew Carla was a better skater."

"Stop it, Lee." Carla frowned. "That's childish. Good grief."

"Just trying to get under her skin a little bit." Lee spun her around and gave her a hug. "C'mon, let's do another throw. You'll be doing the double in no time. You always were a quick learner."

"Hey, you two." Vlad leaned against the gate, and he didn't look happy.

When they skated over to him, he glared at Lee. "What do you think you're doing? Cassie told me you did a throw-jump out there. I told you not to try that with Carla yet. She hasn't done throws in nine years, Lee. Don't be stupid."

Lee grinned. "Just having some fun. She's ready. It's not like she doesn't know how to skate. And we've been practicing all week."

"What do you mean you've been practicing?" Vlad glared. "Maybe you need to decide if you want a coach or not."

Carla bit her lip. Lee had always been a rebel and never followed instructions well. Funny she hadn't remembered that.

After a session with Vlad, the rest of their practice time consisted of simple turns and crossovers. Carla could feel Lee's impatience, but she had a sense of relief that they were returning to some basic pairs moves. She'd felt rushed and unprepared when Lee had insisted on doing the throw-jump.

Lee wanted to take her sightseeing after lunch, so Carla asked if they could drive by the Broadmoor. She remembered very little about it, except that it used to have a grand ice arena and the World Championships had been held there for several years. Carlo Fassi had once coached there. But the rink had been torn down soon after she started skating, to make way for a new wing on the hotel, if she remembered right. Now she was curious, because the luxury hotel was where she and her cousins would stay next week. Although she vaguely recalled something about a lodge. She shrugged. Her cousins would know.

As they drove by, the sheer beauty of the place almost took her breath away. The historic building, with its backdrop of the magnificent Rocky Mountains and a private lake, looked like a picture postcard. It was midafternoon when Lee dropped her off at her car back at the arena. As she drove to the hotel, her glance kept roving to the mountains. She'd missed them and hadn't even realized it. She pulled into the parking lot and got out, locking the car behind her. She breathed in the fresh mountain air. Maybe she wasn't meant to leave. After all, this was her home. Or had been. Could it be that her future did lie here?

If the skating didn't work out, she could finish her education here. She could find a job in Colorado Springs as well as in Kansas.

But as she stepped into her room, a sudden loneliness washed over her. She knew she'd miss her friends. And the diner. She loved the Berry Patch. She grinned at the memory of Todd's shaking his head whenever she called it that. Todd. She sighed. She'd miss him most of all if she didn't return home. He'd been a close friend and, she had to admit, lately her feelings had run deeper than friendship.

Then what about the attraction she'd felt for Lee when she'd first seen him again? A sudden discomfort ran through her at the thought. Whatever it had been, it had dissipated soon enough. If she did decide to be his partner again, it would be a business venture only.

But Todd? Although she'd managed to keep the memory of his kiss at bay, there was no way she could deny the warmth she felt when she thought of him. He'd been there for her through thick and thin the past few years. And the thought of his rugged good looks sent a shiver down her spine.

Carla, stop being so double-minded. She laughed and grabbed her robe and headed to the bathroom. A hot shower was what she needed. Maybe it would wash away her confusion as well as soothe her sore muscles.

The hot water felt so good that every other thought drifted away with the fragrant suds from her shampoo and body wash.

Afterwards, wrapped in the thick terry robe, she grabbed a bottle of water from the fridge and stretched out on the bed.

She glanced at the clock. Not quite four. Maybe she'd give Todd a call before his evening run got too busy. A loop of excitement knotted her stomach as she punched in his number.

He picked up on the second ring. "Hi, Carla. How are you?"

Her eyes filled with tears at the sound of his voice. She blinked them back.

"I'm okay, I guess." She sniffled.

"You guess?"

"Yeah, I'm all right. I drove by the Broadmoor Hotel where I'll be meeting my cousins. Almost passed out at how fancy it is. I guess I'd forgotten."

His chuckle made her want to reach through the phone and hug him.

"Nothing's too fancy for you, Carla. You deserve the best."

She sighed. "There are a few people here who don't think as highly of me as you do, Todd."

"What do you mean?" Tension filled his voice.

"Oh, just silly stuff." She told him about Cassie's attitude. "It's just the usual stuff. Happens a lot around competitive skaters."

"I miss you." The sudden huskiness of his tone clutched at her heart.

"I miss you, too." She bit her lip. "I have to go, Todd. I'm starving. I think I'll grab something to eat and go to bed early."

"All right. Get some rest. Will you call me tomorrow?"

"Yeah, I sure will. Good night." She sighed as she sank bank onto the pillows. How could she make a decision when she was so torn? The possibility of fulfilling her Olympic dream caused a thrill of excitement to run through her. But then, why the stab of pain at the thought of leaving Todd?

Todd stared at the phone. He took a deep breath and crammed it into his shirt pocket. There was something going on she wasn't telling him. He wasn't sure how he knew. Maybe a slight hesitancy in her voice. But something.

He shook his head and went back to chopping onions. She'd tell him when she was ready. In the meantime, he'd pray for her and try not to worry.

The kitchen phone rang and Alan, his fry cook and Hannah's husband, grabbed it. He glanced at Todd. "Do you have time to talk to Mr. Harrington?"

Todd wiped his hands on a towel and caught the phone

when Alan tossed it to him. "This is Todd."

"Todd, Jacob Harrington here. I was wondering if you've thought more about my offer."

"Still thinking, Mr. Harrington," Todd said. "I haven't decided yet."

"Hmm. That surprises me. I would think you'd jump at the chance to be the owner of a nice uptown restaurant." He paused then went on. "You know, my grandfather had a restaurant when I was a boy, and I've always wanted to own one. I'd like to give you this opportunity, because I've heard a lot of good things about your food and your management skills. And of course, you're a friend of Julie's. But I do have a couple of other small café owners in mind, and I'd like to get this deal moving soon."

Even though he was tempted to tell the man to go ahead and find someone else, Todd took a deep breath and said, "I'll have an answer for you soon."

"Good. Glad to hear it. Perhaps we can discuss it at Julie's dinner party. See you then."

Before Todd could say he wasn't sure he was going to the party, Harrington hung up.

Todd washed his hands and went back to his preparations for the dinner run. As much as he liked the thought of expanding the diner, did he really want to sign a deal with someone he didn't know very well? He probably needed to find a good business attorney before he even gave it more thought.

"Hey, Todd. Why so glum?" Alan threw a towel his way, and he caught it and tossed it in the laundry cart.

Hannah stepped out of the cooler with a bowl of lemons. "He misses Carla. That's what's wrong."

Todd gave her a grin but didn't deny it.

"Why don't you drop by our place when we close up tonight?" Alan said. "I got some guys coming over for cards. No money involved. Just fun."

"Maybe I will. I need to have some fun."

"Yes, sir." Hannah grabbed a lemon and placed it on a clean cutting board. "And it'll get your mind off our Carla. You know you don't need to worry about her. She's got her feet on the ground. I don't believe she's going to go and do something stupid, like getting involved in figure skating again."

"It's not stupid to her, Hannah. I guess she was pretty good when she was a kid."

"And that's the key word. Kid. She's twenty-four years old. That wouldn't be so bad if she'd been able to stay with it all these years. But to start out again at twenty-four? How long could she stay with it?"

"Well, it's her decision."

"I know, I know. Sorry. But I still think Carla's got better sense than that." She scraped the lemon slices into a bowl. "Anyway." She turned and looked him straight in the eye. "That girl loves you, whether she knows it yet or not, and before another week is over, she's going to miss you too much to stay away."

Todd grinned. "I sincerely hope your prophetic gifts are working tonight, Hannah."

She laughed. "They are. They are."

After the dinner run, Todd took care of the register while Hannah and one of the fill-in waitresses cleaned the front. He helped Alan finish the kitchen cleanup, and then they all walked out the front door together.

"Whew. I'm glad this one is over." Hannah grabbed Alan's arm.

"It was a busy night all right." Todd glanced at the car pulling up to the curb and groaned. Julie. "You two go on. I'll be right behind you."

Hannah frowned in Julie's direction. "You sure you don't want us to stay?"

Todd laughed. "I think I can handle her, Hannah. But thanks."

He walked over to Julie's car and around to her opened window.

She pursed her lips in a coy smile. "Hi, Todd."

"Julie. Did you need to see me about something?"

"Yes, I want to invite you over to Daddy's for cocktails." She flashed another smile.

He frowned. "You know I don't drink."

"Oh, I forgot. Well, then, you can have coffee or something."

"Thanks for the invitation, Julie, but I have plans for the evening."

"Oh. Well, it was actually Daddy who wanted me to invite you." She wrinkled her nose in a way he supposed she thought was cute. "I sort of invited myself along as well."

"I see. Well, tell your father I appreciate the invitation, but as I said, I have other plans."

She frowned. "Oh, all right. What he really wanted me to tell you is that he has important information for you about the restaurant plans."

He eyed her for a moment. Was she telling the truth? Or was this another ploy?

"He said it really is important for him to see you."

Chapter 6

Hope you don't mind shooting pool while we talk. It relaxes me." Harrington racked the balls then straightened and glanced at Todd. "Want to break?"

Todd shook his head. "To be honest, Mr. Harrington, I'd as soon get on with our business so I can leave. I had plans for the evening and friends are waiting for me."

Harrington frowned. "I see. It was my understanding that you and my daughter were spending the evening together. She suggested bringing you here so we could discuss business." A look of annoyance crossed the older man's face. "I must have misunderstood."

Anger washed over Todd, but he pushed it down. What did Julie think she was doing? He thought he'd made it plain he wasn't interested in her. Apparently, he hadn't.

Harrington put down his cue. "My daughter is used to getting what she wants. My fault, I'm afraid. She's an only child and I've spoiled her rotten. Sorry for the inconvenience. We'll talk another time."

"If you have new information you wish to share with me, I can take the time, sir."

"No, no. You run along. Don't keep your friends waiting. How about coming over tomorrow night after work? I promise it will just be you and me and business."

Todd nodded and smiled. "It's a deal."

Harrington held out his hand. "And call me Jacob. After all, I hope we'll be partners soon."

Todd preceded Jacob out of the room, nearly running into Julie in the enormous foyer.

"Oh, are you finished with your business so soon?" She placed a hand on his arm. "Well, good. We can spend some time together."

"I have to leave, Julie."

"But I'd hoped to introduce you to some of my friends."

"Sorry. As I told you before, I already have plans for tonight. Perhaps another time."

Todd saw the fury in her eyes as he said good night to her father and walked past her toward the door. He was glad he'd followed her in his own car instead of riding with her as she'd suggested.

He glanced at his watch. Maybe he shouldn't go to Alan's. It was after ten, and they all had to be at the diner early to prepare for the breakfast shift. He punched in Alan's number and made his excuses, then headed home.

Carla nibbled on a slice of dry toast then took a sip of grapefruit juice. What she really wanted was a stack of pancakes dripping in butter and syrup with sausage on the side. Seemed like her days of indulgence were over.

The day before, Lee had complained about her weight during a lift. Although Vlad was still angry with Lee, he had nevertheless marched Carla to the scale and then told her she needed to lose ten pounds. One more thing she'd forgotten about training.

At least she'd gotten a good night's sleep and felt well rested.

When she arrived at the arena, Vlad and Lee were already there. She hurried to her locker and grabbed her skates.

Lee took her hand and they stepped onto the ice. Halfway around the arena, Carla felt her skate wobble. The next thing she knew, she landed hard on the ice.

"Carla, are you all right?" Lee caught himself from a stumble and knelt beside her, his eyes concerned.

"I think so." She jumped up. One of the first things she'd learned when she started to skate was that if you fell, you got right back up.

"Lee!" Vlad's voice was sharp as he skated over to them. "Why did you let her fall?"

"Man, she was on the ice before I knew what was happening." He looked at Carla. "What happened?"

"Not sure. My skate feels strange."

Vlad knelt beside her, and she bent her leg back so he could look at her skate. "This blade's loose. Didn't you check them before you put them on?"

Carla's stomach tightened. "I checked them last night before I put them in my locker."

"Never, ever go out on the ice without checking your blades."

Carla felt her face grow warm. She should have remembered, but on the other hand. . . She glanced at Lee. "How could the blade get loose just sitting in my locker?"

"Someone tampered with it." He pressed his lips together. "Someone trying to stop you before you even get started."

Vlad shook his head. "Don't be ridiculous, Lee. She simply forgot to check them and doesn't want to admit it." He gave

Carla a tight smile. "It's all right. It's naturally going to take a little while to remember all the safety rules."

"But. . ."

Before Carla could voice her protest, Vlad had skated away.

Lee took her arm and helped her off the ice. "Never mind him. He has his head in the sand. It's easier to blame you than investigate the matter. Let's leave your skates with Anton and grab something to drink."

Anton had been taking care of skaters' equipment for many years. They found the white-haired man in a large, equipment-filled room near the back door.

They left the skates so Anton could tighten the blades and went to the coffee shop. They carried their coffees to a booth and sat across from each other.

"Try not to worry about it." Lee patted her hand. "I'm sure it's just Cassie or one of the other girls up to their tricks."

"A loose blade is a little more than a trick, Lee. I could have been injured." Carla blew her hair out of her eyes and took a sip of her iced coffee. "Anyway, that sort of thing is what I'd expect from a pre-teen. Good grief. We're adults now."

"I know, sweetie. But you're a threat to them. They can see how quickly you're picking everything up again. And they remember how good you always were. I'm sure we'd have made it to the Olympics if we'd continued skating together."

"Do you really think so?" Excitement ran through her. "Were we really that good?"

"You bet we were." He grinned. "Don't you remember how Tom used to brag on us to everyone?"

"Well, yeah. But he was our coach. He had to brag." She threw him a wink and grinned.

"But it was true. And baby, we can get there again."

She straightened and frowned at him. "Please don't call me that, Lee."

Surprise crossed his face. "Okay, honey, I won't. Didn't know you minded."

"I don't, when it's meaningful. But you and I are *maybe* skating partners and, I hope, friends." She bit her lip.

"Oh. I see." He tapped on his coffee mug. "I'd hoped we could be a little more than that. I care for you, Carla."

She shook her head. "No you don't. You don't even know me. Maybe there's some attraction. I felt it, too, at first, but that's all it is."

He nodded and lifted one eyebrow. "You sure?"

Carla couldn't help the laughter that bubbled up. "Yes, I'm sure. And stop flirting. It'll do you no good."

He sighed. "Can't blame a guy for trying. You've grown into a beautiful woman."

"Thank you. You're not half bad yourself."

"But your heart belongs to someone else?"

Carla's breath caught. "No. . .well, maybe. There is someone. A friend."

"But maybe this friend is more than a friend?"

She ducked her head and sipped through her straw.

"Hmm?"

"Maybe. I don't know yet." The thought of Todd's kiss flashed into her mind and she blushed.

Lee laughed. "All right, Carla. Skating partners and friends."

"*Maybe* skating partners. I haven't decided yet."

"But you're leaning toward yes. Right?" His eyes gleamed, and he took her hand. "I know we can go places."

"You really believe that, don't you?" Could he be right? A picture of Lee and her standing on the top podium wearing their gold medals rushed into her mind. They'd won a few firsts at minor competitions. Could they have really made it to Nationals and Worlds and maybe even the Olympics? And was there still a chance? They'd have to go through Regionals first. Could they even do well there?

"I really do." Lee stood. "We'd better get back before Vlad comes looking for us."

They retrieved Carla's skates and returned to the ice. This time, Vlad told them to do a side-by-side single jump. Carla tightened up and stepped out of the jump, nearly falling. They skated around for a while then tried it again, both landing perfectly.

"Okay, I want you to do two more of those then no more jumps for today. Just skate. Get used to each other again. Tomorrow you can work on spins. You have a long way to go."

When they finally left the arena, snow was gently falling.

"Oh, it's beautiful." Carla lifted her mittened hands and caught some flakes.

"And cold." Lee shivered.

"I like the cold."

Lee walked her to her car and stood beside the window while she started the engine. "How about if I pick you up for dinner later? I know this great sushi place."

"Thanks, but I'm so tired, I don't think I want to come back out. I'll probably have something delivered." And she wanted some time to herself to collect her thoughts.

When she got to her hotel, she tossed her bag on the bed and headed for the bathroom. The hot shower felt wonderful to her sore muscles. She dried off and slipped into warm flannel pajamas, sank into the deep recliner, and got the phone book out of the nightstand drawer. Yawning, she rifled through the pages, looking for restaurants that delivered something besides pizza or Chinese. It was already after five, so she'd have to wait and call Todd later. She yawned again.

She jerked up, blinking her eyes. The room had darkened. She must have drifted off. She glanced at the clock. After nine. Todd would be finished at the diner by now. She punched in his number. After six rings, she pressed END.

She picked up the phone book that had slid onto the floor from her lap while she slept. She found the restaurant section and pursed her lips. There probably weren't too many choices for delivery this late. She called a local pizzeria and ordered a chef salad.

She tried Todd's number again and bit her lip as she listened to it ring. She checked her messages in case she'd missed a text or call while she was sleeping. Nothing.

She stood and went to the coffeepot. She shouldn't drink it this late. Hadn't she seen a packet of decaf? She scrambled through the drawer and located it. When the coffee was brewing, she tried Todd's number again.

A tap on the door announced the arrival of her food. She'd eat then try to call Todd again.

She choked down half her salad and tossed the rest into the trash. Sighing, she poured a cup of coffee and returned to her recliner.

She picked up her phone and punched in Todd's number again. Nothing. She flopped back onto her pillow, frowning at her phone. She really wanted to hear his voice tonight.

Where are you, Todd?

Chapter 7

Todd punched in Carla's number. It went immediately to voice mail. Which meant she'd turned her phone off. It had been late when his meeting with Jacob Harrington ended last night. By the time he'd seen the missed calls from Carla, he hadn't wanted to chance waking her.

His thoughts whirled as he drove to work. The ideas and possibilities Jacob had tossed his way sounded really good. But Jacob knew enough about restaurants to realize any new venture was risky. In normal times, the new place wouldn't support itself at first. Todd would need to have enough money, either his own or his backer's, to cover expenses, including his own salary, for at least a year. And with the economy the way it was, the risk was increased. He was tempted, but didn't intend to jump into it without a lot of thought and prayer.

Carla still hadn't returned his call by the time he arrived at the diner. She was more than likely busy at the arena. The very probable idea that she'd decided to stay in Colorado to train tightened his stomach and sent dread running through him. Before he sank into depression over the situation, he went out through the back door and leaned against the building. He needed to put everything back in God's hands. It seemed like he kept taking things into his own.

Father, I give her back to You once more. You have Your own plan for Carla's life and for mine. Please give me peace and increase my faith. In the name of Jesus. Amen.

He didn't immediately experience a feeling of faith or jubilation, but he knew that sometimes even peace had to be received by faith, regardless of feelings. He knew in his heart God was in control.

The morning practice had gone well. No loose skates and no one running into her. And wonder of wonders, Lee had followed Vlad's directions and hadn't argued with the coach even once.

"Good job, kids," Vlad threw over his shoulder as he left the building.

Carla glanced after him. "Doesn't he have other skaters to train?"

Lee gave her a quick look and focused on removing his skates. "I think he just ended a couple of contracts and decided to move here for his health or something. I believe we're his only ones at the moment." He pulled her braid. "Which makes it better for us, right?"

Carla laughed away her momentary unease. "I guess it does."

"Sure it does."

"Lee, I've made a decision." Carla held her breath as he stared at her.

"Well, don't keep me wondering."

She smiled. "In spite of sore muscles; blistered, swollen feet; and someone possibly sabotaging my skates, I realize I want this. But I also want to get my degree. So if you're willing to work around my college schedule, I think the answer is yes."

"You *think*?" Disappointment rang out in his tone.

"Come on, Lee. I do have some things to tie up, and I've got this week with my cousins coming up soon. I'll have a week to think about it without you around trying to make up my mind for me." She laughed. "My decision is that if I still feel the same at the end of next week, I'll stay."

He whooped and grabbed her around the waist, whirling her around. "I can handle that. But in the meantime I plan to do everything I can to sway you in the right direction. Starting now."

"Lee! Put me down, or I just might back out."

He set her down gently. "Sorry, I got carried away. But I'm serious about swaying you. Did you know there's an ice show in town?"

"Yes, I saw the flyers."

"Well, I thought maybe we could grab some lunch then take in the matinee performance."

"Anyone we know skating?" She'd only glanced at the flyer. It was an ice show out of Denver.

"You'll probably recognize a couple of skaters. But I've heard it's a good show." He grinned. "Some ballet on ice."

"Sounds good. What time is the matinee?"

"Three o'clock. We'll have to forgo an afternoon practice."

Once more, a little unease tried to worm its way in, but she shoved it aside. They'd been training hard for a week and a half. She couldn't expect him to keep it up constantly.

"Okay. I'm heading for the showers, but let's skip lunch. I'd rather go back to the hotel for a couple of hours and grab something there. Can you pick me up? I'm not sure if I know the way to the Ice Palace."

"Sure, I planned on it anyway. See you around two-fifteen."

Butterflies danced in Carla's stomach all the way back to

her room. She looked forward to the ice show, and just telling Lee her intention had made it seem real. She was a skater again. Maybe not a great one yet, but she'd work hard. She'd make it.

She curled up in the easy chair and opened her lunch, feeling a little guilty over the burger and fries, but she was hungry, and she'd been practically living on salads and fish the last few days.

She bowed her head to give thanks and suddenly Todd's face flashed in her mind. She'd had such a busy and exciting morning, she'd forgotten to turn her phone back on after practice.

Oh no, a half dozen calls from Todd. She sighed. She couldn't call him now. It was the busiest time of the day at the diner. She'd have to wait until after the ice show. She sent him a quick text promising to call later then ate her sandwich. She gave her parents a call, and by the time she got off the phone, it was time to get ready.

The ice show was fantastic, and Carla was mesmerized. She hadn't seen a live ice show or competition in years, and she'd forgotten how entrancing they could be. Several times, Lee glanced at her and smiled. He hadn't forgotten her love for the artistic side of skating, and she could see the satisfaction in his glance.

As they walked out of the building, he took her hand. She started to withdraw it but decided she was being silly. They held hands for hours on the ice, not to mention other intimate moves. It didn't mean anything. And she didn't want to ruin the magic of the evening.

As they drove back toward her hotel, she turned to him and smiled. "Thanks for taking me to see the show, Lee. It was so beautiful. I loved every minute of it."

"I know. I could tell. And I loved watching you loving it."

She laughed.

"How about stopping somewhere for supper before I drop you off?"

"Oh, I'm sorry. I'm still stuffed from lunch. And I have some phone calls to make."

Surprised when he didn't argue, she breathed a sigh of relief. She wanted to hear Todd's voice and hoped he hadn't gotten busy yet.

The first thing she did when she walked into her room was to toss her jacket on the bed and head for the easy chair. She pulled out her cell phone and called the diner. The sound of Todd's voice sent a surge of relief through her. She wanted to reach through the phone and pull him to her. Her heart sped up at the thought of being in his arms. She inhaled deeply then let the air out slowly. She had to get her emotions under control so she could think clearly.

"Hi, Todd. How are things at the diner?"

"Pretty much the same, except we're all missing you. How are you?"

She told him about her day at the rink. As she talked about the ice show, some of her joy came back. But she knew she needed to be honest with him.

"Todd. . ." She paused. "I'm pretty sure I'm going to stay here and continue my training."

She heard him draw in a deep breath.

"What about your college plans?"

Surely he didn't think she'd give up her plans to get her degree. "I'll enroll here. They have a very good business college nearby. And Lee and our coach will work around my schedule."

"You already have a coach?"

"Yes, I thought I told you."

"I don't think so. But that's okay." Another indrawn breath. "I'll miss you."

A pang of sadness hit her. "Please, Todd, don't sound like our friendship is over. It's not that far. We can still see each other."

"Of course we will." A long silence. "Well, Carla, I need to get busy. We'll talk tomorrow, okay?"

"Can't we talk after you close up?"

He hesitated. "I'm sorry. I'll be tied up tonight. I'm going to be talking to Harrington. But I'll call tomorrow. Gotta go now. 'Bye. And I'm happy for you, Carla."

The call disconnected. Carla sat and looked at the phone in her hand. She was making the right decision, wasn't she? Then why did she feel so empty and sad?

Todd's decision to go to Julie's dinner party had been made on the spur of the moment. It was born out of his pain and the thoughts running through his head. How could he compete with the hope of gold medals and fame? Maybe, if he had a fancy restaurant that brought in some real money, he'd have a better chance.

It only took about five minutes for Todd to discover that the main attraction at this party was the liquid refreshment. Well, he should have expected it. But it wasn't what he was used to. By the time dinner was over, most of the guests were noticeably drunk. Todd glanced around for Julie to make his excuses and leave. He saw her across the room and headed in her direction.

"Todd." She grabbed his arm. "I want you to meet some friends of mine."

He drew back from the blast of alcohol on her breath. "Julie, I have to go now. Thanks for inviting me to dinner."

He managed to slip away despite her protests. He'd almost made it to the door when Jacob's voice stopped him.

"Todd, my boy. Where are you going? We haven't talked business yet."

Although Jacob wasn't as drunk as some of the others, it was obvious he'd had a few too many. And the blond hanging on his arm certainly wasn't Mrs. Harrington.

Todd stopped long enough to shake his hand. "Jacob, after thinking it over, I've decided to pass on your generous offer. I think I'll just stick with my diner for now."

He headed home, thankful that God had opened his eyes before he'd signed anything. He admired Jacob as a businessman, but he didn't want to be under obligation to someone who didn't share his values. *Thank You, Lord, for Your protection. And Lord, it's been a long time since I've thanked You for the diner. I'm thanking You now. Lord, if there's something You want me to do about the situation with Carla, I ask You to show me that, too.*

Chapter 8

For the first time since arriving in Colorado Springs, Carla had no joy in skating, no excitement at the thought of competing again. She glided across the ice, hardly noticing the moves she and Lee were doing.

"Carla! Get your head out of the clouds. I've told you twice to get ready for a throw." The irritation in Lee's voice jerked her back from her thoughts.

She tensed. "Wait. I'm not ready. Let's go around a couple more times."

He sighed. "All right. But pay attention this time."

Carla forced herself to focus on what she was supposed to be doing for the rest of the morning. When Vlad called a halt, Lee dropped her hand and skated off by himself.

Fine. He'd pout the rest of the day. She'd found that out. Of course, he had a right to be upset with her.

"Oomph." Carla landed on the ice, hard. She popped back up and glanced around to see her nemesis glide away with a grin on her face.

Carla sighed. It was her own fault. She hadn't been paying attention, so it was easy to get rammed.

By the time she left the ice, there was no sign of Vlad or Lee. Oh well. She didn't want to talk to them anyway. She showered and decided to stop at the coffee shop and try to get her head clear before she drove. She hadn't hit her head when she fell but she was jarred nevertheless.

She took a sip of her hot mocha, relishing the bitter but sweet chocolaty goodness. She'd had them add an extra dollop of whipped cream and wasn't feeling a bit guilty. Maybe she wasn't so sold out on being a competitive skater after all.

She glanced up and saw a framed picture of Michelle Kwan. The one whose career she'd followed since she was a little girl. Injury had sidetracked Michelle, the most decorated skater in the United States. Carla still remembered crying along with her angel when she'd had to pull out of the Olympics because of a hip injury. At least Michelle had tons of World and National medals to console her.

But it wasn't just about winning or losing competitions. Carla loved to skate. But did she have the drive she would need to compete? Was it the most important thing to her?

Todd's face popped from the back of her mind to the front. She almost gasped. She missed him. She missed the diner and her friends at home.

She stood and glanced at Michelle's photo again. She'd thought Michelle would skate forever. Sure, she did an occasional show, but she'd finished her education, and she seemed to be moving on to more important things.

I still don't know what I'm supposed to do, Lord. Would You please show me?

She drove around for a while and then with a jolt realized she hadn't even thought of taking flowers to Grams's grave.

With a purpose for the first time that day, she drove to a florist and bought a beautiful arrangement then drove to the cemetery.

It took her a little while to find the right plot. She was pleased to see it well cared for. A pewter vase was empty.

Well, no wonder. Who would bring fresh flowers when it was likely to start snowing again?

She gave a little chuckle and placed the flowers in the vase. She attempted to arrange them nicely and smiled at the crooked bouquet. It would do. At least it was straighter than the stitches on her quilt square. Which she still hadn't finished. "I'll finish it this afternoon, Grams. I promise," she whispered.

Feeling a little better, she left and drove to a small restaurant near her hotel. She ate salad because she wanted it, not because someone thought she needed to lose weight, and added a bowl of cheddar broccoli soup because it was her favorite.

When she walked into her room, she found herself humming an old country song that Todd played in the diner sometimes.

She retrieved her squares from her suitcase, including the one she was trying to finish. She'd do the best she could. She held up her square. Actually, her stitches didn't look as bad as she'd thought. She zipped the suitcase and carried the squares to the easy chair.

Three hours later, she held up her square again and gave a sigh of satisfaction. *Thank You, Lord.*

It wasn't perfect, but it was good enough. At least she wouldn't have to be ashamed. And she knew her cousins would help her with the rest. It was time for her to start being herself and stop comparing herself to everyone else. After all, everyone couldn't skate as well as she could. She cringed at that thought. Was that why she'd decided to return to figure skating? So she wouldn't feel inferior to her cousins?

She closed her eyes. Yes, if she were to be honest with

herself, she'd dreaded telling Eve, Danni, and Zoe that she was a waitress in a diner. Again, she cringed. Such ridiculous self-pride. As if they would care. And even if they did, so what? She'd always had a special feeling for the diner. The shame had come when she thought of her older, successful cousins. *Father, forgive me.*

Had she ever even liked training and competing? She remembered the early mornings when she'd just wanted to sleep a little longer. The tears when her mother would soak her blistered feet. Now that she thought of it, Grams had never once encouraged her to skate. She'd only said Carla should do what made her happy.

She drew in a deep breath. And suddenly peace flooded her, and she felt lighter than she'd felt since she found out she was coming to Colorado Springs.

Now that the decision concerning Harrington was made, Todd felt like a ton of bricks had been lifted off him. Even the uncertainty about Carla couldn't detract from his overall sense of well-being. He knew God was in control.

Of course, Hannah kept bugging him to tell her why he was suddenly in such a good mood after moping around for a week and a half. And when she started guessing, it didn't take her but one try.

"You talked to Carla, didn't you?" Without waiting for an answer, she whooped. "That's it. I knew it. I knew she wouldn't stay away. I sure hope when she gets back you have the sense to ask that girl to marry you."

Alan tossed a dish towel at her. "For crying out loud, Hannah Marie, leave the man alone."

"Don't call me that." She tossed the towel back at him.

"Why not? It's your name." Alan threw her a wink. "And a very pretty name for my girl."

"Oh, you." She laughed and looked at Todd. "Well? Am I right?"

"I don't know, Hannah. When I talked to her yesterday, she was leaning toward staying in Colorado. But I haven't given up hope."

She snorted. "Well, do you wonder why? Have you ever given her even a hint of how you feel about her?"

The good-bye kiss flitted across Todd's mind but he shoved it back. "I think she has at least a hint of an idea, yes."

"Well, maybe it's time you came right out and told her you love her."

"Hannah!" Alan frowned. "Mind your own business."

The phone rang and Hannah picked it up. "Carla! Girl, when are you coming home? I can't run this place without you." She paused and then laughed. "Okay, let me give the phone to Todd. I know you didn't call to talk to me. You take care of yourself. Bye."

Todd took the phone and carried it into the storage room. "Hi, Carla."

"Hi, Todd. It was nice to hear Hannah's voice. I didn't realize how much I miss her."

"Well, as I'm sure you can tell, she misses you, too. We all do." There, he'd said it without sounding pitiful.

Carla hesitated a moment. "Todd, I don't think I'm going to pursue a skating career after all."

He stiffened to control the shout of joy that wanted to explode from his throat.

"Oh, so you've decided against it?"

"I think so. Would you please pray for me? I don't want to make a mistake, and you know how impulsive I can be." She gave a nervous little laugh. "Yesterday, I was almost sure I was going to compete. So you see, I really need prayer to make sure I do the right thing."

"You know I'll pray for you, Carla. I want God's best for you, whatever that might be." Oh, but he wanted to shout, "I think God's best for you is to come home to me." He swallowed. "Do you want me to ask Hannah and Alan to pray, too?"

"Would you please?" She sniffled. "I have to go now, Todd. Can we have a long talk tomorrow?"

"Of course. I'm here if you need me. Call me before work, in between shifts, or after closing. You know the schedule."

"Okay. Thanks, Todd. You're a wonderful friend."

"I always will be, Carla. You can count on that."

The call ended, and Todd stood for a moment, his eyes closed. "God, help her. Please help her make the right decision."

Carla looked at the phone in her hand. Her throat was tight, and she blinked back tears. Had she lost Todd? Or had he ever been hers? She'd probably imagined that he cared for her. She'd built up the good-bye kiss to be something he'd never intended.

But at least she had his friendship, and she knew he would pray.

Chapter 9

The locker room was empty when Carla walked in. Should she change into her workout clothes or wait until she talked to Vlad and Lee? She still wasn't a hundred percent sure what she should do. But she'd prayed and committed the situation to God. She'd trust Him to guide her. She only hoped He didn't wait until the last minute. Her nerves were so on edge.

The door opened and a skater she'd seen around the rink came in. The girl paused when she saw Carla, then smiled and walked over.

"Hi, I'm Dana Saunders. You're Carla Daniels, right?"

Carla nodded. "It's nice meeting you."

Dana hesitated, then took a deep breath and let it out. "Look, Carla, this isn't any of my business, but there's something I think you need to know, if you don't already."

"Oh? What's that?" Was this going to be another smart aleck trying to get under her skin?

"What did Lee tell you about his split with Susan?"

Uh-oh, another gossip. "Just that she left because he'd messed up at Nationals."

A sound of exasperation came from Dana. "That's not what happened."

Carla tensed. Had Lee lied to her? Or was this girl trying to stir up trouble?

"All right, you might as well tell me."

"Look, I don't go around gossiping, but if you're going to be Lee's partner, you need to know a few things. I trained right here for the last year they skated together. Susan and I weren't best friends, but I knew her pretty well and could see her frustration."

Carla couldn't help but see the girl's sincerity. "Okay, I'm listening."

"I don't know what Lee was like when you were his partner, but since I've known him, he's been undisciplined. When he trained with Susan, he wanted his way about everything, and he ignored his coach most of the time. He was late to practices, if he made it there at all. He tried crazy moves that their coach advised against. And he wanted to be in complete control of Susan. The reason he fell at Nationals was because he was careless with a throw and lost his balance. Susan could have been injured badly. Luckily she wasn't, but it really shook her up and she couldn't handle it anymore."

Carla nodded. "But if he's so bad, why was Vlad willing to coach him?"

"Vlad is Lee's last chance. He's been turned down by several coaches. And Vlad doesn't have that great a record either. He was pretty much in coach limbo until Lee came along." She stepped over to a locker and pulled out leotards. "Look, everyone knows this. It's no secret. I just thought someone should tell you. You seem like a nice person, and you're doing really well on the ice, considering how long it's been since you trained. I have to get ready now. See you later."

Carla thanked her and left the locker room. She stood a moment in the hallway, her eyes closed, then headed for the coffee shop. As she'd hoped, Vlad and Lee were there. She ordered a mocha latte and walked over to them. Lee made room for her on his side of the booth.

Vlad frowned and jerked his head toward the latte. "I hope that's sugar and fat free."

She smiled. "As a matter of fact, it is, Vlad. I've decided I've been eating entirely too much sugar and saturated fat."

He nodded and gave her a little smile. "Good girl." He turned back to Lee. "Now, this is what I'd like for you to work on today."

"Just a minute, Vlad." Carla bit her lip. "I have some news for you both. I've made my decision. I've decided not to return to competitive skating."

Surprise crossed Vlad's face, but the look on Lee's was something else. "You can't do that! You promised."

"Lee, you know that's not true. I was leaning toward a yes, but I was wrong." She lifted her chin and looked in his eyes. "I love skating, Lee. But I never did like to compete. I don't think I realized that until last night. And I know I have other things I want to do. Things I'm not willing to give up for the uncertainty of a gold medal."

"Carla, please reconsider." Lee's eyes were begging.

"I'm so sorry. But to be honest, even if I wanted it, which I don't, I can't trust you, Lee. You lied to me about the breakup with Susan, and you've already been careless on the ice." She stood. "I do want to thank you for inviting me to partner with you again and for the nice things you said about my skating. I wish you all the best in your career. But it's not for me."

She offered her hand. "Good-bye." For a moment she thought he'd ignore it, but finally, he reached out and briefly took her hand.

She turned to Vlad. "Thanks for your willingness to work with me."

He smiled and nodded. "I hope you're not making a mistake."

"I'm not."

She returned to the locker room with a lightness in her step that had been missing for nearly two weeks. She looked at her watch. If she hurried, she could call Todd before he got busy.

Todd whistled as he filled the pans for the lunch buffet steam table. The daily fried chicken lay crisp and golden brown in one large pan. Slices of meat loaf lined another, and spaghetti and meatballs filled the third entrée pan.

He was thankful he'd had most of the dishes prepared when Carla called. Otherwise, he'd have been so distracted there was no telling how things might have turned out. He laughed as he scooped the mashed potatoes into their slot and then poured gravy.

Alan was already getting the salads and desserts in place.

All Todd could think about was a certain beautiful blond. She'd sounded happy but perhaps at loose ends when she called. As though she'd burned one bridge and wasn't sure how to build another.

Her voice had sounded different when she said his name. Almost like a caress. Whew. Better stop that. He might go off the deep end and do something foolish. Like hop a plane to Colorado. He stopped in the middle of transferring the green beans. Maybe that wasn't such a bad idea.

"Here. Better let me do that." Alan took the pan from his

hand. "Good thing I got back here when I did. There'd be green beans all over the floor."

Todd gave him an absentminded smile and went to the grill. One ticket hung on the rack. Just for a cheeseburger and fries. He pulled a tray of hamburger patties from the walk-in.

Should he go? He'd been careful not to interfere the past week, preferring to leave things in God's hands. But she'd made her decision to come back. There was nothing wrong in him going there now for a day or two, was there? Just to let her know he was there for her? And maybe propose?

He chuckled. Better not get ahead of himself here. And better get his mind back on his grill before he lost a customer. He'd also better get his head together before the rush hit.

After the lunch run, Todd waved good-bye to Hannah and Alan and drove home. He had a few hours before he'd need to be back at the diner. He took coffee and his phone out to the deck and checked out flight schedules. He could get a plane out of Wichita at eleven tonight. That would be the best bet. He'd need to be back home in a couple of days. Alan and Hannah could manage without him, but he didn't want to put the responsibility of the diner on them for any longer than that. Especially on such short notice.

He made a quick call to the diner and talked with Alan. After being reassured he and Hannah would be happy to run the diner for a few days, he ended the call, got on his computer, and took care of his airline ticket. Then he made reservations at a hotel in Colorado Springs and made sure he could gain admittance that late at night.

Finally, he ran upstairs and packed a suitcase.

By the time he'd brought his suitcase downstairs and set

it by the door, it was time to return to the diner. He'd need to take off a little early to shower and shave, so Alan and Hannah would have to close up.

As Todd drove back to the diner, it suddenly occurred to him that his impulsive action might backfire on him. What if Carla resented his showing up unexpectedly? *Lord, go with me.*

Carla glanced at her cousins' photos lying on the bed beside her. Eve was the one closest to her in age. By the time they'd all scattered, the two of them had grown apart because they were both busy with their own interests, but for a while when they were little kids they'd been stuck like glue. She remembered them playing dress-up at Grams's house.

Danni and Zoe had been several years older, and Carla remembered practically worshipping them from afar. They'd pretty much ignored their younger cousins back then, but there had also been some kind moments. Such as the time Danni had found her crying in the elm tree in Grams's backyard after she'd climbed up and was afraid to come back down. Danni had climbed up in her brand-new designer jeans and rescued Carla. But even better, she hadn't told anyone about her young cousin's fear.

Carla smiled and picked up Zoe's photo. Carla must have been about nine the year she'd talked sixteen-year-old Zoe into letting her ride with her on the Ferris wheel. Carla, frozen with fear, had held onto the bar for dear life, and by the time she'd gotten off the ride, she'd been white as a ghost and shaking all over. A neighbor boy who'd gone to the fair with them had made fun of her and Zoe had threatened to smack him if he didn't stop. Then she'd bought a snow cone for Carla.

Carla laughed, and anticipation rose up in her for the coming reunion. Just two more days. She could hardly wait.

Chapter 10

Todd took a deep breath and offered up a quick prayer before he punched in Carla's number. It rang three times. Maybe she was still sleeping. He glanced at his watch and groaned. Only seven o'clock. He should have waited.

He was about to end the call when a groggy "hello" stopped him.

"I woke you up."

A yawn. "Todd? Is that you?"

"Yeah. Sorry. I should have checked the time. I thought it was later."

She laughed. "It's okay. I need to get up anyway. I want to do a little more sightseeing today. I meet the cousins tomorrow."

"I know." He cleared his throat. "Want some company on your sightseeing tour?"

"What?" A squeal reverberated off his ear. "Todd! Are you coming here?"

"Well, actually, I'm already here." He held his breath.

"Oh, that's great! Have you had breakfast yet?"

He grinned. She sounded like she was glad. "No, I was hoping we could go together."

"Yes. Wonderful. Give me a half hour. Where do you want me to meet you?"

The happiness in her voice about bowled him over. Maybe he should have done this sooner.

"I'm not really familiar with the restaurants in town. What do you suggest?"

"Well, there's a big pancake house in town, but if you want some local color, I know just the place." She rattled off the address to a place called Mac's Chuck Wagon.

Twenty minutes later, he parked in front of the café, which was sandwiched between a small museum and a bookstore.

He locked his rental car and waited another fifteen minutes for Carla to get there.

When she drove up and parked, he opened her door for her and she almost sprang into his arms. Without thinking, he pressed his lips to hers.

"Carla." His voice was shaky.

She blushed and stepped back. "Sorry I almost knocked you over. I don't know what got into me."

"Well, I'm not sorry. I wasn't sure how you'd feel about me coming here unannounced." He grinned and took her arm, guiding her toward the door. "Let's get inside. You didn't wear a very warm jacket."

"I didn't realize the temperature had dropped. It must be twenty degrees colder than yesterday." She stepped through the door and Todd followed her.

A waitress dressed cowgirl style smiled and directed them to a booth. She left menus and promised to be right back.

Todd glanced across the table. Carla's hands were folded on the tabletop, and it seemed the most natural thing in the world to wrap them in his.

"I can't believe two weeks could seem so long."

She nodded. "I know. Even in the midst of all the excitement, I was lonely. How is Hannah?"

"She's fine now that she knows you're coming home. I was half expecting her to come to Colorado and kidnap you."

She giggled. "She would have, too. Can't you just see that?"

They spent the next hour eating bacon, eggs, and biscuits and cream gravy, and enjoying each other's presence. Todd breathed a sigh of relief. He needn't have worried. Carla was still Carla.

He glanced at her as they stepped outside. "Okay, where to now?"

"How would you like to go ice skating?" She flashed an appealing smile in his direction.

"Are you serious? I haven't skated in years." He frowned. "You're not serious."

She laughed. "No, but I thought you might like to see the old rink where I trained when I was a little girl."

"That, I can handle."

Todd followed Carla to her hotel so she could leave her car. They drove to the rink and after she showed him around, they went for a drive.

She directed him to the Broadmoor where she and her cousins would be staying. "Grams arranged it all ahead of time. We'll be staying at a fancy expensive cottage on the grounds here somewhere."

Todd whistled. "I've heard of this place, but you have to see it to believe it."

She nodded. "I was nervous at first, but now I can't wait to see my cousins again. When we came for the funeral, everything seemed so rushed and unreal. I can barely remember even talking to them."

He started the car and they continued their tour, stopping for lunch at a little mountain cabin that had been converted to a restaurant.

It was no wonder she'd wanted to stay here. The place was beautiful, with the magnificent mountains as a backdrop to it all.

"I can see now why you were eager to come back. But are you sure about not moving here? I'd hate for you to regret it later."

"I'm sure. It drew me for a while, and I wouldn't mind coming back for a visit once in a while, but I'm ready to go home. Although I'm looking forward to seeing Danni, Zoe, and Eve, I can hardly wait until it's time to go." She gave him a wistful look. "When do you have to leave?"

"Tomorrow afternoon. When are you going to the Broadmoor?"

"We're supposed to meet with Grams's attorney there tomorrow morning at nine. I guess I'll go ahead and check in then."

He nodded. "Let's have breakfast together before you go."

"Okay. That'll be nice."

He'd already called and made reservations for dinner that evening. He hoped he hadn't been presumptuous.

"Are you free tonight for dinner?"

"Is this an invitation?" Her lips curved in a teasing smile.

"It is, if you're free. I know it's short notice."

"I'm free. I've burned my bridges with the one person I called *friend* in this town." She shook her head. "And I think the term *friend* was stretching it a little where Lee was concerned."

"In that case, can I pick you up around eight?"

"Of course. Should I dress fancy or wear my jeans?" She grinned.

"Not formal, but something nice, I guess."

He slipped his hand into his jacket pocket and tapped nervously on the small box. He wouldn't care if she came in her bathrobe with her hair in curlers. As long as she gave him the right answer.

Carla dabbed at the wisp of hair that wouldn't stay where she wanted it. She wasn't sure if what she was feeling was nervousness, anticipation, excitement, or a combination of them all. She'd felt like an idiot when she'd thrown herself into Todd's arms that morning.

Butterflies began a dance in her stomach. Of course, he hadn't seemed to mind. That kiss about knocked her socks off.

She gave herself another once-over in the mirror. She'd chosen a simple black, knee-length dress with a single strand of pearls and small pearl earrings. Her hair was pulled back and held with a pearl comb. Maybe a little old fashioned, but the pearls combination had belonged to Grams, and for some reason, she felt like wearing them tonight.

Todd arrived promptly at eight, looking handsome in a brown plaid sweater and tan pants. He tucked her arm through his and gazed deeply into her eyes. When he spoke, his voice was husky. "You look so beautiful."

"Thanks. So do you." She felt heat rise to her face. "Handsome, I mean."

He laughed and held the car door for her.

They drove for a few blocks to a small, but very nice restaurant. Carla was surprised when they were led to an enclosed patio that only had one occupied table. A fireplace roared in the corner and candles graced their table. Soft music played in the background, broken only by the clinking of silver on china.

Todd held her chair for her, and she smiled up at him. He bent and touched her lips with his then sat across from her. She felt almost dazed for a moment, as though she were floating on a cloud of dreams.

"This is lovely, Todd."

"I hoped you'd like it." He touched her hand and smiled. A waiter arrived to fill their glasses from a pitcher of water. He told them his name and left their menus.

After they'd ordered, Carla looked at Todd. "We were so busy sightseeing today, you never did tell me what you've decided about Harrington's offer."

"I turned him down." He frowned. "It turned out he wasn't the sort I wanted to do business with. But aside from that, I wasn't comfortable with the idea of having someone else's money tied up in my business. I've been thinking of fixing up the diner. Making it a real fifties-style place."

"Todd! That's a wonderful idea. I saw a diner like that in Kansas City once. It was so much fun." She laughed. "Don't know how Hannah will take to wearing a pink uniform."

"Maybe we can come up with something else." He grinned. "Want to help me make some decisions about the place?"

"I'd love to."

They spoke quietly while they dined then sat back as their dishes were cleared away.

The other couple had left the patio, so they were alone. Todd leaned forward and took her hands in his. "I was afraid you wouldn't come back. That I'd lost you forever."

"But you didn't argue with me about it. You let me decide. Thank you for that." She blinked back the tears that threatened to escape.

"Only with God's help. I knew I had to trust Him to lead you. As much as I wanted you back home, I wanted His best for you."

She nodded. "I'm ashamed to say I didn't think to pray about it until a couple of days ago. Once I prayed, it wasn't long before I knew I didn't want to stay here. As much as I love skating, I finally realized competition wasn't for me."

"It looks like we both needed to put our futures in God's hands."

"That's right. We each had a decision to make, but our emotions, and in my case at least, some pride got in the way of my thinking clearly."

Todd smiled, his eyes crinkling in the way she loved so much. She'd finally admitted to herself that she was in love with him. Even if he didn't feel the same way, at least she hadn't lost his friendship.

"I'm just happy we both listened to Him." He gently squeezed her hand. "And that we're here having this conversation."

Carla said a silent amen to that. She looked into his eyes and saw longing there. Could it be he did love her?

"What is it, Todd?" Her heart beat rapidly as she waited.

He took a deep breath. "I love you. I've loved you for a long time. Even if you don't feel the same, I want you to know how I feel."

"Todd." She tried to stop the tears, but they rolled down her cheeks. "Oh, Todd."

"It's okay." A dejected look crossed his face. "You don't need to feel bad about not loving me back. Please don't cry."

"Not loving you?" She gave a little laugh that was half cry. "I love you with all my heart."

The joy that crossed his face matched what was in her heart. He stood and pulled her to her feet. "Let's get out of here."

They laughed all the way to his rental car. He opened her door, and she scooted over to the middle. He grinned as he walked around the car and got in.

They drove out of town, and he parked at a rest area with a fantastic view of the mountains.

"Todd, it almost looks like you could reach out and touch them, doesn't it?"

"It does." He glanced down at her and smiled, then took her hand, rubbing his thumb across it. A tingling sensation ran up her arm, and she closed her eyes and breathed a sigh. "Todd, you said you thought you'd lost me. I felt the same about you."

He took a deep breath. "And I thought you'd fallen for that skater."

She shook her head. "Hardly."

"And you'll marry me?" He grinned. "I know you want to get your degree, and I want you to, but after that, will you marry me?"

"Yes, of course I will."

"Or better still, marry me first, then get your degree." He grinned. "How does that sound?"

Laughter bubbled up inside her. "Well, it's established we're getting married. We can work out the details later."

"You're right. Details later. But for now. . ." He reached

in his jacket pocket, and the next thing she knew, he was slipping a ring on her finger. The most beautiful ring she'd ever seen. She smiled. Maybe she'd be the only cousin wearing an engagement ring. A little laugh escaped her lips. There she went again.

He frowned. "You don't like the ring? I'll exchange it."

She reached up and touched his cheek. "It's the most beautiful ring in the world. I was laughing at myself."

Her heart beat wildly as he gazed at her. Then their lips met and Carla knew that no Olympic flame could burn brighter, and that Todd was more precious than any gold medal. And helping him turn the Berry Patch into something special? Now that would be true success.

Frances L. Devine grew up in the great state of Texas, where she wrote her first story at the age of nine. She moved to southwest Missouri more than twenty years ago and fell in love with the hills, the fall colors, and Silver Dollar City. Frances has always loved to read, especially cozy mysteries, and considers herself blessed to have the opportunity to write in her favorite genre. She is the mother of seven adult children and has fourteen wonderful grandchildren.

UNRAVELING LOVE

by Cynthia Hickey

Dedication

To God, for never failing to give me story ideas, to my husband and children for their support, and to my grandmothers who instilled the love of quilts in me.

And we know that in all things
God works for the good of those who love him,
who have been called according to his purpose.
Romans 8:28 NIV

Chapter 1

The 1965 Mustang sputtered, coughed, and died on the side of the road like a chunk of metal roadkill.

Zoe Barnes groaned and banged her forehead on the steering wheel. No. This could not be happening. Not now. She had less than a week until Saturday, the designated day to meet up with her cousins. Less than a week to fulfill Nana's dying wish.

She pounded the dashboard then swung the door open. No cars passed in either direction. Served her right for taking her ancient rattletrap of a car down the back roads. She thought it'd be easier not dealing with traffic. Now look at her. Stranded in the middle of Nowhere, New Mexico. Her cell phone sat, dripping and unusable, in the car's console where her soda cup had left a puddle of condensation. Where was a girl's knight in shining armor when she needed one?

Climbing from the car, she studied the lonely highway stretching toward a gray landscape in one direction and disappearing into the sunset in another. On the horizon loomed mountains she knew Old Suzy would never make it over, and Zoe couldn't find a way around no matter how many times she studied the map. She hadn't planned on the car croaking on a straight road.

She popped the hood and stared at the engine. What was she doing? She didn't have a clue what to look for. Tears sprang into her eyes as she leaned against the car. When she'd attended Nana's funeral a year ago, she never thought she'd return to Colorado Springs, much less at Nana's dying wish that the four cousins reunite to piece together a heritage quilt. Fear had struck Zoe with the force of a tornado. Go back home? The place she left with her tail between her legs while she and her mother watched the horizon from the rearview mirror?

Zoe hadn't been sure she could, even for Nana. She'd learned quilting from Nana, although she was never good enough at it to sew one. But God's persistent nudging spurred her into pulling the old car out of the garage and heading west. She'd planned a couple of days to sightsee before reuniting with her cousins. But now it didn't look like the excursion was a good idea.

No help for it, she'd have to start walking. She fingered the tiny diamond ring in her pocket and glanced at the setting sun. Then again, maybe it'd be better to sleep in the car until morning. She didn't want to get caught on a lonely highway at night.

A coyote howled, its mournful sound drifting across the desert. Zoe shivered and lunged inside the car. Standing outside made her a tempting dinner for a hungry beast. She glanced in the rearview mirror and frowned at the absence of headlights or the setting sun glinting off automobile windows. If she walked, should she head in the direction she wanted to go, or back to the one-horse town she'd passed through last? The coyote howled again. Nope. She'd stay put. Eventually someone would come by, and please, God, let it be a good guy. Or a woman. Yeah, a woman would be nice.

Horrible visions of atrocities heard on the nightly news flitted through her mind. Stories of women traveling alone who disappeared, never to be heard of again. Why hadn't she been more careful? She thought of her drowned phone. Her vulnerability at staying in the car scared her, but walking the deserted road frightened her more.

She pulled a nappy, faded Indian blanket from the backseat and draped it across the front of her against the evening chill. Surely, God would send someone to help her. She just needed to wait. *Please, God, don't let it be long.*

The sun disappeared and blackness engulfed her. Zoe was tempted to turn on the dome light, but the last thing she needed in addition to whatever was wrong under the Mustang's hood was a dead battery. She closed her eyes and dreamed of sunny days and how close she was to opening Zoe's Garden.

After saving and scrimping every available penny, all she needed now was a building. Oklahoma City had plenty of empty spaces for rent. A new city where no one knew her or her mother.

A knock sounded on her window. Her eyes snapped open, and she shrieked before shielding her eyes from a flashlight's blinding glare. The light clicked off, and a shadowy form took a step back.

Should she open the window? Get out of the car? Her heart pounded, threatening to burst free from its cage. She opted for cracking the car window. "Who are you?"

"Get out of the car, Zoe."

She gulped. "How do you know my name?" She fought to see through the night and the colored spots floating in front of her eyes. "If you're the police, I need to see your badge. If you're not the police, I want to see some identification."

The stranger slid a driver's license through the small slit in the open window. Zoe stared at the picture of the boy, now a man, who had haunted her dreams for the last twelve years. Dewayne Hofford.

"Do you need help? I noticed the hood's up." Footsteps crunched to the front of the car.

With a quick prayer for strength, Zoe opened the door and slid out, keeping the blanket tight around her. With slow steps, she joined the man studying her engine. He straightened and turned. Zoe's knees weakened. "Hello, Dewayne."

The last person Dewayne expected to see outlined in his flashlight's beam was Zoe Barnes, the girl who ditched him the night of high school graduation. He'd been tempted to leave her stranded, but the sight of her pretty face, peaceful in slumber, changed his mind. "One and the same. Didn't expect to see you out here."

"The feeling's mutual." From the surprised tone in her voice, he didn't have a hard time imagining the look of astonishment on her face.

He wished he could see her better. See whether her eyes were filled with gladness to see him or guilt over the way she'd left him waiting at the park with a picnic basket on an old quilt and a little velvet box in his pocket.

"Do you know what's wrong with it?" Zoe stepped closer, and Dewayne closed his eyes as her familiar perfume, something floral and musky, teased his nostrils.

"What did it do before it died?"

"Steam came from beneath the hood and it clunked. Then stopped."

"There isn't much I can do in the dark. Where are you headed?"

"Colorado Springs."

She was going home? He wanted to ask why, and decided it would be better if he didn't know. He'd help her get back on the road, and then walk away. That was the best way to protect his heart. "Where have you been all this time?"

"Oklahoma."

Obviously she was going to be stingy with information. "I can give you a ride back to Mesquite and take a look at it in the morning."

She sighed. "Is that the little town about twenty miles back? Do they even have a hotel?"

"If you want to call it that. They have one small motel with eight rooms. I'm sure they'll have a vacancy." He reached up and closed the hood then marched to his tow truck. "Grab your suitcase," he tossed over his shoulder. "I'll hook up your car. I was just returning from a tow."

Within minutes she'd placed her case in the back of his truck and climbed onto the passenger seat to wait for him. Twenty minutes later, the Mustang hitched up, he joined her.

He was tempted to turn on the light to see whether she'd changed. Not much, from the little he saw through the window. Well, he had. He was no longer a teenage boy with stars in his eyes and big dreams with her by his side. He turned the ignition and steered back onto the highway.

Zoe sat as close to the door as possible and stared out the window. Dewayne shook his head. He didn't mind the silence. Better than the alternative. He didn't want to know what she'd done in the last twelve years. Whether she missed him or not and if she cried when she'd deserted him.

"I'm surprised to see you moved out of Colorado Springs." She spoke softly, and he barely heard her over the country music on the radio. If she hadn't turned to look at him, he doubted he would have.

"Nothing left for me there." He gritted his teeth at the sarcastic tone coming from his mouth. No way would he let her know how much she'd hurt him.

"What kind of town is Mesquite?"

"About two hundred residents. I don't live there. Just passing through."

"Where do you live?"

"Anywhere between Denver and Albuquerque. I travel a lot, and stay in small rooms built onto the backs of my shops."

"Interesting."

He shrugged. Most likely she thought him a traveling vagabond. Well, he didn't care what she thought. He glanced in the rearview mirror, catching a glimpse of the suitcase leaning against the truck's bed. "How long are you staying in Colorado Springs?"

"Only a couple of nights." She stared back out the window. "I'm meeting my cousins."

"Have you kept in contact?" Dewayne steered for the access road.

"I haven't seen any of them since Nana's funeral." She faced him. "Why all the questions?"

"Just trying to pass the time. Doesn't matter. We'll be there in five minutes, and I'll take a look at your car."

"I appreciate this, Dewayne. I apologize if I'm keeping you from something."

He glanced sideways at her. Did he detect a trace of remorse in her words? "It's no problem." He pulled into Hofford Motors.

Her eyes widened. "You work here?"

He grinned. "I own it. This one and ten more. I'm in the process of buying number twelve. My lucky dozen."

Dewayne owned eleven automobile shops? Zoe glanced at the dark blond hair brushing his collar, the flannel shirt with sleeves rolled to his elbows, and faded blue jeans with the knees torn out. She'd thought he hadn't risen much above his simple childhood. How mistaken could one person be? Her cheeks heated, and she was grateful for the darkness.

At least, as the owner, he ought to be able to fix her car. Then she could get back on the road and get the family reunion over with. She couldn't deny seeing her cousins would be nice, but they'd asked too many questions at Nana's funeral. Questions Zoe didn't want to answer.

They pulled in front of a white stucco building with giant stalls lining the front. The rolling metal doors were painted in what Zoe thought might be a bright blue in the daylight. A sign, HOFFORD MOTORS, hung unlit above the building. Looked like Dewayne had managed to do all right for himself.

She glanced up and down the street. A coffee shop, a bookstore, and a corner grocery. That was about it. Across the street, she could see a pink blinking neon sign that shouted MES UITE MOT L. Wonderful.

She shoved open her door, slid out, then went to retrieve her suitcase. Dewayne pulled the truck inside one of the stalls and exited. He popped the hood on Old Suzy, rummaged around a few minutes, then straightened to wipe his hands on a greasy rag.

"Needs a new radiator. When was the last time you put antifreeze in?"

"I took it to a mechanic a couple days ago. Right before starting this trip." Zoe set down her bag and stepped toward him. "Can you fix it?"

"Yep. Have to order the part though. Will take at least three days." He grinned. "Won't be here before Thursday."

Did he think this was funny? "Can't you do something? Is there a bus station in this town?" She had really wanted time to explore her old haunts in Colorado.

"Yeah. But it's closed. You can see about getting a ticket in the morning." Dewayne tossed the rag on a wooden counter. "The motel most likely has a vacancy."

He'd said that before. Zoe frowned. "Most likely." She sighed. No help for it. She'd spend the night in a rundown motel and take the bus in the morning. If getting together with her cousins to sew a quilt had been important to Nana, then that's what Zoe was determined to do.

She turned as Dewayne stepped from the shop, his muscled form outlined by the streetlamp. Staying in the same town as him was not a good idea. The more time she spent with Dewayne Hofford, the more likely she'd have to explain what happened all those years ago. She didn't think her heart could take it.

Chapter 2

When Zoe exited her motel room the next morning, the parking lot sat empty except for a battered Toyota and an ancient Ford truck. She pulled the door shut behind her and clutched her suitcase. She was thankful the town wasn't large. Wouldn't take more than five minutes to walk to the bus depot. She wouldn't have to wait on the car part. She'd come back after her visit to Colorado Springs and pick up Old Suzy then.

Not wanting Dewayne to think she skipped out again without saying good-bye, she scanned Main Street. No sign of him or his tow truck. She shrugged. Maybe she'd have time to look him up and thank him for his help after she purchased a bus ticket. She stuck her hand in her pocket and fingered the ring. She wasn't sure how she felt about landing in probably one of the only towns where they could bump into each other. God definitely had a sense of humor.

Dewayne had always been good looking, but the years had been very kind to him. As impossible as it seemed, he'd gotten better with time. Shoulders wider, jaw more square, hair darkened to the color of ripe wheat. She gave herself a mental shake. They couldn't go back to what they'd once had. Some hurts ran too deep, and from the tone of his voice last night, she'd given him major pain.

She pulled her denim jacket tight against a chilly morning

breeze and marched to the bus depot. The motel manager had told her it was one block over and shared space with the post office. Overly warm air assaulted her as she stepped inside. The navy blue plastic seats filling the waiting area sat empty. Approaching the counter, Zoe pasted a smile on her face.

"Good morning. I'd like to purchase a ticket for Colorado Springs, please." She set her suitcase down and dug in her purse for her wallet.

"Bus doesn't come for another three days." The gray-haired woman behind the counter pushed wire-rimmed glasses farther up a red nose. "Will that be all right?"

"No." Zoe's smiled faded. "I need to leave today."

"Can't help you. Sorry." A phlegmy cough erupted from the teller's throat.

"But. . ."

"Sorry. Come back in three days." The woman sneezed, closed her window, and rolled her chair back.

Zoe was going to be late for the reunion with her cousins. She rolled her head on her shoulders, trying futilely to un-kink the stress knot. At least she had planned a few days of sightseeing. Not that Mesquite seemed to have a lot to offer.

If Zoe hadn't offered to work overtime at the flower shop, well. . . Excuses didn't matter, and she needed every spare dime to open her floral shop. Late was late. She'd need to call her cousins and let them know they might not be able to fulfill Nana's dying wish on the anniversary of her death after all. Her heart sank. Why couldn't one thing in life go as planned?

She stepped outside and squinted against the sun's glare. Coffee sounded good. She stepped off the curb and made her way down the street to a storefront that stated simply, MESQUITE COFFEE. She doubted she'd get a java up to her usual standards, but today she couldn't afford to be picky.

Frozen mocha drink in hand, Zoe chose a wrought-iron chair by the window and sipped her drink while watching the occasional car drive by. How did any business thrive in this town? Why would Dewayne build an automobile repair shop here? There couldn't be enough traffic to make the investment worthwhile.

Not like her plans of opening a floral shop in Oklahoma City. Plenty of business there.

Her thoughts turned to Colorado Springs and the quilt pieces she carried. Several of them were older than Nana had been. Nana hadn't been able to piece the quilt together, not with the feud between her daughters. Said she was waiting on the pieces from them and the granddaughters. Her dying wish was for the cousins to bring them all together and piece together not only the family heirloom, but the family itself.

On top of the stack in her suitcase sat Zoe's personal square. She'd labored over the design for weeks. She sighed. Who would get the completed quilt? Would it be another chasm between her mother and aunts? Would it cause problems between the four cousins?

Zoe glanced around for a phone. Nothing. And she hadn't seen a cell phone shop anywhere either. Maybe the clerk at the motel would let her make a long-distance call. She reached for her purse, and froze. Where was her suitcase?

Oh, no. She must've left it at the depot. Slinging her purse strap over her shoulder and clutching her icy drink, Zoe dashed across the street and barreled into the door. It didn't budge. Her coffee slipped from her hand and splashed to the sidewalk. She jumped back and glanced at the sign on the door. Closed due to illness? She glanced at the post office sign. It didn't open for another hour. What kind of town was this?

Cupping her hands around her eyes, she peered into the dim recesses on the other side of the window. No sign of her polka-dotted suitcase containing her precious quilt squares and clean clothing.

God, why'd you bring her back into my life? Zoe, with her dark hair shot with strands of gold and copper. Eyes that changed from blue to green with her change of emotions. He couldn't deny he still harbored feelings for her, but they belonged buried; shoved deep, where he'd stuffed them a long time ago.

Dewayne wanted to punch something. Instead, he pressed the button to open the stall door and listened as it rattled its way to the top. He climbed behind the wheel of his Explorer, backed the vehicle out, then closed the large metal door. He was a day behind schedule on checking his other shops. Why he chose to personally run the one in Mesquite when the manager needed time off to have surgery, only God knew. Maybe it was the peacefulness of the sleepy little town that saw more tourists than he could understand. People interested in the Mesas, canyons, and Indian ruins surrounding the area. Or maybe just people wanting to escape the hustle of city life. His home in Espanola wasn't much different. Both had small-town charm.

He steered down Main Street and turned at the town's one light. He slowed at the sight of Zoe on the sidewalk, hunched over, face buried in her hands. When he stopped and rolled down the passenger window, she lifted a tear-streaked face.

With a groan he closed his eyes, not wanting to be drawn

into another one of her disasters. But, he couldn't leave her there like a child who'd dropped her ice cream cone. He pulled into the nearest parking spot and within seconds stooped beside her.

With his hands dangling between his knees, he peered sideways at her. "What's up?"

"I've lost my suitcase." Zoe sniffled then pulled a Kleenex from her purse. "I accidentally left it at the depot, they don't have a bus coming for three days, and when I returned, my bag was gone. There's a sign saying they're closed because of illness. What kind of town is this?"

"So, you're set back a few days."

She glared. "You don't understand! There are quilt squares in my case that need to be in Colorado Springs by Saturday." Her sobs began anew.

"Why?" What could be so important about a few scraps of fabric?

"Nana's dying wish was that the cousins and I get together on the anniversary of her death and piece together the last quilt she designed. She divided the pieces between her daughters, hoping they'd get together and make up over a stupid fight they had. They didn't, and now it's up to us to bring them back together." She jumped to her feet. "I don't expect you to understand. It's sentimental."

His neck heated. "I understand sentimental." Most likely more than she did. He stood. "Come on. Let me buy you a burger."

"It's ten o'clock in the morning." Zoe blew her nose.

"Then I'll buy whatever you want." He gripped her elbow and steered her toward the Mesquite Café.

"Is everything in this town named after a tree?" Zoe

yanked free. "I'm not hungry, Dewayne. I'm upset. I have to find my bag and meet my cousins!"

"Call them and tell them you'll be late."

"My cell phone is temporarily out of service." She brushed past him and into the diner.

Man, she was full of gloom today. The sun disappeared behind a cloud as if hiding from her. Dewayne followed her into the diner and waved her toward a booth. The aromas of bacon, eggs, and biscuits filled the air, along with the soothing sound of murmured voices and the shouts of food orders. "You'll feel better with something to eat."

"No, I won't." She slid onto the red vinyl seat.

"We'll find your bag. It's probably waiting behind the counter for you to claim." Dewayne waved to the waitress, Doris. The woman seemed stuck in the sixties, with a beehive hairdo teased so high there was no telling what hid in it. "Two burger specials, please."

"Sure thing, sweetie." Doris nodded and disappeared through a swinging door.

Zoe laid her head back against the seat. "There are more people in here than I've seen in the entire town."

Dewayne chuckled. "Yeah, the diner does a good business. The locals use it mostly, but there are plenty of tourists visiting Indian ruins to generate enough income to keep it open."

She propped her chin in her hand. "I'm sorry for being so rude and hard to get along with."

"That's all right. You've had a setback and lost something important to you."

Doris arrived with sodas and plunked them on the table then left to get the rest of their order. Zoe twirled her straw in her cup, looking dejected.

Grabbing his own drink to hide behind, Dewayne allowed himself the freedom to study her. She was beautiful and belonged in the past. Not sitting at a table with him, looking like she'd lost her best friend. "Tell me again what's so important that it can't wait a day?"

"My Nana's quilt." She gazed up with red-rimmed eyes.

His gut lurched.

"I'm meeting my cousins to fulfill Nana's dying wish." Zoe took a sip of her soda. "She wanted us to reunite and stitch the pieces together, along with squares that each of us made personally. How can I let my cousins know I've lost everything? I'm always the one who messes up." A tear escaped and rolled down her cheek.

Dewayne clutched his cup tighter in order to prevent himself from wiping the tear away. He didn't know what to say. He couldn't tell her that she didn't mess everything up, because she did. She'd broken his heart twelve years ago. He didn't want to care that she was hurting now. But he did. He sighed and reached across the table to lay his hand on hers.

She pulled free, like a turtle returning to its shell, and shoved her hand in her pocket. He'd noticed her fiddling with something earlier. Maybe one of those worry stones. The Zoe he used to know was a little high-strung. Maybe she'd found something to help calm her.

He'd let her have it her way. He crossed his arms and leaned back, the vinyl seat creaking under him. She squirmed under his gaze, not looking at him even after the waitress brought their orders.

Snatching a french fry from his plate, he sighed. "So, are you going to tell me why you ditched me graduation night, or not?"

Chapter 3

Zoe spewed soda across the table and down the front of Dewayne's T-shirt. She grabbed her napkin and blotted the mess from the table. "Why now, Dewayne?"

"Why not?" He swirled his fry in a puddle of ketchup, piercing her with a stare.

How could he look so calm? She couldn't think with his sky-blue gaze fixated on her like she was a goldfish in a bowl and he was the sinister cat. "Graduation was a long time ago."

"Exactly. So, there shouldn't be a problem with you clearing up a few things." He popped the fry in his mouth.

Zoe tore her gaze away from his lips and wadded up the soaked napkin, diverting her attention to the sprays of soda across his shirt. No way would she reach across and wipe them from his chest. His hand on hers moments ago was physical contact enough. She let out a shuddering sigh and pushed her plate aside.

"Remember the man my mother was dating at the time?"

Dewayne nodded. "Vaguely. A mean drunk."

"Well. . ." How could she tell him how rotten her life turned so quickly? "He turned abusive after he lost his job. Then with the falling out between her sisters and her, Mom packed up and we shipped out. I had to go or be left behind." Zoe lifted tear-filled eyes. "I couldn't let her leave alone. She's always been unstable. You know that."

"You could've told me something!" Dewayne slapped the table. "Not a word, a note, a phone call. Nothing."

"I'm sorry." Zoe hung her head, appetite completely gone.

"We were going to get married, Zoe." His face reddened. "Don't you think I would've helped you and your mother?"

"I was embarrassed."

"Why?"

"You wouldn't understand."

"Then help me understand." He shoved his plate against hers.

"There's so much I didn't tell even you, Dewayne." What would he think of her once he heard what she had to say? "I lied about my father dying. Mom doesn't know who he is. Do you know what that's like? Wondering if every man you see on the street could be your father?" She rubbed the tears from her eyes hard enough to see spots.

"I wouldn't have cared."

"I cared. Then, when Mom wanted to break off with her latest, he said he'd kill her." Zoe waved a hand. "Not that I think he would have, but Mom was scared. She wanted to leave and have a fresh start. At least that's what she told me. In reality, she just went from one man to another. She needed me to protect her from herself."

Dewayne upended his soda and drained the plastic cup before slamming it back on the table. He stood. "I'll be back." He whirled and slammed through the door of the men's restroom.

Zoe choked back a sob and stared out the window. A rusty Ford truck rumbled down the street. An elderly couple, hand-in-hand, strolled outside an antique store. What would that be like? To be with someone until old age and still be in love? Her mother hadn't been a good role model in the love between a man and a woman department. Zoe propped her chin in her hand. Dewayne was right. She should've told him. But by the time they settled in Oklahoma, too much time had passed, and she didn't know what to say.

If not for God and the words found in Romans 8:28, Zoe wasn't sure she wouldn't have followed in dear Mom's footsteps. She sighed. Mom cleaned up, Zoe almost had the funds to start her own business, and life turned out okay after all, right?

Dewayne stormed out of the restroom. Well, almost all right. Seeing Dewayne again brought back all the love and pain she tried to shove away.

Sliding onto the seat across from her, he released his breath in a heavy puff that ruffled Zoe's bangs. "So now what?"

"What do you mean?"

"You go to Colorado, then return here when your car's fixed, and that's it? You leave again forever?" A muscle jerked in the corner of his eye.

Was it? Did she want to try to salvage what they once had? Could they? She studied the face she'd loved above all others. Eyes that could see to her soul, broad shoulders, strong arms that held her during many crying jags, and that cleft in the chin she loved to kiss. It would be impossible. A fleeting dream.

She fingered the ring in her pocket. *Wouldn't it, God?*

Dewayne glanced out the window at the bus stop. Three more days? No way. She had to go before then. First thing would be to find her suitcase. Then he could drive her to the next town and put her on a bus there. In a few days, the new radiator would be in, he'd fix her car, and when she returned for it, they'd part ways and he'd never see her again. His stomach sank. Wasn't that what he wanted? To go on with his life, not worrying about Zoe? No, he might ping-pong between wanting her to go and wanting her to stay, but he was really hoping if she spent time with him, she would want to stay. Any idea other than that was a lie. He wanted to continue their conversation. Demand she explain why she left him, but something held him back. Possibly the tears in her eyes, the major thing that always made him back down during an argument with her. No, he'd asked his questions. It was up to her to answer or not.

"Remember my dream of opening a floral shop?" Zoe smoothed the white pieces of her torn up napkin into a mound beside her plate.

How could he forget? They'd spent many hours during high school talking about her dream. "Yes."

"It's almost a reality. I'm waiting on financing approval. Not that they can get a hold of me without my cell phone." She waved a hand. "Sorry. You must be getting tired of my doom-and-gloom attitude." Picking up her burger, she shrugged. "No sense in letting good food go to waste."

"What's your company's name?"

"Zoe's Garden." She bit into the bacon cheeseburger. "Mmm. Good. You never mentioned wanting to own repair shops."

He chuckled. "Remember that street rod I had?" At her nod, he continued. "I got addicted to axle grease. There's nothing better than taking a car that doesn't run and making it purr. God smiled on me, and now I own several shops."

"Looks like we've both achieved our dreams." Zoe's smile didn't reach her eyes. She stuck her hand in her pocket again.

"What do you keep fiddling with?" Dewayne handed his plate to the passing waitress.

Her face paled. Slowly she withdrew her hand and opened her fingers. Sparkling from the center of her palm, rested the promise ring Dewayne gave her their senior year.

Chapter 4

"You still have my ring?" Dewayne's heart beat faster than the country swing dance at the VFW hall on a Saturday night. His mouth went dry.

Zoe shrugged. "Funny, huh?"

"Why?" Dewayne ran his fingers through his hair. The sight of the simple diamond chip set in a silver band threatened to steal his mind. *What are You doing to me, Lord?* He had long ago faced the painful fact Zoe wasn't meant to be his. Now here she sat, mere inches away, his ring glittering in her hand.

She rolled the glistening circle. "I wasn't ready to give it up. I knew I had to help Mom. I spent more time taking care of her than she did me. I knew it would hurt you, but I couldn't give it back." She closed her fingers and thrust her fist forward. "Here."

"I don't want it!" He lunged to his feet and marched out the door. No way could he survive three days in her company, nor could he drive away and leave her behind. Glancing over his shoulder, he realized he'd left Zoe to pay for their meal.

Dewayne pounded his thigh. What an idiot, leaving her to pick up the tab. She stood at the counter, wallet in hand.

The sun shone bright, despite a slight autumn chill. Golden oak leaves skittered across the cracked asphalt and rested against the office door of the motel. Dewayne straightened when Zoe exited the diner. "Come on. I bet your suitcase is at the motel."

"Why?"

"Because if I know Wanda, when she closed the bus depot due to illness, she stashed it there, thinking you'd wait the three days."

She followed him to the motel, where they were greeted with a sign stating the clerk would be back in an hour. The joys of small-town life. Now what was Dewayne supposed to do with her?

He glanced sideways at her. "Want to go into Espanola to see about getting you a cell phone? I mean, it'll take an hour, but the clerk will be back by then."

"Sure." Her fingers wiggled in her pocket.

Dewayne grimaced. He ought to demand she toss the ring in the garbage, but couldn't bring himself to do so. For twelve years she'd used it as a worry stone. He wouldn't stop her now. His emotions wavered from wanting to spend time with her to wanting to ditch her at the first opportunity. His head didn't know if he was coming or going where Zoe was concerned.

"I've got a bike in the garage. Wanna ride that?"

Her face lit up. "I haven't been on the back of a bike since high school. I'd love to."

"Wait here." Dewayne sprinted across the road and unlocked his scarlet red Harley Fat Bob. Maybe not the most elaborate or bad boy motorcycle, but he loved zipping down New Mexico's highways on his Bob. Grabbing an extra helmet and a leather jacket that would provide more warmth than the hoodie Zoe wore, he rolled his baby into the sunshine.

Zoe's squeal pierced his eardrum. "You just made my day, Dewayne. I'm so excited." She hitched her purse more securely over her shoulder and climbed on.

It wasn't until she was perched up there like a smiling canary that Dewayne realized he'd be riding with Zoe plastered against his back. He froze.

Zoe frowned. "Come on. What are you waiting for?" The man stood there like a marble statue. She almost clapped her hands. On the back of a Harley! It'd been such a long time. The leather seat cradled her bottom. There wasn't a back rest so she'd have to. . . *Oh, Lord, help me.* She'd be against Dewayne's back the whole time. No wonder he looked dumbstruck. Maybe it wasn't such a good idea after all. She moved to slide off.

"What are you doing?" Dewayne pulled a helmet over his head.

"I thought you'd changed your mind."

"Nope." He handed her a fire-engine-red helmet. "This might be a little big, but it ought to still protect you. And this jacket is warmer than what you're wearing."

"Thanks." Obviously, he'd gotten over whatever bothered him. Zoe donned the protective gear. She must've been mistaken. The fact she'd be glued against him for more than an hour didn't seem to have any effect on Dewayne. Fine. She tightened her chinstrap. She wouldn't let it bother her either.

Dewayne slid on in front of her and gunned the throttle. Zoe rested her hands lightly on his waist. Nothing said she needed to be glued to him, right? But when the cycle shot forward, she yelped and tightened her hold. She was doomed.

He hadn't bothered to don a jacket, and his cologne, something woodsy smelling, teased her nostrils. The feel of his strong back beneath her cheek and his taut abdomen under her hands thrust her into the past. Somewhere she had no desire to go. Then why did she keep his ring all these years? She'd asked herself that a million times to no avail.

Mesas and cacti zipped past her line of vision as they roared down the highway. A silver sports car honked and raced ahead. Zoe closed her eyes, lost in memory of her in shorts on the back of Dewayne's Yamaha. Back when innocence and youth ruled their lives. They'd ride to the river to picnic, neck, and dream. Until her mother told her they were leaving, and Zoe allowed fear to rule her head.

Well, she was here now. Let God do what He would.

She shook herself from the memories when Dewayne slowed in front of a cell phone store in Espanola. It wasn't her normal carrier, but it would at least give her the opportunity to call her cousins and let them know of her predicament. Of course, she could have probably used Dewayne's phone, but not having her own cell phone made her feel disconnected. She slid from the motorcycle. Her Jell-O legs threatened to give way.

"I'll hurry. I'll get one of those pay-as-you-go phones then duck into that clothing store next door for something to wear besides these jeans, and we'll be all set." She removed the helmet and handed it to him.

He gave her a lopsided grin. "No hurry."

She rolled her eyes and marched into the store. Thirty minutes later, she emerged with a new cell phone then went into the clothing store. After purchasing two changes of clothing, she exited to see Dewayne eating an ice cream cone at a café across the street. She frowned.

"Don't worry. I've got you a swirl one right here." He

pulled his hand from behind his back and handed her the cone. "Saw you checking out. It's the least I can do after leaving you to pay for breakfast."

"Thank you." Her face heated as their fingers brushed. She sat in a black wrought-iron chair across from him and hated how he still affected her. "Kind of chilly for ice cream, but very thoughtful."

"Never too cold for ice cream."

She averted her eyes from his mouth as he took a bite. What was wrong with her? The last thing she needed was to resume a relationship with a past love. And in the last twenty-four hours, they'd spent way too much time together. Maybe she didn't want the Lord to lead where He would after all. Not if it meant chancing another broken heart.

Zoe focused on her mix of chocolate and vanilla. What if he decided to hurt her in retaliation for her leaving him twelve years ago? Pain radiated from him every time their gazes met. But could the kindhearted boy she knew have turned into a hard-hearted man? She cut him a sideways glance.

No. Revenge wasn't in Dewayne.

"Now that I have a phone, I need to call my cousins and let them know the situation." Wouldn't it blow their minds to know she was hanging out with Dewayne? Finished with the ice cream, she wrapped the waffle cone in her napkin and tossed it in the nearby garbage can.

She needed her suitcase and a bus ticket. Those were the only things that could protect her. With those in hand, she'd leave Mesquite, and Dewayne, far behind. Now, to convince her heart it was the right thing to do.

Chapter 5

Zoe lay in bed the next morning, blinking eyes gritty from a restless night between scratchy sheets. Who decorated these highway motels anyway? Orange paisley bedspread and green shag carpet? Ugh. Just as ugly the second night. A picture of the seventies, and not a favorable one at that. She glanced at her phone. Nine o'clock! When was the last time she'd stayed in bed past seven?

She'd left phone messages with her cousins the night before, explaining her predicament, that she still planned on being there by Saturday, then flipped aimlessly through the few channels available on the television. Her mind returned time and again to wondering what Dewayne was doing. What his house looked like. Was he thinking of her? Until she'd wanted to throw something at the wall.

The morning didn't promise to be any better. Remnants of last night's dreams left her wanting to shake herself. How was she going to survive two more days—and nights—before the bus traveled through Mesquite?

She groaned and tossed aside the blankets. Next time she had somewhere to go, she'd definitely think twice about taking the scenic route. And so much for keeping Old Suzy in what she thought was mint condition. What could God possibly mean by stranding Zoe in Mesquite? He works all things for the good of those who love Him, who are called according to His purpose. She knew that. So what good could possibly come from being stranded in the middle of nowhere? Was having her stranded God's plan for her and Dewayne to resume their relationship?

Moving to the bathroom, she reached up and turned on the shower. A barely lukewarm trickle splashed over her fingers. Zoe sighed. What she wouldn't give for a five-star hotel and hang the cost. She rolled her neck on her shoulders then pulled off the oversized T-shirt she'd slept in and let it fall to the floor. At least the cold water would help her wake up to face the day.

After her shower, Zoe toweled off, pulled on jeans, her new long-sleeved T-shirt, and a black hoodie before sticking her wet hair into a ponytail and shuffling to the shabby lobby for a free cup of coffee. Two more days of this?

"Miss Barnes?"

Zoe turned to see the motel manager headed her way with her red-polka-dotted suitcase bouncing on the cracked sidewalk. "You found it?" With a bounce in her step, she fairly skipped to the middle-aged woman.

"Someone turned it in this morning. Said it was left at the depot, and since you said you lost yours, well. . ." She handed it over. "I assumed it's yours."

"Thank you so much!" Zoe's heart leaped. Now, if only she had a way to Colorado Springs.

Dewayne's Hummer pulled into the parking lot across the street. Zoe grinned. Maybe there was a way, if she paid him to drive her. Coffee forgotten, she rushed across the street, her suitcase bumping behind her. "Someone found my suitcase!"

He turned, truck keys dangling from his hand. "Wonderful!" His smile lit up his eyes. "You're all set, once you get a ticket." His smile faded.

"Oh." Her shoulders slumped. Did she really have to ask? Of course she did. Why would Dewayne offer to drive her after all she'd put him through? Suddenly, her idea didn't sound like such a good one. "Two more days until the bus comes, right?"

"That's it. Then you can do what you've got to do, come back when I've replaced your radiator, and never have to step foot here again."

She stiffened at the coldness in his voice. Had dreams of what they'd once had plagued him last night, too? "Yeah, I guess so."

"You don't sound too excited." Dewayne unlocked the door to his office. "Want some coffee? I'm getting ready to put on a pot."

"Yes, please." She set the suitcase right inside the door and glanced around the sparsely furnished office. A metal desk, clear of clutter. A matching filing cabinet filled one corner beside a rickety table on which sat a coffeepot and Styrofoam cups. Two vinyl green chairs finished off the decor. "You don't spend a lot of time here, do you?"

He shook his head. "I actually live in Espanola, when I'm not traveling, which isn't very often. The man I hired to manage this location is on sick leave." He measured grounds, stepped out of the room, and then returned with the pot filled with water and set it all to work. "Won't take but a few minutes. Have a seat."

"Thanks." She plopped in one of the uncomfortable visitor chairs. Did no one in this town have an inkling of decorating sense?

Dewayne reclined behind his desk, arms crossed, avoiding her gaze. An uncomfortable silence filled the room. Zoe's palms began to sweat despite the coolness of the day.

"How's your mother?" he asked.

"She died of liver failure last year." Something else Zoe failed to change. Her mother's drinking habits. She'd stopped running around with men, even attended church with Zoe, but couldn't stop the drinking. The knowledge still pierced. Zoe felt as if she had failed somehow.

"I'm sorry." He leaped up to grab two cups and filled them with coffee. "Cream and sugar?"

"Please." She sighed. She needed to just blurt out her question. She'd opened her mouth to do so when Dewayne handed her a cup and spoke again.

He nodded at her suitcase. "Are the quilt squares in there?"

"I haven't checked." How could she not after going on about them the way she had? She set her cup on the desk then reached for the case and pulled it toward her. Opening it, she pulled out a handful of embroidered squares in multiple patterns and every color of the rainbow.

"Here's mine." She showed him the white square with Romans 8:28 in red, and roses embroidered around the edges.

"Why that verse?" Dewayne lifted his drink for a sip.

"It's my life verse." Zoe replaced the quilt pieces then zipped the bag closed again. "After Mom and I left Colorado, a new friend invited me to church. The pastor spoke about God turning everything to good. I've found out that He actually does. Even leaving everything I knew turned out for the good. Mom changed her life, for the most part, I found God, and I'm very close to opening my own business."

He stared at her without speaking, shrugged, and moved

back to his desk. "I've got work to do. Feel free to hang out, but I won't be much company."

"Did you find God in the last twelve years?" Zoe's heart rate increased. Why did she insist on keeping the conversation going when obviously he didn't want to talk? Because she had nowhere to go, that's why. And if Dewayne had managed to find God after Zoe left, then she could resume her life knowing someone greater than her cared for him.

"Yep. Joined a young men's group after you left." He opened a drawer and pulled out some papers.

Wow. The Dewayne she once knew didn't have time for church or God.

She sighed. Might as well get it over with. "I'll pay you to drive me to Colorado Springs."

"Storm's coming."

She was absolutely clueless. How plainer could Dewayne get that he didn't want to be thrust into her company? Her presence dredged up feelings he'd rather leave buried.

She glanced out the window at the darkening clouds. "Just looks like rain."

"Could be different in the mountains." Dewayne flipped through the service receipts on his desk.

"Please. I really want to get to Colorado Springs without arriving at the last minute. My cousins said they'd wait, but it really isn't fair to them." Her amazing eyes widened.

He closed his eyes, knowing he'd lost the battle before it began, and released a heavy puff of breath. He never could deny her anything. He'd give her the moon, and a new ring, if she'd let him. "You don't have to pay me. I guess I could check on the possibility of opening a shop up there. I've been toying with the idea for a few months. When do you want to leave?"

"Now? It won't take me but a few minutes to check out of the motel." She grinned. "You're a lifesaver. I'm know I'm putting you in an awful bind." She took a sip of her coffee. "We can wait a while to leave. Let you get things straightened away here."

"I've got no jobs other than yours. It won't hurt to close the shop for a day. Go check out."

She set the coffee mug on his desk then dashed out the door, leaving Dewayne feeling like a lost fool and hating how his heart responded to her smile.

If he thought being in the same town was tough, how was he going to survive for hours with her in his Hummer? He needed his head examined. *Lord, what am I doing?*

He glanced out the window to see Zoe disappear into the motel lobby. So much for catching up on paperwork. He tossed their cups in the garbage, grabbed her suitcase, tossed it in the back of his Hummer, and then leaned against the car to wait for her. He eyed the clouds overhead and prayed they wouldn't get stuck in a mountain storm. He called his shop in Espanola and asked for one of the guys to drive over and watch the one here in Mesquite. Finished, he glanced back toward the motel.

Zoe dashed out of the lobby and into a room three doors down. Minutes later, she appeared with a paper grocery sack in her hand and raced across the street without checking for traffic. "I'm ready. Do you need to grab anything?"

"Nope. Always keep a change of clothes in the truck." He took the bag from her and set it in the backseat.

"I really appreciate this, Dewayne. More than you know."

She opened the passenger door and slid inside.

"No problem." He climbed behind the steering wheel.

"Don't lie. It's a big inconvenience to you, and I'm sorry. Maybe you could just drop me off at the next town and I'll take the bus from there."

"Fine. It's a big inconvenience, but I said I would do it, and I will."

She snapped her seat belt. "Can't you accept my thanks? What's wrong with you? I've made you mad."

"Nothing's wrong, and I'm not mad." He was terrified. Scared to death of a several-hour drive with Zoe. He hooked his own seat belt, started the engine, and backed from the shop garage, glad he'd filled the vehicle's tank earlier that morning. He was acting childish, but even knowing that, he couldn't stop. Torn between wanting her to stay and wanting her to go, he didn't know which end was up. "I didn't sleep well last night."

"Me either," she mumbled, turning to look out the window.

Guilty conscience, maybe? Dewayne gave himself a mental shake. Stop being so petty! What was done, was done. Twelve years ago. They had their own lives now, and clearly Zoe didn't want to resume a relationship with him. Maybe someone waited for her in Oklahoma.

He had to know. "Do you have a boyfriend?"

She jerked around. "Why would you ask that?"

"Just making conversation." He steered the Hummer toward the freeway.

"No, I don't. You? A girlfriend, I mean?"

He shook his head. "I travel too much for a serious relationship." He pulled into a convenience store.

"Do we need gas?"

"Nope." He turned off the ignition and pushed open his door. "I hadn't planned on taking a trip. We'll need snacks and drinks."

She shoved open her door. "I'll get it—in payment for your driving, which I insist on reimbursing you for, plus your time." She bounded into the store.

He shook his head and closed his door, hoping she'd get something other than pastries.

When she returned with loaded arms, he exited the car to help her, and peered into the bags. Chips, bottled water, protein bars, energy drinks, candy, she'd thought of everything. "Good job."

"I grabbed a variety of stuff." She returned to her seat as the first raindrops splattered the windshield. "I remember how you like to snack when you're driving."

Chapter 6

Boredom forced Zoe to open a bag of chips before they'd gone thirty miles down Interstate 25. She really needed to think about eating healthier.

Dewayne's silence filled the car with ice and Zoe with dread. How was she going to survive the drive with someone who clearly resented her? By now, she would've thought he'd have managed to put the past behind him.

She stole a glance at his rock-solid profile. A muscle twitched next to his eye. Obviously breathing the same air as her set him on edge. Her feelings on the matter were as tangled as the threads on her first quilt. One moment she wanted him to keep his distance, the other she wanted them to resume some kind of friendship. After all, they'd loved each other once. At least she had. She stuck her hand in her pocket. Still did, if she were honest with herself.

Glancing out the window, she sighed. No chance for a rekindling of what they'd once had. She'd hurt Dewayne too deep. Besides, he most likely wouldn't want to move to Oklahoma, and she wasn't sure she'd want to start over somewhere else. Not that he'd ask.

"Stop playing with the ring." Dewayne's words cut to her soul.

Zoe snatched her hand out of her pocket. "Sorry."

"I don't understand why you've kept it." The Hummer surged forward.

She leaned to look at the speedometer. The needle crept toward eighty-five. "Should you slow down?"

He growled and eased off the pedal. A gust of wind shook the Hummer and pelted the windshield with raindrops. His knuckles whitened on the steering wheel. Zoe glanced again at the speedometer, relieved to see it lower again.

Why did she keep the ring? Something from a happier time she loathed to part with? Probably. A sign she still had feelings for Dewayne? Most likely.

The rain came across the plains in a gray sheet of water. Old Suzy would've died of fright with the ferocity of the winds. Zoe chuckled at how she thought of her car as a living thing. Still, the Mustang wouldn't have braved the winds like the larger Hummer.

"Well? Why did you?" Dewayne said, reminding her that avoiding the question wasn't an answer.

She shrugged. "You gave it to me in love. I don't toss that away lightly."

"No, you only toss away people."

"That's not fair. I explained my reasons for leaving."

"You could've told me then. Or called. Something. Maybe I would've gone with you."

"By the time we got to Oklahoma, I didn't know what to say." Tears threatened to clog her throat. "I'm sorry."

He grunted.

"You still love me." She stared at him through blurry vision.

"No." He cut a quick glance in her direction. "I'm in love with what could've been."

Her fiddling with his ring ate at him like termites in an old house. With bad weather coming in, he didn't need the distraction of the ring or the perfume that drifted his way every time she moved. He couldn't be positive, but he thought it was the same scent she wore in high school. Something floral and musky. Totally Zoe.

"Can you grab me a Coke?" He motioned his head toward the bag at Zoe's feet. The drink wouldn't be cold, but he needed the caffeine after the sleepless night he'd just had. "Wait," he said as she plunged her hand into the bag.

A gas station loomed ahead of them, and Dewayne steered the Hummer to the side of the building. "Be right back." He shoved open his door and dashed through the increasing rain toward the restroom.

Once inside, he locked the door and planted his hands on each side of the chipped porcelain sink. With head bowed, he stared at the rust stains around the drain. What made him think he could do this? He wanted to grab Zoe and shake some sense into her. Make her see that he still loved her, despite what he said. But every minute spent in her company ripped him apart. *God, what do You want me to do?*

Dewayne pounded the sink. Shards of pain ripped through his fists. He'd tell her. Sometime between here and Colorado Springs, he'd lay his heart open and let her know he still loved her. He'd open a business in Oklahoma, or she could move to New Mexico. Or they could start fresh in Colorado. Having that ring in her pocket meant something. Meant she still felt something for him.

Resolved, with a plan in place, he splashed cold water on his face and raced back through the rain to his car. Zoe glanced at him then transferred her attention back to the window. Another thing he liked about her. She didn't always feel the need to talk, like some women did. But today, he *needed* to fill the silence with words. Get to know the woman he could've spent the last twelve years with.

"Tell me about your store." He headed north on the interstate.

She gave him a puzzled look then shrugged. "I got a job in a florist shop right after Mom and I settled in Oklahoma. It's relaxing. All I need is my share of the inheritance from Nana, and my dream becomes a reality. I don't know how much Nana left us, but it will help sway the bank in my favor."

"Have you signed a lease on a store front?"

"No, just have a place chosen."

Good. Dewayne smiled. With her mother passed on and no lease signed, Zoe had no obligations keeping her from moving. And they had several hours ahead of them for Dewayne to convince her to stay.

"When was the last time you saw your cousins?"

Zoe ripped open a candy bar. "At the funeral last year. We talk on the phone sometimes and e-mail. Why all the questions?"

"Just passing the time. Was there ever. . .anyone else? Besides me, I mean?"

She sighed and looked out the window again. "No." After a moment, she spoke, her question barely heard over the increasing storm outside. "You?"

"Nope. Dated casually a few times." He increased the speed on the windshield wipers. "If this keeps up, we might have to pull over for a while and wait out the storm."

Zoe narrowed her eyes and leaned forward to peer out the front window. "It's getting really dark outside."

"Not looking good." Dewayne frowned. He should've listened to his instincts when he'd seen the clouds earlier.

"How did you know from the clouds in a town hours away that this would happen in the mountains?" Zoe finished her candy, tossed the wrapper back in the bag, and crossed her arms around her middle, still studying the sky.

"I've pulled lots of stranded motorists off this interstate."

"Can the Hummer handle it?"

Dewayne chuckled. "This baby can handle anything."

"Okay." She didn't sound convinced, but leaned against the door and closed her eyes.

For the next hour, the wind continued to buffet the Hummer like a cat with a toy. Headlights shone through the back window and reflected off the rearview mirror. A large truck barreled down the interstate behind them, sending plumes of water from its tires. Dewayne steered closer to the shoulder of the road to let the maniac pass. Only idiots drove like that in bad weather.

"What's wrong?" Zoe cracked an eyelid. "How long have I been sleeping?"

"About an hour. There are signs signaling construction ahead, so we might arrive later than originally planned." Dewayne drove back onto the asphalt. "It doesn't help when you have a moron speeding on a wet highway."

"You've been driving for a while. Do you want me to take over?" Zoe straightened.

"No, go back to sl—" He cut a sideways glance.

"Look out!" Zoe braced her hands against the dashboard.

Taillights loomed in front of the window. Dewayne yanked the steering wheel to the right, and prayed.

Chapter 7

Zoe grabbed the strap above the passenger-side door and screamed as the Hummer bounced off the asphalt, hit something solid, and rolled. Her eyes popped open as her head banged against the window, illuminating the darkening afternoon with multicolored spots in front of her eyes. "Dewayne!"

The vehicle slammed into the side of a hill and leaned against a large dirt mound. Muddy water dripped through cracks in the window. From Zoe's left and slightly above her, she heard Dewayne groan. Using her door as leverage, she unhooked her seat belt and straightened, gasping at a pain in her side where her body had slammed into the door handle. The door was caved in from the impact with the mound of dirt outside. "Dewayne, are you all right?" Her head pounded.

"Yeah. Are you?"

"I think so. Where are we?" She put a hand to her head, feeling something warm and slick.

"Raton Pass. Near the Colorado border." He groaned again and shifted. "There should be a flashlight in the glove compartment. We'll need it soon. I'd turn on the overhead light, but don't want to waste the car battery. Hopefully, we'll be able to leave when the traffic is cleared."

Zoe scooted around until she could reach the glove box. After some banging, it popped open. No way would she get it closed again. She fumbled around inside until her hand closed around a heavy-duty flashlight. *Please work.* She pressed the button and illuminated the interior of the cab.

Dewayne clutched his ribcage. A purplish knot rose on his forehead. "Come closer. Lean your weight over here. Maybe we can set the car back on four wheels."

Ice water ran through her veins. What if they couldn't? What if they slid farther in the other direction? She scooted closer, all but sitting on Dewayne's lap. The Hummer fell back with a thud.

"Feels like we've got a couple of flat tires," Dewayne said. "Look out the window. See if you can tell what happened."

"We almost plowed into somebody, last I remember." Zoe climbed to the backseat and shoved open the door enough to peer out into the pouring rain. If she hadn't whined so much about getting to Colorado, they wouldn't be in this fix and Dewayne wouldn't be moaning in pain.

She shone the light through the opening in the door, and gasped. Cars lay crooked and tossed as if a young child had finished playing with them. She searched in the opposite direction. The same scene mocked her. No one would go anywhere anytime soon. Where had all these cars come from? She pressed the button to light up the face of her watch. Weekend travelers? Thank God, Dewayne's quick reflexes on sending them into the ditch kept them from taking out someone else's car.

Pulling the door shut, she climbed back to the front seat and transferred her attention to Dewayne.

He waved a hand. "I'm all right. My ribs are sore, and the breath got knocked out of me, but I'm okay. You're not." He brushed his fingers across her forehead. "You're bleeding."

"And you might have a concussion." She'd forgotten her head's contact with the window. Now the pain came back in a throbbing rush. Maybe they both had concussions.

"No, I'm fine. There are napkins in the console." He struggled to a sitting position, lifted the lid of the console between the bucket seats, and pulled out a handful of paper napkins. Then he grabbed a bottle of water. "Let me take care of you."

Tears stung her eyes. When was the last time somebody had said those words to her?

"Oh, baby, don't cry." Dewayne wrapped his arms around her and pulled her to his chest. "Are you hurt anywhere besides your head?"

She wanted to say yes. Instead, she shook her head. "Just the adrenaline wearing off, I guess. It's a mess out there. The Hummer looks okay, from what I could see, now that we're back on all four tires, but we're blocked in by other cars."

"We'll hold tight until morning. Things will be cleared by then. I'll call 911 and a tow truck, and we'll get back on the road." He wet a napkin and dabbed at her forehead.

She winced and pulled back to give him easier access. "Do I need stitches?"

"I don't think so."

"What happened?" She moved back to the passenger seat. "All I saw was the back of a semi in the front window."

"Good news is we didn't hit it. My best guess is, someone lost control. When I saw cars scattering and colliding, I barely had time to yank ours off the road." He leaned his head back against the headrest. "We should probably save the flashlight batteries. I'm going to need it when I go out." He shifted his position and pulled a cell phone from his pocket. "I don't have a signal. Do you?"

Her heart seized. "Why would you go out? It's still raining." She checked her phone. "No signal either."

"Darn. I'm going out to see whether anyone needs help. And to look for a phone."

"But what about your head? You could hang a potted plant on the lump." She should've thought of helping others, but Dewayne's apparent pain and her own aching head kept her wanting to stay inside where it was at least dry, if not warm. She shivered, glad for the jacket she wore.

"There's a blanket behind the seat if you're cold."

"Thank you." She fished it from the floorboard and wrapped it around the front of her. "Are you cold?"

"There's another blanket. I'll get it when I come back. I'll be wet." He took the flashlight from her lap then wrenched his door open. Icy rain blew inside. "Stay here. Flash the lights and honk the horn if you need me." His gaze locked on hers. She nodded, and he was gone, leaving her as alone and frightened as a child locked in a dark closet.

Dewayne directed the light in the windows of the four-door sedan behind the Hummer. Wide eyes stared from the faces of two young children. He yanked open the driver's-side door and felt for the pulse of the unconscious woman behind the wheel. A steady beat met his fingers. "Your mom?" One of the boys nodded. "She's okay." He hoped. "Let her rest. Help will be coming." He moved to the next vehicle in line, a semi, its engine still rumbling.

The driver sat slumped over the wheel. No seat belt. Dewayne climbed inside and felt for a pulse. This time, nothing but chilly skin met his touch. He closed his eyes and sighed. How many more would he find dead before completing his trek down the long line of cars? Using the man's CB radio, he called in the accident then turned off the ignition and climbed from the truck.

He pulled the collar of his denim jacket higher on his neck and flashed his light down the road. A few people huddled around their vehicles. Only two were moving from car to car. Maybe, like Dewayne, they searched for survivors.

The next vehicle, a small model truck, had the engine smashed into the cab. The driver and passenger, dead. Dewayne said a prayer that he wouldn't find any more dead bodies and kept moving. Two hours later, he'd tied a tourniquet on a man's leg, handed a newly orphaned infant to an elderly woman to care for, and cried more tears than he could number. Cold and despondent, he trudged back to Zoe, his clothes clinging to his shivering body.

She woke when he wrenched open the door and slid inside, his teeth chattering so hard he thought they'd crack. He held up a hand when she started to speak. "Not now, please. Fetch me the other blanket, okay?"

"Use this one. It's warm from my body." She draped it over him, enveloping him in her scent. He closed his eyes and breathed deeply. He could hear her scrounging for the other cover. How could he tell her about the devastation outside their cold little world?

"How bad is it?"

"Very." He pulled the blanket over his nose and willed the shaking to stop.

"Is there anyone that needs, well, a woman's touch?"

He cracked open an eye. "I don't want you to see what's

out there. I used a CB radio and called for help. Just wait."

"I can handle it, Dewayne. I watched my mother die."

He groped for her hand and squeezed. "Please, stay with me. Pray for those out there. That's the best thing you can do. And pray that help arrives soon. With the wet roads and congestion, it'll take emergency vehicles a while."

Zoe wanted to help. Not be treated like a fragile flower that would wilt under devastating circumstances. She and Dewayne were fortunate. She wanted to use the gift God gave them to minister to others. There were people she could sit with and pray for. She moved to climb over the seat, her own door still pressed against the hill.

"Don't even think about it."

"Why?"

"A woman alone shouldn't be traipsing around after dark." He turned his head to look at her, color returning to his face. "Yes, we've all been in a horrible accident, but there might be others out there who will prey on innocent people. I can't protect you if you aren't here."

"Can I at least get you something to eat or drink? I've got ibuprofen." She reached for her purse.

"That would be wonderful. And one of those granola bars."

Zoe used the water in the bottle he'd opened to down three ibuprofen before handing the bottle over to Dewayne. He smiled his thanks and popped four of the little orange pills.

"The rain has stopped. Try to catch some sleep," he mumbled, closing his eyes. "No telling how long we'll be here."

She scooted her back against the door and watched as the moon, playing hide-and-seek with the clouds, illuminated his face. Already the lump on his forehead promised a colorful array of blue and purple. She pulled down the visor mirror. So did her own. She smiled grimly. What a way to see her cousins for the first time in over a year.

Pulling her cell phone from her pocket, she checked for service again. Still no bars. She was thankful Dewayne had found a CB radio and called for help. How bad was the pileup that prevented help from coming? She thought to ask Dewayne but decided not to when she noticed his steady breathing. What had he witnessed outside that would leave those deep furrows in his forehead? How many people sat in their cars, paralyzed with fear and injury? How many dead?

Tears spilled down her cheeks as she tried to find the good in the night's circumstances. Sometimes, her life verse was hard even for her to hang on to.

How long would she be confined to a car with the man who wanted her gone as quickly as possible?

Chapter 8

Zoe woke to loud voices as the sun peeked over the horizon, spreading fingers of gold and magenta across the dented metal of a rainbow hue of automobiles. She rolled the kinks from her neck and glanced at the empty driver's seat. Where had Dewayne gone to so early? She crawled from the Hummer.

She saw two men, one holding what looked like a crowbar, shove Dewayne into the muddy ditch. They both wore baseball caps, one blue and the other red. Dewayne sprang back to the road like a striking mountain lion, landing a punch on Red Hat's chin. The man staggered back while Blue Hat struck with the bar, catching Dewayne behind the knees and dropping him to the ground.

Zoe screamed and rushed forward. "Stop! Leave him alone!"

Red Hat grabbed her arm and yanked her forward. Tobacco fumes washed over her. "Give us your money. All of it."

"I will—I'll get it." She hated the tremor in her voice. "Just stop hitting him."

Dewayne made a move to get to his feet, and Blue Hat whacked the bar across his shoulders, felling him like a tree. Sobs clogged Zoe's throat as the man drew back a leg and kicked Dewayne in his side.

"Stop! I'll get the money. There isn't much." She pulled free and backed toward the Hummer. From the corner of her eye, she caught a glimpse of red and blue lights flashing as a police cruiser maneuvered around the stalled cars. A siren wailed. *Thank You, Lord.* As the men dashed away, Zoe ran and fell to her knees beside Dewayne.

Blood trickled from a gash in his head. He groaned and opened his eyes.

"Let me help you up." She planted her shoulder beneath his arm, only for him to fall back to his knees. She needed help. "Stay here."

He nodded.

Zoe sprinted to the squad cars and waved her arms. "Help!"

Another traveler leaped from his car and stepped in front of her. "Lady, a lot of people need help. Wait your turn."

She ducked under his arm and ran to one of the officers, who was just getting out of the car. "Please, some men just beat up my friend. They tried to rob us."

The officer nodded, motioned to his partner that he'd handle it, and followed Zoe. "Did you get a look at the attackers?"

"They wore baseball hats—one red and one blue. They wore flannel shirts and stained blue jeans. They ran toward the front of the line." She swiped a hand across her tearing eyes. "My friend is Dewayne Hofford. I tried to help him get up, but he's too heavy for me."

"How badly is your car damaged? Can you drive?"

"It has a flat. Dewayne's in no condition to change it."

"Did he lose consciousness?"

She shook her head. "No, but he's bleeding."

The officer—Zoe noticed the name Castell on his name tag—turned as an ambulance weaved its way through the traffic toward the front of the line of vehicles. Another followed close behind.

Officer Castell pushed a button on his radio. "I'll take care of this. Have the other officers arrived? Good. Send them after the ambulances, and I'll need a tow truck." He smiled at Zoe. "Now, let's take a look at your friend. We'll have you on the road in no time." He waved at the closest ambulance.

"I'm sorry. I'm sure there are others hurt worse," Zoe said. "But if the EMT can clear Dewayne, and we get the tire changed, I'll drive him to the hospital myself."

"No problem, ma'am. Let's see what we've got."

"What took you guys so long to get here?"

"Mud slide buried the road about a mile back. We got it cleared, but traffic is backed up over five miles to get through this pass. We did the best we could."

By the time Zoe, Officer Castell, and a paramedic made their way to the Hummer, Dewayne had managed to scoot against the front bumper, his face pale beneath the blood trickling from a cut above his left eyebrow. Zoe tried to decipher the look he gave her. Whether of pain or frustration, she wasn't sure.

"I'm fine," he insisted as a paramedic shone a light in his eyes. "Just need to catch my breath. There are dead people, children, they need your help more than I do."

"We've plenty of help arriving." The paramedic felt Dewayne's side. Dewayne winced. "Concussion and possible fractured rib. Not life threatening, but it's hard to tell under these circumstances. You need to seek medical assistance."

Officer Castell sighed. "Ma'am, I'll get the spare tire and

have the tow truck move some of these vehicles so you can leave." He speared her with a glance. "Are you sure you're able to drive? You've got your own bump on the head to deal with."

"I'm positive."

"I can drive," Dewayne insisted. "Just give me a couple more ibuprofen."

The paramedic shook his head. "I don't think so."

Officer Castell helped move Dewayne away from the Hummer. "I'll change your tire, sir, you rest."

"It's a regular-sized tire. I don't carry one of those little ones."

"Even better." He nodded at Zoe.

She reached beneath the dashboard and released the latch so the officer could get the tire. How would she have managed herself if the officer hadn't helped? Tears pricked her eyes. God never failed to come through in a pinch. Even when the need was out of the ordinary.

While Officer Castell changed the tire, the tow truck crew worked on pulling aside vehicles that wouldn't run and helping to start others that would. Paramedics ushered the walking wounded to a safe waiting area and moved the more severely wounded directly into the waiting ambulances.

A paramedic reached into a car then pulled back, shaking his head before moving on. It seemed the dead had to wait.

With the spare tire mounted in place, Officer Castell climbed into the driver's seat and turned the key in the ignition. The Hummer roared to life. "Good thing you managed to steer for the ditch. Some folks' cars are too banged up to drive." He closed the door and maneuvered the Hummer clear of the hill blocking the passenger door then climbed out. "I'll have an officer meet you at the hospital to take your statement."

A few minutes later, Dewayne sat in the passenger seat, still insisting he felt fine enough to drive, and Zoe sat behind the wheel of the biggest vehicle she'd ever driven.

Dewayne hunched in the passenger seat, careful not to make any sudden moves. Every time the car jostled, his head throbbed and stabs of pain shot through his side. Once clear of the multicar pileup, Zoe drove like a mad woman. Good thing all the cops were busy at the accident site.

She kept her knuckle-white grip on the steering wheel and her eyes glued on the road. The sun streamed through the window, touching the ends of her hair with fire. He remembered the feel of her hair, alive in his fingers. He sighed.

"Are you all right? Is the pain worse?" Zoe cut him a sideways glance. "We'll be at the hospital in Trinidad soon."

"I'm fine. Don't worry every time I make a sound."

"Stop saying that." She rolled her eyes. "Why do you always have to be so. . .so macho? Those men could've killed you."

"But they didn't."

"Thank God they didn't. You helped a lot of people last night." Her voice shook. "I don't know what I would have done without you."

She was right. If he were injured worse than he thought, and something happened, the tire, the work the police officer did getting them back on the road, all would've been in vain. Except for Zoe. She would've been okay. Back on the road to Colorado by tomorrow at the latest. She still had time to make her meeting with her cousins.

"Just drop me off. You can borrow the Hummer. I'll have

one of my employees come and get me."

"Don't be ridiculous. You went out of your way to help me, now I'm returning the favor. I'll still make it. I've got two days."

"Day after tomorrow."

"That's still two days. I can show up late on Saturday and still make it. We aren't meeting until three, I think." She flashed him a grin.

"Okay, Pollyanna." He returned her grin, the gesture pulling at the split on his lip. "We almost got there early."

"What happened, Dewayne? I woke up and two men were pounding you in the mud."

"That's pretty much it." Holding his breath against the pain in his ribs, he shifted in his seat to get a better look at her. "I stepped outside for some fresh air, and they jumped me. Wanted all our money or they were going to bash in the windows. So I hit one of them."

"Why didn't you give them the money? You can always buy new windows. You only get one head, hard as it is."

He shrugged. "It wasn't the smartest thing I've ever done." His actions weren't based on whether or not he'd have to purchase a new windshield. The thought of what the men could do to Zoe if they wanted—if they put him out of commission—that's what spurred Dewayne to take them on. From what they'd said during his beating, he figured they'd gone up and down the line of crashed vehicles, looting what they could, using violence if necessary. Maybe no one else had the stubbornness to stop them. Especially after the catastrophe they all had to deal with. Besides, he hadn't wanted Zoe to have to deal with another stressful situation. So much for being her knight in shining armor.

Here he was, wounded, barely able to move, and on his way to the hospital, while her face still showed signs of her tears, not to mention the beginning of a colorful bruise on her forehead. Had she cried over him?

Conflicted emotions coursed through him. One of elation that she might be receptive to rekindling their relationship, another that she'd suffered through a horrible night. He closed his eyes. Remembering her life verse, he vowed later to ask her how God turned the multicar pileup into a good thing.

Chapter 9

After three hours in the emergency room, Zoe finally got Dewayne to take a painkiller and lie down in the hotel room adjoining hers. Now she stood in the doorway between the two rooms and watched him sleep, amazed at how much he still resembled the young man she knew from high school.

A lock of hair fell forward across one eye. A two-day's growth of stubble gave him that GQ look some men strived to attain.

She slipped her hand into the pocket of her jeans and ran the ring through her fingers. She'd caught his calling her "baby" while she cried in his arms. Had the word slipped out from habit, or did it mean he still considered her his baby? She sighed. Too much confusion. Too many conflicting emotions. They needed to sit down and have a serious conversation. But not now. Not with him doped up on painkillers. She needed time to work up her nerve and let them both have clear heads when the conversation occurred. Maybe they could talk when she returned to Mesquite for her car?

Stomach rumbling, she turned back to her own room and grabbed the keys to the Hummer. Locking the door behind her, she marched across the parking lot and took in the sight of Dewayne's pride and joy bashed in on the passenger's side.

He had to be heartbroken. Good thing he owned an auto repair shop.

Not familiar with the town of Trinidad, Colorado, she drove to the nearest fast food place and ordered two chicken dinners and two large Cokes. With the smell of fried chicken filling the Hummer, she drove back to the hotel.

With her purse slung over one arm, one hand balancing a holder for drinks, and the other clutching the bag of food, she unlocked the door to her room and stepped inside.

"Zoe!"

"I'm coming." She dropped her purse on the bed and carried their dinner into Dewayne's room. His eyes were closed, blankets tangled around his jean-clad legs.

"Don't go." He rolled his legs from side to side. "Why do you have to leave? Let me go with you."

He was dreaming. Talking in his sleep. They hadn't had a conversation the night she'd left. Like a thief, she'd escaped in the dark, leaving him and the life she loved behind. She set the bag of food and the drinks on a small round table and approached the bed.

"I love you, Zoe. Don't you see that? I want to marry you."

Her heart stopped. She needed to wake him before he said more. Would he remember the words he spoke and be embarrassed? She touched his shoulder. He grabbed her hand, crushing the bones beneath his fingers.

"Dewayne! Wake up, you're hurting me." She pried his grip loose.

"Zoe?" His eyes fluttered open. "How long was I sleeping? I feel like I've been run over by a truck." He struggled to a sitting position. "This is why I never take pain pills."

She turned away, running her tongue over dry lips. "I've brought supper."

"Great. I'm hungry."

Thank You, God. He didn't seem to recall a word he'd said. She closed her eyes, halfway wishing he had. "Is chicken all right?"

"Perfect."

She handed him his soda then dragged the table closer to the bed. "Other than feeling run over, how are you?"

"Fuzzy, and I've got a killer headache."

"Do you want another pill?" She glanced at her watch then made a move toward her room. The doctor had said he could take another if the pain was bad enough.

"No. Sit down and eat with me." He motioned toward a chair under the window. "Pull that closer, and we'll share the table." He swung his legs over the side of the bed.

Zoe dragged the striped chair to the table. Pulling out boxes of chicken and plastic containers of slaw and potatoes, she grinned. "A home-cooked meal."

He chuckled. "Did you ever learn to cook? I remember the spaghetti you made once, when you put in cinnamon instead of chili powder. Yum."

"You're teasing." She remembered, too. It'd been terrible. "And yes, I did learn to cook, and learned well."

"You'll have to prove your cooking skills to me sometime."

Did he mean it? He wanted her to cook for him? Like in the future?

She brought a forkful of potatoes and gravy to her mouth and studied his face. Purple and blue decorated the receding bump on his forehead. Furrows, most likely from his headache, lined his brow. She looked toward the door adjoining their rooms.

Here she was, a single gal with an attractive man, alone in his hotel room. Once, a few nights before high school graduation, they'd almost succumbed to their passion in their favorite "parking" spot. Instead, friends roared up, honking their horns, and saved Zoe and Dewayne from a mistake. She glanced at the bed.

Dewayne caught her look and his eyes darkened. If he wasn't injured, would they act on what had been interrupted years ago? No, not with their newfound faith. Even if they weren't Christians, they weren't ready for a physical relationship. Too many emotions needed to be sorted through. She jumped to her feet. "I'm really tired. I'll see you in the morning."

He grabbed her hand. "Wait."

She searched his eyes.

"There's no need to rush, Zoe. I know what you're thinking. We're safe. I'm in no condition for. . .that. Even if I were, I wouldn't put you in that situation."

Maybe she was in no danger from him, but what about the other way around? What if she were weak enough to go against her moral convictions about what was right in God's eyes? With the heated thoughts burning through her mind, retreat seemed the best option. She shook her head, picking up her dinner. "I should go. I really am tired and achy. A hot bath will help me sleep. See you in the morning." She ran to her room and slammed the door, flipping the lock as if wild dogs chased her.

She leaned against the paneled wood and closed her eyes. What an idiot she was! She'd shown Dewayne how she felt about him as effectively as if she'd put it into words.

Dewayne smiled and grabbed another drumstick. Yep, she still had feelings for him whether she wanted to admit to them or not. He leaned back against the headboard. All he needed to do was get her to realize that fact and act on it. Not the way she could have by being in his room, but a kiss wouldn't have hurt anything. Maybe he'd try kissing her tomorrow, when his head didn't pound so much.

The shocked expression on her face had been priceless. He chuckled at the way she scurried from the room like a mouse running from a cat. And he was the cat.

The sound of a shower came from the room next door, reminding Dewayne how much he, too, needed to clean up. He tossed his half-eaten chicken leg onto the table then gingerly pulled his T-shirt over his head. He might as well take care of hygiene while nausea from his concussion was momentarily relieved.

He'd just settled his aching body in a tub of water as hot as he could stand when the shower shut off next door. What would she put on? An oversized T-shirt like she used to wear? He'd stopped by her home early one morning years ago. His teenage heart had almost stopped at the sight of Zoe's tanned legs beneath that faded shirt. Or did she actually wear pajamas now? Dewayne closed his eyes and leaned his head back against the tub. He shouldn't allow his thoughts to run in such a direction. The Bible advised taking each thought captive.

Using his toe, he turned off the spigot. Slowly, the water soothed his aches and pains. If only it could soak into his head and his heart and clarify which direction he ought to go. His heart wanted Zoe. His head said he'd get hurt again.

Theme music from a sitcom vibrated through the wall. Would Zoe be offended if he knocked and asked to join her? Most likely. They'd spent a lot of time together the last few days. He'd let her be.

Dewayne jerked awake and shivered. He'd fallen asleep in the tub and now sat in water as cool as the room. He clamped his chattering teeth and reached for a towel. The room next door was silent. His head pounded and spots danced in front of his eyes.

It wasn't until he'd dressed for bed in a pair of worn-out basketball shorts that he realized Zoe had his painkillers. He slipped on a T-shirt and padded to the door separating their rooms. He rapped three times on the laminate door.

Zoe opened the door, wearing an oversized shirt and cotton shorts, her hair mussed and still damp from her shower. "Are you okay?"

"I need a pain pill." He leaned against the doorjamb. "I fell asleep in the tub and woke up with a killer headache."

She gasped. "I'm sorry. I should've checked on you." She rushed to her dresser, where his prescription bottle sat. Clutching it in her hand, she hurried back and thrust it at him. "If you need to rest another day, we can—"

"No. We'll leave in the morning as planned."

"Not at the risk of your health." She crossed her arms.

"You can drive. I'll take a nap if I have to." It took all his willpower not to kiss her, pounding head or not. To see whether her lips felt the same as twelve years ago. Did her curves fit his angles like a puzzle? He shook his pounding head. Now was not the time. One thing he did know for sure, he wouldn't let her disappear again without telling her how he felt. Then, if she wanted to walk away again, he'd know he'd done everything he could.

Zoe steered the Hummer onto the highway. Dewayne sat in the passenger seat nursing a coffee and staring out the window. She wanted to ask him about his thoughts, but the fear that he might be glad their time together was drawing to a close stopped her.

The ring in her pocket threatened to burn into her leg. Should she give it back after all this time? She couldn't. The small silver circle was the only reminder of what might have been. Somehow, she needed to tell Dewayne she still loved him and let him make the next move. But what if he turned around and left her as she'd done to him? It'd be what she deserved.

She powered her window down an inch to let the fall breeze inside. Maybe she should just blurt out the feelings in her heart, lay them out there to see whether he accepted them or trampled them like dry autumn leaves. Or tell him how her life verse applied even in their current circumstances. What the good was to be found in this particular circumstance. Because she didn't regret God bringing her and Dewayne back together again. Not for one minute.

The idea that she might have to continue on for the rest of her life with his ring in her pocket, comparing every man she met to the one she wanted, sent rivulets of fear through her veins.

From the corner of her eye she could tell he slept, or

pretended to. His head rested sideways against the window, eyes closed, mouth set in a firm line. She wanted to smooth away the frown lines between his eyes.

She was the biggest coward she knew. Maybe she could tell him how she felt while he was asleep. Like a practice run before they reached Colorado Springs. "Dewayne? Are you awake?"

Not even a twitch. She took a deep breath. "I kept the ring all these years because I never stopped loving you." There. Not too bad of a beginning. "I didn't have the heart to tell you about Mom taking me away. If you'd tried to talk me out of going, I would've left her to go without me, and I don't think I could've lived with the guilt." Tears stung her eyes and she wiped them away with the back of her hand. "I know you're not going to hear a word of this, but I've got to tell you. And maybe, hopefully, I'll get up the nerve again when we get to Colorado Springs."

She cut a sideways glance to see whether he'd moved. Nope. Still good to go. "I'm sorry I dragged you all the way out here. If you hadn't been so generous, your truck wouldn't be smashed, you wouldn't be injured, and I wouldn't have this lovely purple knot on my head. I should've waited for the bus." But then she wouldn't have spent the last couple of days with him.

"You want to know how God brought good out of this situation? I've come to terms with my feelings. I love you, Dewayne Hofford, and I have no intention of letting you go. I'll set up my flower shop wherever you are until you realize you still love me, too." Whew. She'd said it. Now, if she could only do a repeat performance when he was awake.

The tires droning on the freeway threatened to lure her

into drowsiness. A sign announced a gas station half a mile ahead. Zoe glanced at the gas gauge. Fuel, a soda, and a bathroom break ought to last them until the hotel.

She turned on her blinker and took the access road. Dewayne mumbled when the Hummer went over a pothole, but didn't waken. Zoe pulled beside a gas pump and cut the engine. She might as well get him something to drink, too. He'd be thirsty when he woke up.

After filling the tank, Zoe headed inside and made her way to the restrooms in the back of the station. She stared at herself in the dingy mirror, wondering what in the world compelled her to spill her guts to a sleeping man. Was she that big of a chicken? She shook her head in defeat, knowing the answer.

Ten minutes later, a diet cola in one hand and a regular in the other, she made her way back to the Hummer. Dewayne sat awake, a puzzled look on his face.

She handed him his drink through the open window then resumed her place behind the wheel. "Did you have a good nap?"

"Not sure. I had the weirdest dream." He frowned at her.

Zoe's blood drained to her feet. Avoiding his gaze, she turned the key in the ignition. "Want to talk about it?"

"No." He turned to stare out the window.

The cold soda felt good on his parched tongue. Did he want to talk about his crazy dream? Not in a million years. Telling Zoe that he dreamed she had spouted words of love to him would probably make the last hour's drive seem much longer.

He turned to study her. What if he did tell her? How

would she respond to his words of love? Most likely stroll out of his life again, even quicker than the last time. Well, he'd see about that. Once he had her settled in Colorado Springs, he'd tell her his feelings and let God handle the outcome.

"Are you excited?"

"What?" She cast him a glance.

"About meeting with your cousins tomorrow." He took a sip of his drink.

"Very. A year is a long time to be away from family."

A knocking sound came from under the hood of the Hummer. Zoe's hands tightened on the wheel. "What now?"

"Most likely damage from the accident." He leaned over to see whether any engine lights were blinking. Nothing. "Just keep driving."

"What if we break down?"

He shrugged. "We'll worry about that if it happens. If smoke starts pouring from under the hood, pull over." No telling what kind of damage was done when they'd run into the ditch. His heart clenched. He loved his Hummer, but it was only a vehicle. The important thing was, neither he nor Zoe was badly hurt. Physically, at least.

Chapter 10

Zoe parked the Hummer in front of the Broadmoor Hotel, handed Dewayne the keys, and slid from behind the wheel. The valet glanced at the truck and raised his eyebrows.

"Yeah, we ran into a little trouble on the road," Zoe told him as she stood off to the side, suitcase at her feet. After losing her precious quilt squares once, she didn't want to let them out of her sight. She studied the gorgeous building in front of her.

The hotel towered above lush, perfectly manicured lawns. What a wonderful place to spend a honeymoon. She peered at Dewayne. Maybe after their talk. Oh, who was she kidding? The expense of the place meant she'd better enjoy every minute of her reunion and not entertain ideas of a happily ever after with Dewayne. But it would be nice to enjoy every minute with him.

He jangled the keys to his truck. "We made it."

Zoe smiled. "Yes, we did, thanks to you. Are you coming in?"

He shook his head. "A little over my budget, I'm afraid. I'll check into a cheaper place and head home in the morning."

She fought to keep her chin from quivering. "I'll see you in a few days when my car is finished. You have my cell phone number?"

"I do." He gathered her in a quick hug. "Take care of yourself and have fun, Zoe." He strode to the driver's side of the car and slid behind the wheel. Without so much as a wave, he left her standing in the Colorado sunshine, a battered suitcase at her feet and her heart shattering into a billion pieces.

After the Hummer disappeared from view, Zoe clutched the handle of her suitcase and wheeled it to the registration desk. "Zoe Barnes, checking in."

"You're in one of our cottages." The clerk handed her a key card and a dentist-brightened smile. "Enjoy your stay, Ms. Barnes." He waved a bellhop over.

"Thank you." Zoe would. Tomorrow, she'd meet her cousins after a long year apart and together they'd fulfill Nana's dying wish. She'd deal with the emotions surrounding Dewayne when it was time to retrieve her Mustang.

The bellhop led the way to her assigned cottage and opened the door. Zoe stepped into a room less like a cottage than anything she'd ever seen. Rich fabrics, plush furnishings, and a lit fireplace welcomed her to a world of luxury she'd never had the fortune to enjoy. By the time she'd stopped gawking and turned to tip the man who'd led the way, he'd disappeared.

Had Dewayne tipped the man when Zoe wasn't looking? No way would the bellhop leave otherwise. One more thing that pointed to Dewayne's gentlemanly and caring ways. She was a fool to let him walk away, and once she'd fulfilled Nana's dying wish, she'd tell him so.

She stepped into the room that would be her home for a few days and plopped on the sofa. This was the life! A large picture window framed a vibrant green lawn. She headed in the direction of the bathroom. All white and glass, with striped wallpaper. With such elegance, what would the bedroom be like?

"Oh!" She rushed toward the padded window seat, bypassing the white bed with rose-accented pillows. She simply had to curl up by the window. She dashed for her suitcase, tossed it on the nearby chair, and pulled out her quilt squares. Finally, situated in the type of seat she'd always wanted as a little girl, she spread the fabric pieces out around her, running her finger softly over the one she'd designed herself. Another, uncompleted, and rather plain, simply had her mother's name embroidered in blue.

Maybe Zoe could finish her mother's square before the meeting tomorrow. The cottage room could be her inspiration. She dug in her suitcase for the small amount of embroidery thread she'd shoved inside. Pinks and reds with a touch of green would set off her mother's name nicely and add another completed square to the mix. She glanced out the window. What better place to do an act of love than this?

Two hours later, stomach rumbling from having skipped lunch, Zoe studied the white linen square in front of her. Roses in two of the corners, her mother's name, and the words "John 3:16" were the entire legacy her mother had left her. *Thank You, Lord, that Mom found You before she died.*

She moved to the living area and picked up the booklet listing the hotel's amenities. She flipped through and decided on Café Julie. A salad and a glass of tea sounded perfect. After a shower and change of clothes, she headed out, careful to take her purse and key with her.

As soon as she stepped out of her room, a couple strolled by arm in arm, and loneliness assailed Zoe with the same force as the thunderstorm days before. What would it be like to spend time with Dewayne in a place like this?

She blinked against the tears. She'd only be lonely for a few hours, and then she'd be meeting up with her cousins. She could survive until then.

Dewayne checked into a run-down motel, a place that suited his mood, and propped himself against the bed's scarred headboard, not bothering to remove his boots. He flipped aimlessly through the few television channels allowed free of charge, with the intention of doing so until his mind went as numb as his heart.

What he wanted to do was storm back to the Broadmoor and confront Zoe with his feelings. Only fear of rejection kept him from doing it. Sure, he'd heard her spout words of love when she thought he was asleep, but she'd professed to love him twelve years ago, too, when she'd run off, taking his heart with her.

He pounded his fist on the unyielding mattress. Could he take the chance of rejection again? If he didn't, would he always wish he had? For the first time in many years he wanted to reach for a bottle of something stronger than soda to drink. How would Zoe react if she knew he'd turned to drinking after she left? Most likely run screaming into the night, considering her mother's alcoholism and death.

He'd only experimented anyway. Never did get a real taste for it. He clicked off the television and stared at the water-stained ceiling. Maybe a walk would help clear his head.

Pocketing his room card, he exited the motel and watched as neon pink highlighted the parking lot. When had night fallen? Zoe could muddle his mind faster and thicker than any concussion.

His legs carried him down the dark street. A cold wind blew, and he shivered. Before he knew it, he stood in front of a jewelry store window, eyeballing a diamond ring that put the one in Zoe's pocket to shame. What would it be like to slip one like that on her finger? Would she scream, cry, run? He shook his head and pulled away from stupid dreams.

He could call her. His cell phone nestled in the pocket of his jeans. What would it hurt to check on her? Make sure she was settled in okay? He pulled the phone from his pocket and punched in her number. When her voice mail picked up, he slipped the cover shut. Stupid idea anyway. Most likely she sat in a lounge somewhere catching up with her cousins, having forgotten all about him and the last few days.

Tomorrow, he'd do the same. Head back to Mesquite and concentrate on fixing her car and his. Then, he'd never see her again. The thought hurt like a knife to the stomach. He couldn't do it. Couldn't let her walk away again. He turned and retraced his steps.

Chapter 11

Zoe sat in the hotel restaurant, scooting her eggs around her plate with her fork. She'd slept very little the night before. Visions of Dewayne as a high school senior, then as a man, ran through her mind like a spool of film. She'd let go of a prize and had no idea how to get it back.

Couples smiled and chattered to each other. One man reached over and stroked the cheek of his companion. A woman brushed a man's shoulder on her way to the restroom. Zoe sighed. That's what she wanted. Tenderness aimed in her direction.

She tossed her fork on her plate. What did she expect? A person couldn't rip out another person's heart and expect to be shown love.

The words she'd heard when Dewayne slept returned to her. She'd take a chance. Grabbing her purse, she dug out some cash, slipped it under the lip of her plate, and then stood and strolled from the restaurant. There couldn't be that many cheap motels in the area. She'd call his cell phone. If he didn't answer, she'd call every motel around until she found him. Then she'd rent a taxi and throw herself at Dewayne's feet. Hopefully he hadn't left Colorado Springs yet.

She stopped in the middle of the hotel lobby. Her cousins expected to meet with her at three. How could she leave now? She took another step toward the door. Nobody could keep her from telling Dewayne how she felt. Not this time. She shoved open the glass door and bolted into the morning sunshine.

Finding a seat beside the fountain, she pulled her phone from her purse and tried Dewayne's number. No answer. She activated her GPS in a search for motels. There were a few really cheap ones, but surely Dewayne could afford better than those. He owned several auto shops after all. Cold calling was futile.

Zoe let her tears fall. She didn't care who saw. Once again she'd made the wrong choice and allowed what was right there to slip through her fingers. She stared at her closed phone. Should she try calling again? Her fingers poised over the buttons. She couldn't. He'd walked away without a backward glance. The best thing was to let him go.

"Are you all right, dear?" An elderly woman with stylish hair and clothes that cost more than the contents of Zoe's entire suitcase smiled down at her.

"No. I made the biggest mistake of my life. For the second time." Zoe's shoulders shook with the force of her sobs. "He'll never forgive me this time."

The woman sat next to her. "Almost everything can be forgiven, sweetie."

"I let him walk away again." She sniffed.

"Go get him now."

"I don't know where he is."

"Call him." The woman nodded toward Zoe's phone. "I'll sit with you."

"I tried. He didn't answer."

"Try again. And keep trying until he answers."

Zoe nodded, wiped her eyes on the sleeve of the pink

hoodie she wore, and dialed Dewayne's number. The phone went to voice mail. She hung up without leaving a message. "He didn't answer this time either. I'm too late."

"God's in control, dear. Remember that." The lady squeezed Zoe's shoulders then stood. "I will pray for you."

Zoe nodded and raised her head to thank her new friend. She was gone. Zoe stood and searched the few people wandering the grounds. The lovely woman was nowhere to be seen. Had Zoe entertained an angel unaware? She smiled. Possibly. At any rate, she felt better, lighter, since speaking with the stranger. She slipped her phone in her purse.

She would try Dewayne again later. After her meeting with the cousins. She turned and headed for the main building.

Dewayne left the Hummer with valet parking and sprinted for the hotel's entrance. Maybe he could catch Zoe before her meeting. He sighed and waited in line for the front desk, one leg jittering, while a family of five checked into the hotel. Each moment he had to wait was one more minute away from telling Zoe how he felt.

Finally, his turn. The pretty blond woman's gaze flicked over his wrinkled clothes and he could tell she forced a greeting. "May I help you?"

"Zoe Barnes's room, please." Dewayne leaned against the counter.

"Do you know the room number?"

"No, I'm hoping you can give it to me." He flashed her his best smile.

Her coldness melted a little, but not enough for her to

budge. "I'm afraid we can't do that. I can ring her room if you'd like."

"That would be great." He didn't want Zoe to have warning he was coming, but at this point, he'd take what he could get.

"There's no answer, sir. Would you like to leave a message?"

Dewayne shook his head. "She's meeting three other women. Do you know where?"

The clerk's tweezed eyebrows disappeared beneath her hairline. "Most likely one of their rooms, sir. I cannot give you—"

"I know." He raised a hand. "You can't give me that information."

"Perhaps she's in one of our restaurants, or walking the grounds?" The woman cocked her head.

"I'll be back." Dewayne speed-walked to the nearest lounge and scanned the patrons. Nothing. One by one, he checked each eating establishment, lounge, and bar. No Zoe. He should've come back early that morning and waited in the lobby for her to appear. She could be anywhere in the huge hotel. They could be going in circles, passing each other, he on a desperate hunt, she enjoying her cousins.

He slumped against a pillar. Who was he kidding? If she'd wanted to see him again she would've called him back yesterday. She wouldn't have let him drive away.

He pulled his cell phone from his pocket. Dead. He'd been too upset the night before to think of charging it. He pushed open the door and stepped outside.

God, let me find her. Please don't let her walk out of my life again.

An hour later, he plopped on a bench beside the fountain.

What could he do until dinner time? Surely, she and her cousins would hit one of the restaurants then. He bowed his head, letting his hands dangle between his knees. Maybe they really weren't meant to be together. Maybe there wasn't anything good to come out of the last few days. Nothing but new heartache on top of the old.

Pushing to his feet, he followed the pathway back to the hotel, being careful to avoid the bars and lounges. In his frame of mind, he didn't trust himself not to give in to temptation.

A nearby elevator dinged. He swiveled toward the sound. Zoe stepped out.

"Dewayne?" Zoe's steps faltered. Her toe caught as she stepped from the elevator, pitching her to her knees. She stared up at him. "What are you doing here?"

Her heart rate increased. He'd come back. He hadn't left town after all. *Thank You, God.* Now she'd have the opportunity to tell him how she felt. "I need to talk to—"

"I, uh, need to ask you a question." He helped her to her feet and glanced around. "Is there somewhere we can speak more privately?"

"One of the lounges?" What could possibly bring such a worried look to his face? She clenched her fists to keep from reaching up and smoothing away his frown. Did he have something so horrible to say that she'd never put back together the pieces of her shattered heart?

"No." He sighed, his breath ruffling her hair. "This is hard. I had a problem after you left. A drinking problem. I try not to frequent those places."

Dewayne was an alcoholic? Her heart pained. Like her mother.

"I've been sober over ten years. My stint didn't last long. I never had to go to meetings." He gripped her hands. "It was just a bad time. A bad choice. I know this is probably not the right time to say this, but with what else I want to say, it needs to be in the open."

She nodded. Because of her, Dewayne had slipped into a bad place in his life. How could he possibly want her after all she'd done to him? "We can go outside. I need to meet with my cousins soon, but fortunately, they're used to me being late." She allowed him to lead her outside, back to the fountain where she'd met her angel. She sat, Dewayne taking a seat beside her.

"Before I go any further, I need to know something." His beautiful eyes searched hers, full of all the love she'd prayed to see again. Her hopes rose. "Your life verse. Romans 8:28. What good did God bring out of the last few days? Besides knocking me upside the head."

"What do you think it is?" She couldn't have pulled away from his intense gaze if her life depended on it. Instead, she was pulled deeper, cemented in the emotions whirling there.

Dewayne smiled. "I want to hear your answer."

She swallowed against the mountain lodged in her throat. "He brought you back in my life."

"Is that a good thing?"

"I hope so." Most definitely for her. "Yes. You weren't dreaming. I really said all those things when you were sleeping. Do you think it was a good thing?" She took a deep breath, afraid to hear his answer, yet aching to.

He pulled a black velvet box from his pocket. "Last

night I went for a walk, trying to run from my emotions. Afraid you wouldn't want me. I saw this." He opened the box to reveal a larger replica of the princess diamond ring she carried in her pocket. "I want to start over. With you beside me for the rest of my life. A new ring. A new life." He sat beside her.

Tears welled in Zoe's eyes, blurring her vision.

"Would you consider opening your floral shop somewhere besides Oklahoma? I mean. . .I'll move there and open one of my shops if you want, but maybe we could move here, set up our businesses in Colorado Springs."

She choked back a sob and covered her mouth with her hand.

"Say yes." He stood and pulled her to her feet. "I don't want to live another day without you, Zoe. Please. Finish your business with your cousins and marry me."

Even after all she'd done to him—the pain, the rejection, the abandonment—he still wanted her. "Yes, Dewayne, I'll marry you." She threw her arms around his neck and let the tears fall.

He cupped her face in his hands and kissed her. Not the timid, exploring kiss of high school teenagers, but the heated, soul-claiming kiss of a man who loved a woman. With everything in her, Zoe returned his affection. She'd do her best not to cause him pain again.

"Do you want to get married now?" Dewayne grinned. "Will you let me take care of you for the rest of my life?"

She was definitely blessed. What had she done to deserve such a wonderful man? He was a gift from God. Truly He worked all things together for the good, even heartbreak caused by a silly teenage girl too afraid to follow her heart and live her own life. She answered Dewayne with another kiss that stitched their hearts and lives together with threads that could never be broken.

Cynthia Hickey grew up in a family of storytellers and moved around the country a lot as an Army brat. Her desire is to write real, but flawed characters in a wholesome way that her seven children and five grandchildren can all be proud of. She and her husband live in Arizona where Cynthia works as a monitor in an elementary school.

STITCHED IN LOVE

by Winter A. Peck

Dedication

To my soldier, Shawn, who served his country and has stood by me through every step of this dream. And to those who served and fought for our freedoms and now suffer daily from the effects of combat related PTSD. Thank you and never forget you're not alone.

God had planned something better for us
so that only together with us would they be made perfect.
HEBREWS 11:40 NIV

Chapter 1

Danni Lindsay glared at the empty luggage carousel. Everyone else on her flight had fled with their bags fifteen minutes ago. The airline company better not have put her duffel bag on another plane. She wasn't sure she could handle one more pain to her already throbbing head.

Closing her eyes, she massaged her temples.

Lord, I just want to get my stuff, head to Mom's, and go to bed. Please, please, please, send my bag around.

She snapped her eyes open. The carousel was still empty. Danni groaned. Now what? She glanced at the quiet terminal. Hers had been one of the last flights to get into the Colorado Springs airport. That's what she got for booking a flight last minute. It wasn't like she hadn't known about the stipulation in the will that she and her three cousins meet on the one-year anniversary of Grams's death.

But who knew that a wrong move during a semifinal volleyball match would tear her ACL? And that Danni would spend the last four months in and out of the hospital and rehab? Her recovery had so preoccupied her mind, she would've forgotten about returning to her hometown if her mom hadn't called to check on her.

She sighed and adjusted the shoulder strap of her carry-on. With thousands of frequent-flier miles under her belt, she wasn't caught unprepared. She knew how to pack for the inevitability of the occasional lost bag. But the quilt blocks, those all-important pieces, were tucked away in her missing duffelbag.

Maybe someone, somewhere in the airport could tell her what happened to it.

"Danica Lindsay, is that you?"

Frowning, she turned. A tall man dressed in the uniform of the United States Army stood next to a nearby carousel. His face, clean-cut and deeply tanned, looked familiar. When he shouldered a dark-green duffel bag she saw the medic patch. A memory of a handsome twenty-year-old in the old green-brown-black uniforms hit her.

"Trace Bryant?"

He gave her a broad grin. "Good to see you didn't forget me."

Guilt twinged in her gut. But she had forgotten him. That brief summer twelve years ago, right before she left for college, he was home between basic training and his medic training. A few short, fun months together. They'd parted with promises to keep in touch.

The promises didn't last.

Trace closed the distance between their baggage claim areas. "Your mom said you've changed."

"You talked to my mom?"

He grimaced. "Actually our moms talked. Unlike us, they kept in touch."

Danni held back the flinch. Mom had never breathed one word about knowing Trace's mom, much less talking to her. What else had she hidden from Danni?

She let her gaze rove Trace's tall frame. She wasn't the only one who'd changed. The young, pie-in-the-sky solider she'd hung out with had matured into a wary-eyed man. Normally,

Danni had to look down at people. Trace was the exception. At six-foot-four, he edged her by two inches. Military-short brown hair enhanced his square jaw and sharp cheekbones, revealing his Arapaho ancestry.

The corners of his mouth twitched as he realized what she was doing.

Danni cleared her throat. "So, where has the Army taken you?" She glanced at the luggage rumbling by.

"All over. Mostly Iraq and Afghanistan."

More people ambled over to the carousel Trace had left. Apparently his plane had arrived recently. As a courtesy the airlines always let the soldiers off first, which explained why he got here so fast.

"How many tours has it been?"

Was that pain flickering in his hazel eyes?

"Too many," he said softly.

The swoosh and thump of luggage hitting the belt drew Danni's attention. More bags slid down the chute on the carousel.

"Um, do you have a ride?"

Jolting, Danni gaped at Trace. "Uh, yeah. My mom was picking me up."

He made a rumbling noise in his throat. "Figures." His long fingers slid along the top of his head. "She's not coming, Danica."

She resisted the urge to correct him on her name. "What do you mean? She said I'd have a ride."

"I'm your ride."

Somebody slap her upside the head. Danni swallowed, took a deep breath. "What?"

"Our moms decided it was easier, since I was coming in at

the same time as you." He chuckled. "Appears they're trying to play matchmaker."

"You've got to be kidding me." She spotted a navy-blue bag with black trim sliding down the chute. Finally! "There's my bag."

Trace moved before she could and grabbed it off the belt. Facing her, he nodded his head in the direction of the parking garage.

She had no other choice. Oh, Mom was going to get an earful. Taking a fortifying breath, she followed him out of the airport.

Her bad knee started to throb. She'd spent too much time on it today and the cramped conditions on the plane didn't help any. Should have gone with the special accommodations so she could stretch it out.

I'm too stubborn for my own good.

She wasn't about to show Trace her pain. Hopefully his vehicle was nearby. They paused to wait for a car to pass.

"Still playing volleyball?"

"Beach. Pro level." At least she was before the injury. With this setback, she and her teammate would have to start at the bottom. Their chances for the Olympics teetering.

Trace removed a slip of paper from one of his many pockets and glanced at it. "My folks parked my truck outside."

Stairs or hills? Anticipated agony screamed through Danni's knee. She scanned the lot for the elevator, spotting one. But Trace headed away from it.

"Uh, Trace."

He paused and looked back at her. "Yeah?"

Clamping her lip between her teeth, Danni glanced at the elevators then him. She should take it, but he carried both bags, so that reduced the amount of weight she had to carry. It wouldn't be too far, right? Maybe the walk would do some good in stretching the tight muscles. She'd missed her last physical therapy session to make the flight to Colorado.

"Never mind." She took off after him.

Danni kept pace with him through the first and second levels. By the time they rounded the corner for the third the throbbing turned into fire. Gritting her teeth, she pushed through it. Way too stubborn.

Where was that odd panting sound coming from? Danni stopped breathing, realizing it was her.

God, please tell me I didn't just ruin months of work.

"Danica, are you okay?"

She looked at Trace. Big mistake. She stepped down wrong, her knee protested, and she stumbled to a stop. Wincing, she dropped her carry-on bag and grabbed her knee. The pain intensified.

Danni stuffed back the cry and gingerly sat down on the concrete. Trace dropped to a knee next to her. Why did he have to see her this way? Another stab of pain made her cringe.

Warm hands clasped hers and gently pulled them away, and then cupped her knee. Danni took a shuddering breath as Trace straightened her leg out.

"Stay still." He unzipped the side of her athletic pants and rolled the pant leg up past her knee. His eyebrows furrowed when the faded surgery scars appeared. "When did you injure your ACL?"

"Four months ago," she said between her clenched teeth.

Trace ran his fingers along the scar, the pressure making her tense. While he meant to check for damage, his touch released a bolt of electricity through her leg. His roughened fingertips chaffed against her soft skin, and she bit her lip.

"Pushed it too far today?" His gaze clashed with hers. "Why didn't you wear the brace?"

"Haven't needed it for the past month. Physical therapist said I was fine."

A hint of a smile played with his mouth. "That was it," he muttered.

"What was it?"

"That's what you wanted to tell me before we came up here. If you needed to take the elevator you should have said so."

Clenching her fists, Danni tried to scowl, but the zap of pain stopped her. "I'm not a weakling."

Pulling a small bag closer, Trace opened it. "Didn't say you were. But a recovering ACL isn't something to mess with, Danica." He dug around inside the bag and withdrew rolls of prewrap and athletic tape. He propped her calf on his duffel and proceeded to wind the prewrap around her knee.

Danni groaned. "I really messed it up."

"Nope. You're just being reminded it's not ready." He tore the sheer synthetic and smoothed down the edge. "I think a night's rest will be enough."

She watched him rip off long strips of white tape. "Did my mom happen to tell your mom why I'm here?"

His hands stilled, and he glanced up at her. "I don't recall an exact reason, no."

Her shoulders sagged. Well, Mom's li'l secret mission was the gift that kept on giving. "Family reunion of sorts."

"This the same family you were trying to avoid that summer we met?"

"I wasn't avoiding them. They sorta ran off."

Trace finished with the tape and rolled her pant leg down. He settled his hand on her ankle, the warmth from his hands seeping into her chilled skin. "How do you sorta run off?"

Danni sighed. "Long story. Can we go? This concrete is cold."

Giving her a curt nod, he gathered up his gear and hers, then stood. "Sit tight and I'll put this in the truck."

"Trace, I'm sitting in the middle of the parking lot—"

He held up his hand then pointed at a gleaming black truck two spaces away. "You almost made it."

Chapter 2

She was still as stubborn as he remembered.

Trace resisted the urge to chuckle. It shouldn't surprise him that Danica held fast to her independence. It was that persistence that drew him to her the moment he watched her beat some of his old high school buddies in a pick-up game of volleyball. Twelve summers ago. The best summer of his life.

The diesel engine roared to life and settled into the familiar and comforting rumble. He gripped the worn steering wheel. His civilian truck smelled like leather and horses. Compared to the metallic odor of the Humvees coated in the sandy dirt of Iraq or Afghanistan, his truck was heavenly. Trace glanced at Danica in the passenger seat and then backed out of the parking spot and shifted into gear. Once out of the parking garage, he directed the truck toward Danica's childhood home.

Dusk had settled in, night's fingers reaching across the skyline. By the time he reached his family ranch it would be dark.

Oh, the comfort of a fat mattress to sleep on tonight, and warm, clean blankets. Even the ground felt better than those rotten excuses for a mattress the Army provided.

Six more weeks. His enlistment would end and he could finish his sports therapy degree. The discharge couldn't come fast enough.

He looked at Danica. She slumped in the seat, her eyes closed as her head lulled toward the passenger-side window. The knee he'd wrapped was stretched the length of the floorboard. Sun-bleached strands draped across her cheek. How many times that summer long ago had he resisted the urge to finger her hair? She'd shortened it, probably to help manage it while she played on the beach.

Tearing his gaze from her, he redirected it on the road. Whatever their mothers were up to, it would prove interesting.

After five tours, five bloody, heart-wrenching tours, he wanted something good to happen for him. Trace swallowed against the tightness in his throat. He'd known what he'd gotten himself into when he enlisted and then re-enlisted as a combat medic. But nothing had prepared him for the sights and sounds of war. And its dangerously strong aftereffects.

His faith, and memories of the good times with his family, kept him afloat. When most medics washed out in one or two tours, Trace kept going. Longer than what was healthy.

Danica pushed herself upright and moaned.

"Do you have any pain meds?" he asked.

She looked at him. "In my carry-on."

Which was behind their seats. Trace sighed. She'd have to wait until they got to her mom's house. Next best thing was to get her mind off it.

"Pro level, huh? Going for the Olympics?"

"Trying. Gotta get this knee healthy before we can start again." Her athletic pants rustled as she shifted. "Are you on leave?"

"Switching duty stations. Visiting my folks before I report for duty at Fort Carson."

"How'd you manage getting stationed here?"

He shrugged. "Pull the right strings and you can get what you want."

"How are your parents?"

Trace slowed the truck and turned onto a residential street. "Good. Just celebrated their thirty-sixth anniversary."

"Wow, that's a long time."

"My grandparents made it to their sixty-seventh before my grandma died."

Facing him, Danica's mouth puckered. "How did they do it?"

Trace's heart constricted. He heard through Mom that Danica's grandmother had passed away a year ago. The woman had been Danica's lifeline to her mother's family.

"Sheer determination. 'Bout sums it up." He turned down the street to her mom's house. "That's what my grandpop always said."

"Hmm." Her attention returned to the windshield.

"I heard about your gram's passing. I'm sorry." Trace slowed the truck, his gaze darting along the street, counting the houses to find the right one.

"In heaven probably dancing her heart out for Jesus."

Trace grinned. "Won't we all be doing that?"

The fourth house on the block stood dark. This was the Lindsay home. Hadn't Danica's mom waited up for her? That summer they'd hung out, her mom didn't seem to care what time Danica returned home as long as she got home. Back then she left the light on. Or maybe Danica had when she left the house. She admitted her mom didn't pay much attention to her, so she was free to do pretty much what she wanted.

Back then she was ready to head off to college. What parent held onto rules at that point?

Trace pulled into the drive and cut the engine. "Is your mom out or something?"

"Uhh. . ." Her mouth drew into a thin line, and she swallowed. "I don't know."

"I'll check." He moved to exit the truck.

Danica grabbed his arm. "Wait." Her hand fell away. "Ah man. She would do it, too."

Rotating to face her, Trace frowned. "Do what?"

She heaved a sigh. "Mom probably skipped town. She complained about being here on the anniversary of Grams's death. Too many memories. But she never told me she would actually leave."

Trace frowned. "You're here alone?"

"Apparently."

His gaze dropped to her knee, then up. "In that huge house, with an injured ACL?"

Her shoulders stiffened. "Excuse me. I've been on my own since I tore it." She popped the door handle. "I can take care of myself, thank you very much."

Before he could bail from the truck and reach her side, she was out of the cab and had her bags in hand, ready to hobble to the door.

"Danica—"

"Trace, I don't go by that name. It's Danni. Always has been."

Tossing a rope around his ire and stuffing it away, he drew in a deep breath and let it out slowly. "Fine, Danni."

Under the streetlight, he noticed the lines in her forehead. She was probably frustrated to no end with him, but she needed to learn to lean on people once in a while. Or maybe he was someone she didn't want to lean on? Two and a half months twelve years ago hadn't given them much time to get to know each other.

"Hold up. Let's think about this before we go off half-cocked."

She tilted her head as if to say, *I'm listening*.

Groaning, he ran a hand over his face. "I can't in good conscience let you stay here alone. If your knee gives out again, you might not be able to get help."

"I'm not an invalid."

"No, just stubborn."

She narrowed her eyes and crossed her arms.

Did she have to prove him right? Maybe it wasn't tenacity he'd seen in her—maybe it was a streak of bullheadedness.

Trace held out his hand as a peace offering. "You only have to stay at my folks' place for tonight. Let your knee rest, get some sleep, and I'll bring you back here tomorrow."

Her features smoothed and her arms slid to her sides. She sighed. "For tonight. But I have to be back here tomorrow. I'm meeting up with my cousins in a few days and I need to get ready."

"Yeah, the family reunion thing."

He picked up her duffel bag and carry on and placed them in the backseat, hesitating at the subtle scent of citrus and coconut tickling his nose. He savored the closeness until she shifted. Stepping back, he shook his head. "Hop in. Then maybe you can tell me what this family reunion deal is about on the way to the ranch."

Danni glanced into the cab, back to him, then hobbled up. He closed the door behind her, catching her irritated grimace. Good. She was going to have help, whether she liked it or not.

Hopping into the pickup once more, he pulled out of the drive and headed for home.

Silence saturated the air around them. Guess she wasn't ready to spill the story yet. She sighed and slumped in the seat.

Trace resisted the urge to drum the steering wheel. "Meeting up with your cousins have anything to do with the anniversary of your grams's passing?"

"Yeah."

"Something special about it?"

"Yeah."

"You want to see them?"

"Yeah."

"Danni, you're going to have to elaborate here."

She looked at him, the streetlights flashing across her face. "Trace, I'm really not in the mood. I'm tired, I hurt, and I'm having a hard time wrapping my head around the fact that you just railroaded me into going to your ranch."

"All right, fine."

She slid farther down in the seat. "There's one good thing about staying at the ranch. It'll be quiet, and I can sleep in."

Oh no. Trace winced, and his gaze darted to her. "Um, Danni."

Her eyes closed and she let her chin drop to her chest. "What, Trace?"

"My family is having a welcome home party for me tomorrow."

"That's fine."

She was not going to like this. Especially with her body

still running on West Coast time. "Danni, this is going to be a big party."

Her eyes snapped open and she gaped at him.

"The house is full. You're not going to get any peace and quiet."

Chapter 3

A soft *whiff, whiff, whiff* dragged Danni out of deep sleep. She pried one eye open and found a white, furry nose in her face. She squealed and bolted upright, startling the black-and-white ball of fuzz. In a flurry of claws and blankets, the thing jumped off the bed into the arms of a blond pixie with pigtails.

"You're not Uncle Trace!"

Danni gaped at the child clad in pink-and-green camouflage from head to toe. "How'd you get in here? I had the door locked."

One arm clutched around the fuzzball, the girl pointed at the closet door. "There's a secret door in there." She stroked the rabbit. "You scared Duchess." The girl set the furball on the bed.

Long, silky black ears perked up, and the pretty little thing scooted closer to sniff Danni's hand. She smiled and stroked its fur. "She's pretty."

"Uncle Trace got her for me last time he was home. Mommy and Daddy said I can't have any more." The girl hunched down beside the bed, resting her chin on the edge. Changing course, the rabbit hopped to her owner and started licking her nose. "I think Duchess needs a friend."

Danni racked her brain. Trace had an older sister, Julia.

Eyeing the child in front of her, Danni estimated her to

be about five or six.

"Misty?" Trace's voice penetrated the door. "Are you in there?"

A screech erupted from Misty, and she grabbed up the startled rabbit. Danni had two seconds to drag the blankets up to her chin before Misty flung open the bedroom door and launched herself into her uncle's arms.

"I couldn't find you. Why aren't you in your room? Mommy said you came home late last night." Misty plopped a fist onto her hip, and her face puckered, Shirley Temple style. "And you didn't give me a come-home kiss."

Trace laughed and planted a raspberry on Misty's cheek. She giggled and squealed, the poor rabbit probably squished to death between them.

"Better?" he asked.

"Yes." Misty wiggled Duchess free and held her under Trace's nose. "Duchess wants one, too."

A pained expression covered Trace's face. Danni hid her grin behind the edge of the sheet. Wouldn't that be something to see—Army-man Trace Bryant kissing a rabbit.

"I think Duchess likes your kisses more." He set the girl down. "Your mom said it's time for breakfast."

She clutched his hand and tried to drag him along. "Come eat with me, Uncle Trace."

"In a minute." He extracted his hand. "Hurry up, or your mom will come looking for you."

Misty took off. Trace watched her go then looked at Danni.

Heat flushed her face, and she sank lower into the bed. "Niece?"

He grinned. "Yeah."

"She's cute."

"Yeah." Red colored his cheeks. "Um, breakfast is ready." He backed out of the doorway. "Hurry if you want something to eat."

"Okay." Danni clutched the blankets as he nodded and closed the door. She let out a breath, stirring stray strands that fell in her face.

This was going to be interesting, to say the least.

Certain she was alone, she slipped from the bed and entered the adjoining bathroom. Last night before going to bed, she'd removed the stabilizing tape on her knee and massaged it like the therapist had shown her. Twenty minutes later, Danni emerged from the bathroom in a cloud of steam. Rummaging through her suitcase, she pulled out a pair of jeans and a yellow short-sleeved blouse and dressed. As she ran a brush through her damp hair, her attention drifted to her surroundings.

When Trace escorted her here last night, Danni didn't bother to look the room over. She'd taken five minutes to get ready for bed and then collapsed, falling asleep minutes after her head hit the pillow.

Her gaze slid from the huge map of Iraq dotted with red pins to the equally large map of Afghanistan with blue pins. She drifted to the maps, squinting at the oddly named towns. Did the pins mark places Trace had been stationed?

A glint to her right drew her to a shelf lined with mementos. A small plastic box was propped against a rodeo belt buckle. Danni picked it up, and her throat tightened. The Bronze Star. What had Trace done to receive this? Cold dread pricked her spine. People who received this star had most likely faced something horrific.

She set the box down. Since the start of the war, she'd verbally supported the troops, going so far as playing in a special match in South Carolina put on for the soldiers. But had it really meant anything to her? Another promotional ploy. A rung up on the ladder to the Olympics. She felt like she'd only paid lip service to her country, when guys like Trace had faced untold dangers to just come home.

Danni hadn't planned on staying for the homecoming party. She dropped the hairbrush on top of her suitcase. Maybe she should stick around. Trace deserved that much from her. The meeting with her cousins was in two days. Plenty of time to ready the quilt blocks and find Mom's piece.

Danni glanced at her suitcase and blew out a breath. A little makeup probably wouldn't hurt. She pulled out her small cosmetic case. Typically, she refused to wear makeup. What was the point when she showered between games all the time? But there were occasional moments when she had to get dolled up for a benefit or charity event.

With a sigh, she returned to the bathroom. This was no charity event.

It was Trace Bryant, a Bronze Star recipient.

Trace grinned at his niece as she chatted with her rabbit like it was a close friend. Duchess munched on a carrot and didn't seem to care. Orange lined the rabbit's mouth, making her look like she wore lipstick. The whole scene was too cute.

"Misty, eat your pancake," Trace's sister said as she passed the table.

"I'm full, Mommy."

Julia sighed and set a stack of boxes on the kitchen counter. "Fine. Put your plate in the sink and go wash the syrup off your hands."

"Okay." Misty hurried the plate to the sink then rushed back to her rabbit.

"Don't pick up. . ." Julia groaned when Misty grabbed the poor thing in her sticky grasp.

Trace chuckled. "Too late."

His sister scowled at him. "Now you can clean it." She extracted the squirming ball of fuzz from a protesting Misty and plopped it in Trace's lap.

He winced as its claws dug into his thighs. "Ow."

A wide smile on her lips, Julia scooted Misty out of the kitchen. "Don't give her a bath. A wet washcloth will do."

Eyeing the matted fur, Trace looked at his departing sister. "Why not a bath?"

" 'Cause then you'll need stitches," Julia called from down the hall.

"Come on, Duchess." He scooped up the rabbit and gingerly carried it to the sink.

Soft footfalls brought his attention to the doorway. Danni entered the kitchen, a bemused expression on her face. Trace did a double take. Was she wearing makeup?

"What are you doing?" she asked.

He glanced at Duchess. "Cleaning syrup out of her fur." He ran a wet cloth over the rabbit.

Danni joined him. "The thing is terrified."

"You would be, too, if you belonged to Misty." He scrubbed a stubborn sticky spot. "I'm surprised she's still alive."

"I'm surprised you gave a—how old is Misty?"

"Seven."

One of Danni's eyebrows rose. "She's seven? I thought she was younger."

Giving her a one-shoulder shrug, Trace dumped the hairy washcloth in the sink and cradled the rabbit against his chest. "I was younger than Misty when I got my first pet."

"A horse doesn't count as a pet." A mischievous smile turned up the corners of her mouth. She rubbed the rabbit's head. "She's adorable."

So was Danni. The yellow blouse brought out the blond highlights in her hair and the rosy tint in her cheeks. She smelled like peaches and cream today. Hard as she tried to be a tomboy, Danni's feminine side often slipped through. Did she realize how pretty she was? And how much it affected him?

Trace's chest ached. He'd hoped and prayed for a second chance with her. Never did he imagine he'd get it. He had to make the most of what little time he had with her today.

"How's your knee feeling?"

"Better." She moved to the coffeemaker. "Can't even tell I overdid it yesterday."

"Good." Trace placed Duchess in her cage, glimpsing Julia and his mother outside hanging red, white, and blue banners. They didn't have to do this again. The four previous homecoming parties were more than enough. But no one said no to Mom and lived to tell about it.

Worry and nerves played havoc on his gut. He needed to tell his family. His secret weighed on him like a millstone. The elated expressions on his parents' faces when he told them he was getting out of the service had stifled any desire to reveal the true reason. So far the triggers that set off his post-traumatic stress disorder hadn't occurred around his family. Hopefully they never would. Hopefully they could bask in their hero worship for a day or two longer.

"Wow." Danni's breathless voice sent shivers down his back.

Trace looked at her. Her green eyes were riveted to the spectacle in the backyard.

"When they throw a party, they go all out."

He hooked his thumbs in his belt to avoid caressing her face. "Fifth time around. Mom and Julia have this down to a fine art."

Danni stared into her coffee mug, the amusement and wonder gone.

"Would I impose if I stayed for your party?" She gave him a hopeful look.

His heart swelled. *Lord, is this a dream? Am I getting a chance to spend more time with her?*

"You're not imposing on anything. We would love it if you stayed." *I would love it if you stayed.*

Her gaze returned to the decorating outside. "It'll be nice to see your family and some of our old friends again. It's been so long."

Trace couldn't help but think that this party would be a lot more beneficial to Danni than it would be to him.

Chapter 4

Country music mingled with the boisterous laughter and conversations of Trace's friends and family. Danni hovered at the back of the party, nursing a lemonade and regret. She shouldn't have asked to stay. Ridiculous sentimentality. There were other ways to show her appreciation for the sacrifices that Trace had made for their country.

She swirled the lemonade, watching it swish around in the plastic cup. Were her cousins in town yet? When they were together for Grams's funeral, they had discussed how to go about fulfilling her request. Grams wanted their mothers to reconcile within a year, but Zoe's mom had been bad off, then passed away. It now fell to the cousins to set right what their mothers had ripped apart.

Mom had been the peacemaker, and she tried to keep the peace between her sisters when the dispute over Gramps's inheritance came up after his death. Things went south fast, and Mom retaliated, driving the wedge between all of them for good.

Pop!

Danni jerked, the cup slipped from her hand, and lemonade splashed on her pant leg. Quickly scanning the now silent group, her breath hitched.

Misty stood horrified in the center of the crowd, a broken

balloon lying on the ground at her feet. Nearby, Trace seemed to grope for something at his waist. People veered out of his path as he swung around.

"Give me a gun! Now! Before they get here!"

Danni's heart stalled. Was Trace having a flashback? She took a step forward. But pulled up short. What if he got violent? She couldn't risk any more injuries to her knee.

Trace swore and reached for his uncle's shirt. "I need a gun."

His dad tried to intervene, and Trace shoved him aside like a rag doll. The older man nearly fell on Misty, who burst into tears.

Trace pointed to the little girl and yelled, "Someone shut her up, or they'll hear us."

Julia swooped in, grabbed up her daughter, and backpedaled as Trace advanced on them.

Determination steeled her body, and Danni rushed in.

Lord, don't let him hit me.

As she drew closer, his rapid breathing seemed to suck the energy from the air. His wild eyes darted from left to right. Sweat beaded on his forehead, his skin turning pale. Danni swallowed hard and eased in front of him.

"Trace," she whispered.

His gaze bounced off her, around the group, then back.

"Trace, it's Danni." She grimaced. "Danica, remember?"

He frowned, the cloud of panic on his face lifting. "Danica?"

"Yeah." She forced a smile. "Remember how much I dislike that name?"

A tentative smile played at the corners of his mouth. "I love it."

"Why is that?"

Slowly, his control slipped into place and the fear cleared from his eyes. "Because it's beautiful, like you."

His words slammed into her like a killer spike to the face from beach volleyball champ Phil Dalhausser. Trace thought she was beautiful? She shook the shock off. This wasn't about her at the moment. Careful not to move fast, she held her hand out to him.

"Let's take a walk. I haven't seen the horses yet."

Trace glanced around, and he blanched. Danni followed his gaze. His mom stood with a hand over her mouth and tears pouring down her face. Julia, her eyes glistening, held a sobbing Misty. Apparently, they didn't know he had post-traumatic stress.

Easing into his line of sight, Danni stared at him. "Trace." It took a moment for him to register her presence again. She smiled. "I want to see the horses."

"Uh. . .okay." He about-faced and marched off.

His family and friends parted like the Red Sea for Moses. Danni hurried after him. Once he rounded the corner of the house, his pace slowed. She caught up with him and stayed at his side, saying nothing.

Talk would come soon enough.

When they reached the horse pasture closest to the house, Trace flopped to the ground and leaned against a post. Drawing his legs up, he propped his elbows on his knees and drove his fingers through his hair.

"I can't believe I did that. In front of all of them."

The torture in his voice pierced Danni's heart. She sat down next to him and dragged his hand away from his face. His skin was flushed. A by-product of the flashback?

"Trace, look at me."

He hesitated a second then looked at her. A wet sheen coated his eyes. His clenched jaw fired spasms across his cheek.

"How long have you had PTSD?"

He moved to turn his head away. Danni grasped his rock-solid chin and forced him to face her.

"I didn't say you could stop looking at me. How long?"

The warmth from his sigh seeped into her hand, sending a chill through her soul. "Since my third tour."

"And I take it by your mom's reaction, you didn't tell anyone."

"What's the point? They can't help me." Words of the defeated.

She released his chin and he dropped it to his chest. "Have you been getting help?"

"Some. It's hard when you're in the field."

"Then get out."

His head jerked up, and his heated gaze bore holes into her. "I am." He flung his hand at the world. "That's why I got stationed at Fort Carson. I've got six weeks and I'm done."

Done? He was getting out for good? After all this time, and two wars, Trace was walking away from the Army.

Danni pressed her back into the fence. Above them, fat white clouds drifted by on a brilliant blue backdrop. The crisp autumn leaves rattled in the breeze. Behind them a horse whinnied.

"Does this have anything to do with how you got the Bronze Star?"

"Everything."

Whatever happened for him to get that medal, Danni

was fairly certain she'd never hear the story behind it. A car engine purred to life, and a couple of doors snapped closed. A few seconds later the crunch of gravel reached them.

"Sounds like the party's breaking up." Trace's chuckle sounded brittle. "I'm getting good at being a downer these days."

She jerked her attention to him and scowled. "Knock that off."

He looked at her sharply.

"I know PTSD is rough, but throwing a pity party for yourself isn't going to make it go away."

"Here comes bossy Danni."

A pang twinged in her chest. Is that how he thought of her? Was that how he'd always thought of her? "That's unfair."

He had the good grace to grimace. "Sorry, that's not. . .I don't mind." He took her hand and squeezed. "You saved me back there. If you hadn't. . ."

An odd sensation blossomed in her stomach and spread. Something inside of her wanted to crawl into his lap and kiss away the hurt and the memories plaguing him.

"This isn't the first time you've saved me."

She jolted at his admission and gaped at him. "What do you mean?"

With his other hand, he reached over and trailed his finger along her jaw. "Thoughts of you got me through." He drew his hand back. "I know we barely knew each other. And we lost contact, but. . ."

Her throat constricted. Why did he have to go and do that? She swallowed hard and freed her hand. "You stopped writing to me first. I figured you'd found someone else."

Trace frowned. He dropped one leg to the ground and

scooted to face her. “Not someone, something. A war started and I got sucked straight into it.” He sighed. “I started tons of letters, but I didn't know what to tell you.” He directed his attention to a long blade of grass and plucked it. Rolling it between his finger and thumb. “Why don't you like the name Danica?”

“You know why.”

His gaze slid to her then back to the blade. “Because you think it's too girly is a lame reason.”

She sighed and massaged her knee. “My dad used to call me Danni. After he died, I wanted to keep a piece of him alive. Mom was the only one, besides you, who refused to give up Danica.”

“Why didn't you tell me that before?”

“It still hurt to talk about him.”

Trace twined his fingers with hers and tugged her close. “Guess we're airing a lot of hurts today.”

Danni leaned against his side and let her head rest on his muscular shoulder. His musky scent enveloped her. She closed her eyes and filed away this moment for later. When she returned to San Diego she wanted to remember every minute with him to pull out when she got lonely.

A vibration in her jeans pocket startled her. She lifted her head from Trace's shoulder and dug out her cell phone. There was a message in her voice mail. She called her mailbox and found out Zoe was running behind, but she'd get to Colorado Springs as soon as she could.

Which reminded Danni. “I need to get to my mom's house.” She crawled onto her feet and dusted grass from her rear.

“Now?” The pained tone in Trace's voice made her turn.

The light in his eyes had dimmed. His gaze flicked to the house then back to her. Danni looked that direction as well. No one stood outside. The few visible party decorations drifted lazily—almost dejectedly—in the breeze. With his secret now out in the open he wasn't ready to face his family alone.

She sighed, thrusting out her hand and wiggling her fingers. "Not at this exact moment. But I really can't stay here another night. I've got to find something at Mom's before I meet up with my cousins."

He stared at her hand a moment. "What would that something be?"

"A missing quilt piece." Danni planted her free fist on her hip. "If you need me for backup I'm here."

Heaving what could have been the most soul weary sigh she'd ever heard, Trace grasped her hand and she hauled him up. He jerked his arm back, knocking Danni off-balance. She landed against his solid chest. The sneak used the awkward position to wrap his arms around her waist and hold her close.

"I've missed you, Danni," he whispered.

His warm breath tickled her ear, sending a shiver down her neck and through her body. All those years in the Army had matured him, mentally and physically. Not a shred of the care-free, scrawny twenty-year-old remained. He was all man.

It felt good in his arms. Drawing strength from someone other than herself. Her volleyball partner's family had been supportive when Danni hurt her knee, but it wasn't the same as having her own family.

The thought of her partner snapped Danni out of her reverie. They needed to get back into training for next season. The Olympics loomed, and they had a shot to make it. She had no clue what Trace planned to do once he was out of the

Army. But if his deep ties to his family were any indication, she'd bet her college national championship trophy he was staying put in Colorado Springs.

Danni wiggled until she broke Trace's grip, and backed away. "Trace, I'm going home to California."

Chapter 5

For a brief moment, Trace relished the feel of Danni in his arms. The subtle scent of peaches in her hair. Her feminine body pressed against his. He couldn't believe they were together. She was here for him and nothing else. All those years of hoping and praying she thought about him the way he thought about her washed over him.

Then she brought him crashing back to earth and the reality that she had something waiting for her in California. And he would be left drifting once he discharged.

He couldn't get attached to her again. This time when she left there would be no coming back.

Trace stepped away from her. "You know, I think I'll be okay talking with my folks." He nodded at the house. "Go get your things. I'll take you to your mom's place."

Danni blinked, her features melding into a frown. "You sure?"

With a shrug, he rammed his hands into his Wrangler pockets. "Don't worry." He forced a smile. "Whatever it is your cousins and you are up to, you need to find that quilt piece."

She remained rooted, her eyes seeming to attempt to peel back the shelter he erected around his emotions. "Okay." Turning, she wandered back to the house.

Trace watched her enter the house. Heaving a frustrated

sigh, he headed to the horse barn, where friendly whinnies greeted him. The heady scent of horseflesh and hay filled his senses as he walked past the stalls, but did little to comfort him. On a wall toward the back of the barn, he scaled a ladder to the hayloft.

Once his eyes adjusted to the dim interior, he wove a path through the bales to the loft door. He settled on the edge of the opening and let his legs dangle. His gaze swept over the view of horse pastures and empty hay fields. The Rocky Mountains towered in the distance, mist shrouding their snow-draped tops. Everything in the world was peaceful. Except inside him.

Danni was right. He had to tell his parents about the PTSD. He'd put it off too long. He didn't have the first clue how to begin, or what to say. How did he tell the people he loved something wasn't right inside his head? That seeing men die in his arms and knowing there wasn't a thing he could do for them had messed him up? Every time he visited, in between tours, he'd managed to put up a good front. Luckily, he didn't suffer from nightmares. As far as he knew, he didn't have them.

It was out there now. And no amount of sidetracking would keep his parents from knowing the ugly truth.

The horrified look on Misty's face flashed through his head. He scrubbed his face and groaned. Would she forgive him for scaring her?

Oddly enough, Danni seemed to handle it well. He couldn't believe he'd blurted out that he thought she was beautiful. Like everything else between them, she took it in stride and moved on.

She'd told him she always dreamed of playing pro

volleyball, especially beach. That dream, and a full-ride scholarship to Southern Cal, had taken her far. But from the looks of her knee, she couldn't play full-out competitive volleyball for another four months, maybe more. One wrong move now and it might mean the end of her career.

And a lovesick fool reeling from the horrid effects of PTSD probably didn't help either.

Trace gripped the edge of the loft and peered down at the ground. Maybe squeezing her like a doll and admitting he missed her had been the wrong move. On second thought, there was no maybe about it. She made it clear his advances weren't welcome. He needed a different approach.

The horses whinnied. Someone had entered the barn. After a few moments the scuff of boots on the ladder rungs reached him.

Trace twisted around and waited. Soon his dad appeared through the maze of bales, a grim expression on his face. It looked like that long-overdue conversation about his PTSD was about to happen sooner than Trace expected.

"Hey, Dad."

His father gave him a solemn nod. "Son, I think we need to talk."

Danni stared at the pictures on the mantle. The one of Trace and her after a long afternoon of playing sand volleyball stood front and center. She couldn't believe his mom kept the photo, much less framed it and placed it where everyone could see.

Did both their mothers hope they'd get together?

Sighing, she left the living room and strolled down the

hall to Trace's room. The time she'd spent with his family today made her heart ache for what she once had with her own. It would be good to see her cousins again and catch up. Their mothers might never mend their rift, but Danni and her cousins wouldn't let that stop them.

All those years of being on her own wore Danni down. Success came with a price. She'd heard the rumors on the pro beach circuit. People wondered about her life and how she managed to keep her family away. Yet no one bothered to ask her personally. Speculation sold news and tickets.

Danni was Orphan Annie who rose to the coveted position of Queen of the Sand Court. On her own and alone.

She shut the bedroom door and flopped on the bed. She stared at the ceiling, trying to make images out of the swirls in the paint, avoiding the job of gathering her things.

A sniffle from the closet drew her attention, and she propped herself up on her elbow. The sniffle came again, louder this time. She rolled off the bed and onto the floor.

Scooting close to the door, she left it closed and leaned against the wall.

"Knock, knock," she said softly.

"Who's there?"

Danni smiled at Misty's muffled voice. "Duchess."

Scuffling sounds came through the door then it creaked open. Misty poked her head out. "You're not Duchess."

"No, but I'm a friend."

The girl studied Danni with watery eyes.

"Do you want to tell me what's wrong?"

Misty sniffed and ran the back of her hand under her nose. Danni grimaced at the thought of what she rubbed on her hand.

"Why did Uncle Trace act like a bad guy?"

Oh, boy. Guess Julia hadn't talked to Misty about what she saw. Danni's gaze flicked to the bedroom door and back to the little girl. Would she cross a line if she told Misty the truth about her Uncle Trace?

"Why are you hiding in here?"

Misty shook her head, her pigtails flying. "Mommy told me to go to my room and stay there until she came to get me. That was forever ago."

Probably more like ten minutes. Danni cocked her head. "Tell you what. Why don't you run into the bathroom and wash those tears away. When you're done, we'll play a game."

Misty's pixie face lit up. "Really? What kind of game?"

"I'll show you when you're ready." Danni nodded at the bathroom. "Hurry up."

Misty scrambled to her feet and skipped into the bathroom. While she ran the water, Danni slipped out of the room, located a wayward balloon, and returned as Misty exited the bathroom. The girl eyed the balloon.

"What are we doing with that?"

Danni grinned. "We're going to play a little game of balloon volleyball."

Girlish giggles drew Trace to his bedroom. What was Danni doing in there? He paused outside the door and listened.

Misty squealed. "I'm winning."

"Not for long," he heard Danni say.

Trace opened the door a crack and peered inside. Danni and Misty sat on the floor facing each other, batting a white balloon between them. Hands clasped together and her arms out in perfect passing form, Misty hit the balloon. Danni had taught her to play balloon volleyball.

As if sensing his presence, Misty spun around on her knees and stared at him. A look of momentary fear swept through her eyes.

Trace entered the room cautiously and squatted down to his niece's level. "Hey, pretty girl."

Her gaze darted to Danni. With a nod, Danni smiled. Misty faced Trace again. She seemed frozen, unsure of what to do. Then suddenly she exploded, running at him and squeezing his neck until he couldn't breathe.

Trace choked back the tears and wrapped her in a tight embrace.

"I'm sorry I scared you. I didn't mean to."

Misty sobbed something. With a bit of maneuvering to unlock her arms from his neck, he drew her back.

"What?"

"I shouldn't have popped the balloon. Mommy told me to be good, and I wasn't."

Trace gave her a sad smile. "Balloons pop. What happened today is not your fault. Okay?"

Her bottom lip trembled and she nodded. He smoothed some of her fly-aways and tucked them behind her ear.

"There's a lot of stuff going on inside my head right now. But you just remember, I love you, and nothing is going to change that. Got me?"

Misty thrust her shoulders back and snapped him a little-girl salute. "Yes, sir."

Trace chuckled and blew a raspberry on her cheek until she squealed with laughter. After another bone-crushing hug, he stood. "Misty, I need to talk with Miss Danni. Can you go find your mom or Grandma?"

A mischievous spark flared to life in her eyes. "Are you going to play balloon volleyball with Danni, too?"

Danni snorted and clamped a hand over her mouth. Trace cleared his throat and shook his head.

"I don't think I'd win."

"Oh." Misty shrugged. "I did." And with that, she skipped from the room.

"Did she?"

Slowly, Danni climbed to her feet and sat on the corner of the bed. "It's hard to move when you're longer than the room is wide." A smile brightened her features. "Future player there."

Trace glanced at the door and closed it. "Maybe. She loves barrel racing, too." He whipped out the desk chair and straddled it, crossing his arms over the back. "You'd make a good coach. Ever considered it?"

"It's a possibility." She shrugged and began massaging her knee. "I found Misty crying in the closet. Figured a li'l game would get her mind off the party."

"Thanks for that."

"I was a little girl like her once." She winced.

"Here." Trace stood, kicked the chair around to face the bed, sat, and patted his thigh.

One eyebrow rose and she frowned. "What?"

"I'll give you a proper massage. It'll help with the circulation and prevent any more strain."

Seconds ticked past as she seemed to contemplate his request. Would she give in? Or would she let that stubborn streak take over?

Lord, for once let her accept my help without a fight.

She sighed. “Okay. But let me change into shorts first. You might want to get an ice pack. I’ll probably need it.”

He pushed the chair back and stood. “Be right back.”

As he left the room, he looked over his shoulder. Danni pulled out a pair of purple athletic shorts from her suitcase and wadded them in her hand. She straightened and met his gaze.

“What?”

“Danni, it’s okay to let someone help you.”

“Isn’t that what I’m doing? Letting you help me?”

He shook his head. “I don’t mean about just this. Something to think about.”

Chapter 6

Danni emerged from the bathroom, trepidation swimming in her stomach. She shouldn't have agreed to Trace's offer to massage her knee. He was supposed to be taking her to her mom's house. A simple drive into town tomorrow to visit a local massage therapist would've done the trick.

Something in his eyes when she looked up and found him watching her and Misty play squeezed in her heart. He was still hurting from his PTSD episode. Danni didn't have the heart to turn him down when he made his offer.

He hadn't returned with the ice pack yet. Danni clamped down on her lip and contemplated putting her jeans back on and forgetting the whole thing. And then Trace strolled into the room carrying a cooler. So much for that idea.

"How are we doing this?"

"Sit on the bed with your leg extended, and I'll sit in the chair beside it." He set the cooler on the floor next to the dresser, rolled the desk chair over, and then patted the edge of the bed.

She could do this. Her knee ached, and a massage would help. She sat on the bed, legs stretched out, and settled back against the headboard.

Pinpricks skittered up her leg at his touch. She watched him as he gently probed the tender areas with his fingertips. Warmth spread from his hands and the pain eased.

"Where did you learn to do this?"

His gaze flicked up to her then back to his miracle hands. "I've been working on my sports therapy degree. As soon as I'm out of the Army, I'll finish one more class and then I can get my license."

"I didn't know you wanted to do that."

"Still don't know if I want to continue." He began rubbing the whole knee and part of her thigh.

"Why not? It's a good career."

He shrugged, continuing to massage. His facial muscles twitched, but Danni couldn't decide if he was upset by her question or by his indecision.

Danni closed her eyes and enjoyed Trace's heavenly massage.

"Say you get your license, where do you plan to work?"

"If I get it I could work anywhere."

She looked at him. "Anywhere?"

His massage focused on the underside of her knee and she tensed when it tickled. Trace paused and frowned.

"Did that hurt?"

"I'm ticklish there."

A glint flashed through his hazel eyes. In the back of Danni's head a voice whispered a warning.

"Don't for one second think you can tickle me. My spiking arm isn't injured."

A wide grin split his face. "Don't worry. I remember what a ball to the face from you feels like." Pressing a little harder, he continued on the back of her knee. "Your surgeon did a good job."

"I would hope so. He's the best in the business." Danni grabbed the extra pillow on the bed and hugged it to her midsection. The attempt to stop the butterflies didn't quite work. "In two months I should be able to start light training with my teammate."

There was a slight hesitation in Trace's movements. Was he still upset over her not staying? Why should he be? They weren't together.

"Trace—"

"What was your degree at USC?"

Danni blinked at the quick change in subject. She got her bearings back on track and squeezed the pillow. "Physical education."

He stopped and rocked back in the chair. "You're a PE teacher?"

"I could be a PE teacher. Training and competing take up all my time, so I never got a job."

"A part of me is surprised by your choice, but another isn't."

Tossing the pillow away, she crossed her arms and frowned. "Am I supposed to be offended by that?"

"No. I think it's great." He removed the cloth-covered gel pack from the cooler and laid it over her knee. "Your knee healed well. The surgeon might bump you into light training sooner than you think."

She swallowed against the sudden tightness in her throat. "Really?"

Trace stared at her, seeming to examine her face, then flipped the cooler lid shut. "Just don't overdo it on my say-so." He stood and pushed the chair under the desk. "Still want to go to your mom's house?"

His movements were sluggish. Today's events had taken a toll on him. Having him drive her into town might drain him further.

Danni sighed. "You know, it can wait until tomorrow. I've got one more day before I meet up with my cousins."

"Are you sure? It's not too much trouble."

"Yeah. Honestly, you look like you need to get some sleep."

Trace gave a one-shoulder shrug. "If you say so." His eyebrows dipped into a *V*. "Are you going to tell me what this family reunion deal is about?"

Danni slid her fingers through her hair, twirling a strand around one. "Guess you deserve that much. Right after Grams's funeral we, my cousins and I, were each given a set of quilt squares for an heirloom quilt. Most of them were done, with the names of each female family member on them. There were four left undone that we were supposed to finish. And on the first anniversary of Grams's death, we four granddaughters are supposed to meet at the Broadmoor and assemble the quilt together." She dropped her hand in her lap. "Mom took the square with her name on it and hid it from me. She refuses to tell me what she did with it. I want to go look for it, since she's not there to stop me."

"Why did she hide it?"

"I think she's still sore over the fight and how her sisters treated her. And apparently ticked at Grams for doing this. Grams said in her will that the inheritance will be paid out to only the granddaughters."

Trace's eyebrows rose. "Just how much money are we talking about here?"

"A lot." Danni toyed with the edge of the quilt. "I've got a stack of medical bills that money could pay off."

"Is that the only reason you're getting together with your cousins?"

She jerked her head up and glared at him. "My cousins

meant the world to me, Trace. They were as close as sisters at one time. Just because our mothers were a bunch of hotheads doesn't mean we have to follow in their footsteps. I just want us all to be a family again."

He placed a hand on her shin and gave a gentle squeeze. "We'll go to your mom's house tomorrow and find the quilt piece."

"You want to help?"

"It's the least I can do after you saved my hide during the party."

Trace stared into the half-empty cup of decaf. Around him, silence prevailed. The only light shining in the house was in the kitchen where he sat at the breakfast bar. After a three-hour discussion with his family about his PTSD, they'd trudged off to bed while he stayed up to pray and think.

His family was satisfied that he had taken steps to get out of the Army and seek counseling. What they weren't happy with was his decision to finish his sports therapy training as soon as his enlistment was up. Both of his parents thought he should take some time off, let his mind heal. But Trace felt certain that if he remained stagnant, the PTSD would worsen. On that note they parted, deciding they all needed to sleep on it.

Well, they all went to sleep. He couldn't get his mind to settle.

The soft shuffle of feet across carpet drew his attention. In an oversized white professional beach volleyball T-shirt and the same purple shorts from earlier, Danni entered the kitchen. Her mussed hair rebelled from the ponytail she'd tried to tame it with. She shuffled up to the bar, dragged out a stool, and plopped onto it.

"What-are-you-drinkin'?"

"Decaf. Want some?"

She harrumphed.

"Does that mean yes?"

She grunted. Fighting off the urge to laugh, Trace stood and headed for the coffeepot.

"Wha' time is it?"

He glanced at the stove clock. "One-thirty." He filled a cup and brought it to her. "What are you doing up?"

"I don't know. Saw the light on and thought. . ." She took a sip then set the cup down. "Why are you up?"

"Praying and thinking."

" 'Bout what?"

He circled the rim of his mug with a finger. "A lot of stuff." Stuff that could change the course of his life. And hopefully hers, too.

"Did you and your parents talk about your PTSD?"

"Yeah."

"How'd it go?"

Trace met her more-aware gaze. "Better than I expected."

A smile tilted up one corner of her mouth. "See, I told ya."

"No, if I recall correctly, you told me it sucks and to stop throwing pity parties."

She rolled her eyes. "Details." She drank more coffee and cradled the cup. "Now that they know, what's next?"

"Finish up my enlistment, get out, continue getting help, and get my sports therapy license. Though my folks don't agree with the last one."

"I can't believe you're getting out. You always talked about being a lifer."

"Yeah, but we didn't know that the world as we knew it was about to end and that the war would go on for so long. It wears on you, Danni. The daily exposure to blood and carnage. I'd do what I could and have to move on."

Images and voices flashed through his head. The acrid stench of smoke and gunpowder filled his senses. He drew in a ragged breath, hoping to cleanse the odor from his nose. It only stirred more memories.

The soft feather-touch of Danni's hand anchored him in the present. Trace fixed his gaze on their joined hands. How did she do that? How was it that the thought of Danni kept him sane through the fighting and the death? And her presence now helped him see past those nightmares.

"One day, will you tell me the story of how you got the Bronze Star?"

He started to pull his hand away. She stopped him, intertwining her long, nimble fingers with his. His heart throbbed and his blood thickened. One act of tenderness had him wanting to drag her across the counter and kiss her senseless.

"I said one day. I know you guys don't like to talk about stuff like that with civilians."

"How do I know there will be another day with you?"

Danni's hand spasmed, but she didn't pull away. "We don't. But there's always heaven."

Smiling, Trace ran his thumb over her knuckles. "Heaven will work. By then I might be able to tell you."

They sat in companionable silence while Danni finished her coffee. Finally, she freed her hand and stood. Trace ached to hold on to her a moment longer. If his plan failed, she would walk out of his life for good. He didn't think he could handle another blow.

She set her mug in the sink and headed for the bedroom.

"Danni." Trace grimaced at the crack in his voice.

She hesitated and faced him. "Yeah?"

"Misty was hoping you'd go riding with us tomorrow. Think you can swing it before we go to your mom's?"

"I think I can." Her gaze dropped to her knee and then met his. "What does the sports therapist say about the status of my bum knee?"

It would never get old, hearing her call him that. "If you wrap your knee, I think a ride won't hurt you any. Might do you some good, actually."

A frown marred her pretty face. "I don't have any boots."

"I think there's a pair of Mom's or Julia's that might fit you."

"All right," Danni said and then left the kitchen.

Trace looked down into his empty mug. Her interest in him completing his training for the license sealed it. He'd make a few inquiries tomorrow before they went riding. Maybe by the time he took her to her mother's house he'd have a solid answer.

Chapter 7

A note on the breakfast bar directed Danni outside. A pair of boots sat on the tiled floor next to the counter. She grinned and slid her feet inside. They felt comfortable.

On her way out the door, Danni grabbed a huge blueberry muffin and ate it while she strolled to the stables. The crisp October air was ripe with the scent of pine, musk, and sun-cured hay. Such a contrast to the smell of ocean and beach she woke to in San Diego.

She popped the last of the muffin in her mouth, tossed the wrapper into a nearby trash can, and entered the stable's dim interior. Once her eyes adjusted, she made her way down the aisle. Misty's chatter guided her to a small area at the end of the stalls. Three horses swished their tails as they waited to be saddled.

Trace emerged from the tack room lugging a saddle, with Misty hot on his heels. Danni's breath lodged in her throat at the sight of him in a form-hugging dirt-brown T-shirt, jeans, scuffed boots, and an old ball cap. Scruff shadowed his face, enhancing his rugged features. She worked at her tight throat until she could swallow.

Time had made her forget how good Trace looked in cowboy mode. Her last memory of him was the day they saw each other before he headed out for his medic training. He'd been in one of those woodland-patterned uniforms. He'd looked good then, too.

But the Trace of today trumped the Trace of yesterday.

"Danni's here." Misty's squeak slammed Danni back to the present.

Trace propped an elbow on the saddle he'd just settled on a sorrel-and-white Paint. His lazy smile was like a drug. "Remember how to do this?"

She exhaled and forced a smile. "Like riding a bike."

He patted the well-muscled rump of the black next to him. "He's yours. Get to work."

While she and Trace saddled the horses, Misty chatted like a magpie about her bunny, her parents, and her horse. Danni stole glances at Trace, feeling liquid heat surge through her veins each time. The man had a pull on her.

Seeming to sense her scrutiny, he paused in tightening the cinch on Misty's horse and met Danni's gaze. His eyes darkened to the color of melted chocolate as they stared at each other.

"Uncle Trace, can we go?"

A muscle twitched in his cheek. "Almost ready." He broke eye contact to look at his niece. "Go get your helmet on."

"Okay." Skirting around the horses in a wide arc, Misty hurried into the tack room.

Free of his pull, Danni jerked her cinch strap a final time then wrapped it around the ring. Double-checking that the saddle was secure, she moved to the black's head with the bridle.

"Danni." Trace's whisper startled her.

She spun and collided with him. Her stomach did a funny flip at the feel of his well-muscled chest. The air whooshed from her lungs. Cornered, she had no choice but to look up.

The expression on his face turned her into a pile of dry sand. He wanted to kiss her.

Fear pulsated from her heart. If she let him, there was no going back. She wouldn't have the strength to leave him.

"Danni, I—"

"Trace, don't." She dared to touch him, pressing her hand into his solid chest and pushing him back. "We can't."

"Why?"

Too many reasons why they couldn't raced through her head. Lots more of why they should competed with the why nots. Closing her eyes, she turned from him. "You know why."

"I'm ready." Never had Misty's return been so welcomed.

With control Danni envied, Trace moved away. He caught up his niece and lifted her onto her horse. "Okay, squirt. You know the drill. No running ahead. No—"

"Ignoring you or the horse. And always be aware of my surroundings. I know." She gave her uncle a sassy roll of her eyes. "I've done this like a thousand times."

"Watch yourself." Trace winked at her then mounted his Paint. "Danni, you might want to use the mounting block because of your knee."

She led her horse to the three-step block next to the open bay doors. "Planned on it."

Once she was settled in the saddle, they left the stable. Trace led their little group with Misty next to him. Bringing up the rear, Danni sat back and enjoyed the ride and scenery.

While the Pacific Ocean was beautiful, nothing compared to the Rocky Mountains. The cloud-covered peaks and the lush valleys were breathtaking. She'd missed looking out her window each morning to stare at them. Her gaze slid to Trace. As much as she'd missed him.

Whoa! Where'd that come from? She'd been an awful friend and forgot about him. Hadn't she?

Looking back over the last ten years or so, she guessed she really hadn't forgotten about him as much as she thought. There were moments like when she played for the soldiers in South Carolina when she wondered if Trace was there to watch her. Or when she was laid up in the hospital the night before her surgery watching the news and saw where a combat unit had been bombed. Fear over the possibility of Trace being with that unit lanced her worse than her surgery.

Misty's hand shot out and they reined in the horses. A mule deer emerged from a stand of trees. It stopped and stared at them, its tail flicking back and forth. Misty giggled and the deer darted back into the dark interior.

"Beautiful," Danni muttered.

"I agree."

She looked at Trace and froze. He was staring at her.

"Come on, Uncle Trace. I want to ride up to the pond." Misty urged her mount forward.

"Wait for us, Misty."

Letting his niece ride ahead of them, Trace lingered next to Danni. "Is someone special waiting for you in San Diego?"

"You mean, do I have a boyfriend waiting?"

He pulled the brim of his ball cap lower. "Yeah."

"No."

"Did you ever date?"

She cut a sideways look at him. "Did you?"

"Kind of hard to do that between deployments." He peered at her. "Your turn."

Danni shifted in the saddle. "I didn't have time. Went out with one of the guys on the USC men's team, but it didn't work." She adjusted the reins, only to return them to the previous length. "Why does it matter so much to you?"

"Just wondered is all." He smooched to his horse and they trotted to catch up with Misty.

Wondered her foot.

"Miss Danni."

She smiled at Misty. That pixie-face beamed back at her. "Yes, Misty?"

"Uncle Trace said you wanted to go to your house, but can you stay for dinner? Mama's letting me help her make dessert. And I'm a real good cook."

Suspicion threaded through Danni and she peeked over Misty's helmet. Trace seemed to find something more interesting off to his far right. The sneak was trying to use his niece as leverage. She returned her attention to Misty.

"Dessert you say? Yum, that's my favorite part of the meal." She leaned forward. "What kind is it?"

Misty leaned toward her. "It's a secret." She pressed her finger to her lips. "Shhhh."

Danni nodded and straightened in her saddle. First their mothers manipulated them into running into each other at the airport; next her mom just ups and leaves, forcing Danni to stay at the Bryant ranch. The party, Trace's unexpected flashback and the subsequent fallout, the request for a trail ride, and now this. Was everyone and everything conspiring to thrust Danni and Trace together?

Her gaze traveled back to Trace. He rode loosely in the saddle, as if he and the horse were one and the same. Misty whispered something to him, and he looked at his niece. His dark eyes flicked up and locked with Danni's. A glint flashed through his, and he gave her a quick smile.

Danni's heart seized. It was the same look he gave her right before he almost kissed her in the barn. Trace was in love with her.

Whipping her attention forward, she squeezed the reins. Unnamed emotions swirled in her gut. How long had he loved her? And why didn't he say anything, ever?

But the biggest question was, did Danni love him?

"Why are we stopping here?" Danni stared at the large building with huge letters across the top announcing it was the Colorado Springs VA. The old brick structure looked like it once housed a school. She faced Trace, suspicion threading through her.

"I have an errand to run inside. Want to come in with me?" He flashed one of his charming grins.

"Are you meeting a counselor or something?"

He checked his watch. "Or something."

Danni peered at the brick building. "All right."

Exiting the truck together, they entered the building. The place smelled like floor wax and aged timbers. The tomatoey scent of lasagna and stale coffee lingered in the air. A chill crept over Danni's skin at the brisk temperature of the building.

Her gaze darted to Trace. Why'd he bring her here? Wouldn't it have been less embarrassing if he'd come alone to talk to a counselor, or whatever it was he planned to do here?

He nodded toward an office. "I'll be in here. You're free to wander. Doubt you want to be bored stiff while you wait on me."

"Okay." She drifted toward a large glass trophy case. She

heard Trace chuckle and the click of his boots on the polished cement floor as he walked away.

Pictures of soldiers, sailors, and marines—young and old—were displayed in the case. All locals. All probably suffering from one repercussion of combat or another. Danni glanced at the closed office door where Trace had disappeared. Would his picture join the others on this wall?

Male laughter drifted up the hall. Interested, Danni moved to follow the sound. The plunk of a ball against wood flooring joined the men's voices. She found a gym. A volleyball net stood in the center of the court. The men she heard were evenly numbered on each side of the net.

Danni rooted herself in the doorway, keeping her body partially hidden behind the open door and watched them.

All eight men were about her age or younger, and each one of them sported a life-changing injury. Missing limbs replaced by prosthetics. They batted the ball back and forth in their clumsy manner, teasing each other when someone messed up.

Smiling at their antics, Danni rested against the doorframe. Had they been healthy and whole, these men wouldn't have been able to play against her and her teammate. The two of them would eat those eight alive. But from the looks of things, those eight were enjoying themselves, getting a handle on what was to be their new lives as disabled veterans.

"Want to introduce yourself?"

Danni jerked at the low voice in her ear and glared at Trace. "Don't sneak up on me like that."

"Sorry." He winked.

Yeah, like he was really sorry. She resumed observing the men. "They won't know who I am." Crossing her arms, she let her head rest against the cool metal frame. "I don't wanna interrupt their fun. It looks like they need some."

"Actually, what they'd probably like more is not to be forgotten."

Scowling, Danni faced Trace. "How would they be forgotten? They're war vets."

A dark look passed through his eyes as he watched the men. "You'd be surprised at the number of men and women who come home wounded and there's no one there to help."

And not all of them came home with visible wounds. Danni's gaze slid back to the men. Out of those eight, how many of them were trying to make it on their own? People like Trace could benefit them. His physical therapy training and his long service record would go a long way for them and for Trace.

"Is that why you're here?" She pushed off the doorframe and blocked his view of the court. "Are you looking to get a job here as a therapist?"

"Kind of. I needed to speak to some people about counseling for myself first."

"Then what?"

"Then—"

"Heads up!"

A ball pinged off the wall and headed for the back of Trace's head. Danni's hand streaked out and caught it. She clasped the ball in her hands, the feel of smooth leather soothing her.

"Sorry about that."

Danni turned to the man gimping toward her and Trace. The man stutter-stepped to a stop, and his eyes widened.

"Danni Lindsay?"

"You know who I am?"

His grin widened, white teeth flashing against dark skin. "I'd know you anywhere. Been following your volleyball career since you were named NCAA player of the year the first time." He swung around best he could on a prosthetic leg. "Hey guys, we've got a legend hanging out."

Danni stepped forward, hand outstretched. "Uh, I'm no legend."

The guy peered at her over his shoulder. "Wanna bet?"

Panic flashed through her veins. She looked at Trace. He shrugged and entered the gym. Swallowing back her trepidation, Danni joined them.

The seven other men crowded around her admirer, their eyes shining.

"Goin' for the Olympics."

Danni gripped the man's shoulder, amazed at the muscles that flexed under her hand as he turned to her. "Wait a minute. If you're following my career you know I'm out because of a knee injury."

He glanced down at her bum knee then slapped his prosthetic. "You've still got your leg."

Next to her Trace snickered. Glowering at him, Danni pasted on a smile. "Are you insinuating something, soldier?"

His buddies chuckled.

"What makes you think I'm a soldier? Maybe I'm a Marine?"

"Naw. Not cocky enough." Danni pointed at Trace. "He's a soldier."

Eight pairs of eyes roved between her and Trace. Danni's admirer stroked his chin.

"Boys, whaddya think about having Miss Danni Lindsay give us a few pointers?"

Expectant faces looked back at her. She glanced at Trace; he smiled back. Blowing at a wayward strand of her hair, Danni nodded.

"On two conditions. One, you call me Danni. And two, you take it easy on me."

They all laughed.

"Danni, we should be asking you to take it easy on us poor boys."

The group moved back onto the court. Danni followed, a new thrill surging through her. Far different than the one she usually got before a match, but exciting, just the same.

Chapter 8

Trace parked his truck in the driveway and leaned on the steering wheel. "We're here."

Danni stirred and moaned. Blinking her eyes open, she peered through the windshield at her mother's home.

Halfway to town she'd dozed off. When he wasn't trying to drive, Trace stared at her, until he nearly collided with a grain truck. He was glad to hear she didn't have a boyfriend. It made what he planned to do a bit easier.

She sighed. "Let's find that quilt block."

Trace trailed her along the sidewalk. Instinct born of too many trips into the field with patrol units had him scanning the area. All seemed quiet. Ahead of him, Danni mounted the porch steps. She took a key from her pocket and unlocked the door.

A sweet floral scent greeted them as the door swung open. Trace entered the sunlit foyer, his gaze bouncing from one end to the other. From what he could see, the house hadn't changed much in the last twelve years. Still decorated in the eclectic classical style her mom was fond of, it remained rooted in a time when Danni's family had been intact.

He fingered a delicate red afghan draped over the back of a loveseat. "Where do you want to start?"

"You can look through the hutches and cabinets down

here. I'll look upstairs." She moved to the staircase.

"Danni, let me look upstairs."

With a hand on the banister, she eyed him. "Why?"

"Well. . ." His gaze flew up the steps then back to her. "You already pushed your knee on inclines."

She rolled her eyes. "Really? Going up the stairs once isn't going to be a problem. And I haven't been confined to a plane for three hours."

"Better safe than sorry."

Dipping her chin down, she looked at him like a stern teacher. "Do you really want to go through my mom's bedroom?"

Heat flushed into his face. "Uh, no."

"Didn't think so." She moved to mount the stairs.

"Oh, this is a waste of time." Trace strode toward her.

Panic flashed through Danni's eyes. "What are you doing?"

"Taking you upstairs." He grabbed her by the waist, slung her over his shoulder, then marched up the steps. "If you're going to be stubborn about it."

"Put me down." The palm of her hand cracked against his back. "I mean it."

"Not happening."

She moaned. "I think I'm gonna be sick."

"Not on me you're not." He reached the landing and gently set her down. Gripping her shoulders to steady her, he stared at her. "One day you'll get over the 'I can do it all on my own' mentality and ask for help."

"You could've asked if I wanted help, instead of going all 'Me Tarzan, you Jane' on me."

Guilt prickled, and he winced at her correct assessment. "Sorry. Old habit."

A tepid smile fluttered across her mouth. "I guess." She glanced down the stairs. "Think I'll be all right going down them alone, or do I need to call you?"

"Play it by ear." He started down the steps. "Then again, you could always slide down the banister."

"Ha! I tried that once as a kid and nearly fell off. Mom went nuclear on me and I never dared it again."

Trace paused halfway down and faced her. "You mean to tell me, independent Danica listened to her mother?"

She cocked her head and shrugged. "Guess I did."

"Well, wonders never cease."

"Oh, get to work."

"Wait. What does this quilt block look like?"

Danni's face scrunched. "I'm not sure I remember. But it'll have Mom's name on it and maybe some lavender and honeysuckle blossoms. Grams knew how much Mom loved those flowers." Danni turned to leave and then stopped. "Oh, and a Bible verse. Not sure which one, but Grams had a verse on the others I have and I had to put one on mine."

Trace reached the floor. "What verse did you use for yours?"

"Why are you so interested?"

"Just making conversation."

Danni rolled her eyes. "The longer we talk, the longer it'll take to find the block." She disappeared around a corner. "Seek and find, Trace."

"Yes, ma'am," he muttered and entered the living room.

He spent the next hour going through drawers, cabinets, and boxes, taking special care to rifle through anything that could hide a thin quilt block. Nothing turned up. Maybe Danni had better luck upstairs.

Standing at the bottom of the staircase, he listened. Except for the tick of the grandfather clock in the dining room, the house was silent. Trace mounted the steps. Which room was Danni in?

He checked in the room directly opposite the stairs, which belonged to her mother. No Danni. Moving down the hall, he found the upstairs bath and a guestroom. The last door at the end of the hall, he struck gold.

Sitting with her good leg tucked under her body and the recovering one stretched out on the floor, Danni stared at an open scrapbook. She looked up at the creak of the hinges, gave him a weak smile, and held up a block of material. "Found it."

"How long ago was that?"

She gave him a sheepish smile. "Not sure. Half hour ago, maybe."

He settled on the floor next to her and flicked the edge of the scrapbook. "What's this?"

"Family pictures." She turned the book for him to see. "Back before Dad got sick."

A lot of the faded pictures were of Danni and her parents at various functions. Some of her and her cousins or grandma.

"You miss them?"

She sighed and closed the book. "Tons. I've been so busy chasing my tail for volleyball I never tried to contact any of them. Mom and Grams were the only ones I talked to on a regular basis. Sometimes I want to go back and smack some sense into our mothers for acting like brats. My cousins and I got the raw end of the deal."

He picked up the quilt block and fingered the soft material. "Where'd your mom hide it?"

"Inside the scrapbook." Danni shoved the book into a

box. "It's like she didn't figure I would actually look in here."

"When she took it, would you have?"

Danni met his gaze. Sadness filled her eyes. "Last year, I wouldn't have touched that box for a million bucks." She bowed her head. "Too many memories of Grams and Dad in there."

He tucked a stray wisp of hair behind her ear. "Maybe your mom didn't hide it so much as send you on a path."

"A path to what?"

"I think you need to figure that out on your own."

Danni drew circular patterns in her mashed potatoes, half-listening to Misty's chatter about seeing the deer and other things on their ride that morning. In the course of the drive back to the ranch, Trace convinced her to spend one more night. She was grateful that he asked. After finding the scrapbook, she didn't think she could face a night alone in her mom's house.

He didn't breathe a word about why he'd gone to the VA. After her enjoyable afternoon with the disabled vets and teaching them some volleyball pointers, Danni didn't want to ruin it by making him talk about something he obviously wasn't comfortable with yet.

Hard as she tried to bury it, the thought that Trace loved her kept rearing to the forefront of her mind. And the questions soon followed. Did she love him in return? Was she reading too much into a few looks and a near kiss? If she did love him, how would they make a relationship work?

Was she capable of coping with his PTSD?

Danni let her fork clink onto the plate. No other guy had ever managed to make her think twice about him. She was wrong to think she'd forgotten about Trace. He had always been there, lingering in the back of her mind, the what ifs creeping into her lonely moments of the past twelve years.

An ecstatic Misty jumped from her chair and bounded into the kitchen, returning with a large pie dish. It clattered onto the table. She hopped over to Danni's chair.

"See! I made pumpkin pie!"

Grinning at the girl, Danni bent forward. "Do I get the first slice?"

"Yup."

Once Misty—with help from her mother—sliced the pie, she passed out a piece to everyone, making certain she gave the first one to Danni.

Danni's gaze bounced to Trace then back to her pie. She was ready to wrap things up here and get back to San Diego. Tomorrow afternoon she'd meet up with her cousins at the Broadmoor. It would be good seeing and reconnecting with them again. Once they fulfilled Grams's request, Danni could focus on her next objective—getting her knee back to full strength and making another go at the Olympics.

Maybe some distance between her and Trace would help clear things up for her.

She pushed her empty plate away. She wanted to look over the quilt pieces once more, especially her mother's, to make sure there were no loose threads or damage she missed. Mom's block had sat in the scrapbook for a year, pressed between pages where glue could seep through.

Her cell phone vibrated against her leg. Frowning, she withdrew it to check the caller ID. Mom.

Excusing herself, Danni headed down the hall to the bedroom. "Hi, Mom."

"How are you doing, Danica?"

She eased the door shut and sat on the corner of the bed. "As good as can be expected, considering where I'm at."

"I'm sorry I didn't stay to see you. It was just so hard, you know? I couldn't be around Colorado Springs and not think about your grandma and knowing she was gone."

"I understand." Danni lifted her mother's quilt block off the bed and laid it in her lap. "Things will get better. I promise."

"You found it, didn't you?"

Her head snapped back. "Found what?"

"The quilt block. I knew you'd figure out sooner or later where I put it."

"Mom, why did you hide it in the first place? Grams trusted it to me."

Silence hovered over the connection. Her mom's sigh broke through a few seconds later. "Danica, I was angry. When I saw those quilt pieces, I lost it. I'd just buried my mom and. . .well. . .I couldn't stand the thought of once more being denied what my parents had wanted for us because my sisters and I couldn't get along."

"But why the scrapbook?"

"Part of me hoped you'd finally come home and stay if you'd look through the old photos. I hated that you were able to move on with your life and I was stuck."

Pain sliced through Danni like the surgeon's scalpel had her knee. For years after Dad's death, her mother was indifferent, passive, cold at times. Sometimes laying on guilt trips to shame Danni into doing what she wanted. And it got worse after Mom and her sisters had their falling out. Mom's admission was like hearing those jabs about Danni being so far away from home, not visiting enough, and the complaints about Danni's life as a beach volleyball player.

Closing her eyes, Danni took a deep breath and let it out slowly. *Don't blow your top. Don't blow your top. This isn't a fight worth pushing. Lord, give me the patience to deal with her.*

Calmed, she opened her eyes. "Mom, we've both lost a lot. And I guess the one thing I learned from you was to bury my feelings and run. When I get back to San Diego, we need to talk."

"Yes, we do. And I'm sorry for everything I did, or didn't do, after your dad died. I wasn't sure how to handle my grief and how to move on alone. In trying to figure it all out, I forgot about you."

Danni's throat tightened. "Mom—"

"Danica, I have something I need to tell you." Silence once more. Danni thought she'd lost the connection. "Danni, I met someone."

Danni's body went slack, like she was nothing more than flesh. "Wha—"

"I've been seeing this man for a year. We. . .I. . . We're getting married."

Danni's grip on her phone loosened, then tightened as she contemplated throwing it. "For a year? And you couldn't bother to tell me?"

"You had your volleyball and life in San Diego. Then you hurt your knee. Danni, I wasn't sure how you'd handle it."

"Well, now you know."

"Danni, please."

"Mom, I need some time to think about this. I'll call you." She punched the End button and tossed the phone at her suitcase.

Laughter drifted into the room. Through a veil of tears, Danni stared at the door. All those years while her mom pushed her away, Danni'd found solace with her cousins. They were there, open and willing to accept her. But there was so much left unsaid between her and Mom.

Danni caressed the quilt block, raised threads rubbing against her fingertips. Frowning, she lifted the piece and stared at the open areas between the embroidered lavender and honeysuckle. Grams had stitched some writing there, white-on-white. Focusing on the raised letters, Danni made out the words *mercy* and *love*. She finally made out the third word, *forgiveness*.

Forgiveness.

Grams knew they all needed it. But why put it in Mom's block?

A knock on the door startled her.

Trace's voice threaded through her like a soothing balm. "Can I come in?"

Wiping any trace of tears from her face, she straightened. "Yeah."

He opened the door enough to poke his head in. Concern etched his face.

Danni gave him a weak smile. "Hey."

"Hey." He entered the room and leaned against the wall. "Who was that on the phone?"

"Mom."

"That would explain the frown. . ." He pointed to a spot near his mouth. "Right there."

Rolling her eyes, she set the quilt block aside and stood. "What's going on out there?"

"Julia's talking about playing a game of some sort, but

Misty wants to go out and groom her horse." He pushed away from the wall. "Want to come?"

Remembering the close encounter that morning in the stable, Danni licked her lips. She should go over the quilt pieces. But the temptation to set everything about her family aside and just spend some time with Trace before it was gone overruled.

"Sounds like fun."

When she stood, Trace held out his hand. She grasped it, strength and assurance flowing from him into her. For once, Danni didn't want him to let go. Ever.

Chapter 9

The comforting smells of leather, hay, and horses wrapped around Trace as they entered the barn. He lingered at Danni's side while Misty skipped ahead to her horse's stall. With Danni's hand in his, Trace didn't want to let go. He could feel the tension shrouding her.

Whatever Danni and her mom had talked about had seriously dampened her spirits. Her good mood from earlier seemed squashed.

"Do you want to talk about it?"

She glanced at him, shook her head, and watched Misty enter the stall with a brush in her hand.

"Misty, use the step stool."

"I am." The sass coming from his niece reminded him of his sister when they were younger.

Trace looked at Danni. She would leave here tomorrow to meet up with her cousins. And he had to report for duty at Fort Carson. Tonight might be his last chance with her. Intertwining their fingers, he tugged her forward. She tripped after him as he led her down the aisle.

"Misty, I'll be at the other end of the stable if you need anything. Got it?"

His pixie-faced niece flashed a smile and nodded, that twinkle in her eyes. Like she knew what he was up to. She'd probably overheard Julia talking about him and Danni. Misty was hoping for a wedding. She wanted to be a flower girl in the worst way.

Danni grasped his hand and put the brakes on. "Should you leave her alone like that? What if the horse—"

"She'll be fine. That horse is an old hand when it comes to kids. Especially if they have treats."

"But—"

"Come on," he whispered and coaxed her forward.

Her face flushed dark pink. "Okay." She trailed after him.

He made a beeline for the opposite end of the barn. Releasing her hand, he unlatched the doors and pushed them open, the rollers squeaking at lack of use. A gasp escaped Danni's lips when the scene came into view.

"Wow."

Trace drew in a deep breath of mountain air. "My favorite view on the ranch." He pointed at the loft. "Looks better up there, but you're not climbing the ladder."

Her gaze slid to him as she moved into the doorway, a wry smile playing at the corner of her mouth.

The urge to kiss her strengthened. Trace swallowed and looked away. One step at a time.

"When are you going back to San Diego?"

"Don't know yet. Figured I'd spend a few days here with my cousins if they can swing it, so I didn't buy a return ticket."

Trace shifted to face Danni. "I have to report to Fort Carson tomorrow." He hooked his thumbs in his belt loops. "I need to know something before I go."

Leaning her back against the barn door, she crossed her arms. "And what's that?"

Free of scrutiny and inquiring minds, he approached her. Momentary panic zipped across her face and her arms dropped. Then understanding dawned in her eyes, and she thrust out her hands, pushing them against his chest.

"Stop right there, Trace Bryant."

The feel of her warm palms pressed into him sent ribbons of pleasure threading through his veins. He wrapped his hands around hers and slowly dragged them down. Standing toe-to-toe, he touched his forehead to hers. So close, the coconut scent of her perfume reminded him of the beach.

Her erratic breathing was the only sound between them. He inched closer to her lips. A hair's breadth between them.

"Trace." Her voice was hoarse. She tilted her face away.

"Why do you fight it?" he whispered. "What's standing in the way?"

Danni swallowed and let her gaze drop to his chin. "I'm scared."

"Of what?"

Her gaze darted up. "I don't know if I love you." Her shoulders slumped, and she hung her head. "I don't want to hurt you, Trace."

"No one said you would." His hands traveled up her arms, and he grasped her shoulders. "I should have told you how I felt a long time ago. There was always one reason or another not to contact you. When the PTSD hit me. . ." He sighed. "I didn't want it to look like I was asking for sympathy."

She touched his cheek then cupped it. "Why do you want to know when I'm going back?"

"Six weeks and then I'm out. For good. You won't start training again in about the same time. Would you stick it out here in Colorado Springs a little longer?"

Danni stiffened. Her hand fell away from his face. "And what if I don't want to? Did you assume I didn't have a life, a place to live, bills, that kind of thing waiting for me?"

"Danni, wait—"

"No, you wait." She shrugged his hands from her shoulders and stepped to the side. "I get that you don't have one clue what you're going to do after you leave the Army. But I can't just hang around here waiting for you to make up your mind."

"That's not what I meant."

"From my perspective, that's exactly what you meant." Shaking her head, she moved past him.

Trace caught her elbow and hauled her to a stop. "Would you let me finish?"

"You know what? It's been a long day, and I've got a lot to do before tomorrow." Deftly slipping free of his grasp, she marched off.

He heard her speak to Misty. Then silence.

Dropping onto a nearby hay bale, he buried his face in his hands and fought the urge to throw something. So much time wasted. Thoughts wasted on her when he could have been looking for someone else.

What was he thinking asking her to stay? Only a fool believed a woman in Danni's position would just drop everything and do his bidding. He'd hoped she'd stick around so they could get to know each other better. Maybe let her find out if she loved him or not.

What a joke.

"Uncle Trace?" Misty's tiny voice floated to him.

"Yeah?"

"Can we go back to the house? It's getting dark."

He glanced out the door. Stars dotted the sky. He pushed up from the bale. "I'm coming, squirt."

After closing the doors, he found Misty waiting by the

stall. He took his niece's hand and led her out of the barn to the house. Light shone in his bedroom window.

There was still time. He had to figure out what it was he wanted. Because this time, Danni would walk out of his life for good.

The quilt pieces looked in order. Now all Danni had to do was meet her cousins and put this quilt together.

And hide.

When had she turned into her mother? And why was she just now realizing it?

Danni sighed and zipped her suitcase shut. She plopped on the floor and drew her good knee up, resting her elbow on it. Were her cousins having similar kinds of headaches? She chuckled. Wouldn't that beat all? Each of them dealing with her own love quandary. That would be a story to tell their kids one day.

Grams's message in the block floated through Danni's head. Love, mercy, and forgiveness. Was there a Bible verse with those three exact words in it?

She straightened her leg along the floor and unzipped her duffel bag again. Rummaging through her clothes, she found her Bible and pulled it out. She scanned the concordance, but the words never appeared together in the same verses. There were plenty for love and mercy, fewer for forgiveness. Danni chose the ones she thought best fit what Grams said and wrote down each reference.

An ache in her neck and shoulders brought her to a stop. She looked up and found two hours had slipped past. Gathering up her Bible and notepad, she climbed onto the bed and continued her reading.

With each verse, a peace settled over Danni.

Mom had been the peacekeeper, the one who showed mercy and forgiveness. But when she lost Dad, she lost her desire to stitch her sisters' frayed edges back together. It seemed Grams wanted her daughter to return to that place. And love was the answer.

Maybe Mom knew about the message. She'd found love again and sounded so unlike herself on the phone. Danni swallowed the lump in her throat. She had thrown her mom's good news and happiness back in her face.

Obviously, those three powerful words weren't for her mother alone.

Closing her Bible, Danni set it on the floor and rolled onto her side, hugging a pillow. The conversation with Trace in the barn haunted her. Had she been wrong about his motives? He loved her; she could see it plainly.

What do I do, Lord? I can't stand this confusion.

Her gaze drifted to the cell phone on the floor. Was it too late to call Mom? Guess she'd find out.

She crawled off the bed and scooped up the phone. She punched three and waited. The phone rang twice.

"Danni?"

Her throat tightened. That was the third time Mom called her Danni and not Danica. "Mom, I'm sorry."

It sounded like her mom sobbed. "Oh, honey, it's okay. I knew you needed some time to absorb the news."

"When can I get the details?"

"How long do you plan to stay in Colorado Springs?"

Danni ran her hand along her pant leg. Should she take up Trace's offer and stick around a while longer? She'd been so frustrated with the thought of staying and not getting back to San Diego, she didn't bother to hear him out. What else did he want to say? She sighed. Even if she decided not to stay here for him, she should still stick around to patch things up with her mom.

"I'll be here as long as you need."

"Really?" Mom's breathless joy infected Danni through the line.

"Yes, I have time."

"Oh, Danni. I can't wait for you to meet my fiancé."

Smiling, she cradled the phone. "I can't wait either. And Mom?"

"Yeah?"

"Thanks for calling me Danni. It means a lot to me."

"I know, honey. I know."

Trace tri-folded a tan T-shirt and laid it on the growing stack in his green duffel. The next time he packed this bag, he would be done with the Army for good. The last couple of days he'd hoped it would also mean being with Danni. But that dream looked like a lost cause.

He folded another shirt and added it to the stack as footsteps sounded on the stairs coming to the basement. His sister flashed him a tight-lipped smile when he glanced at her.

"Misty wants a good-night kiss from you."

"I'll be up in a few." He tightly rolled a set of ACU pants and slid them in beside the shirts.

"You just going to let her go?"

His head whipped toward Julia. "I don't see how it's any business of yours."

"Oh, it became my business when my little girl decided she wanted Danni for her aunt." Julia placed her hands on her hips and eyed him. "Now you try telling that stubborn child it's a hopeless cause."

Heaving a frustrated sigh, Trace moved closer to her. "Sis—"

She wagged a finger in his face. "Don't 'Sis' me. That woman is good for you. What she did at the party when you had a flashback is a miracle. And now you're just going to let her run off to San Diego."

"I never said I was going to let her run off."

"But I bet you haven't told her how you really feel, have you?"

This was nonsense. He couldn't believe he was having this conversation with his sister. Turning, he marched back to the bed and his packing.

"Julia, let me be. This is what Danni wants, and I'm letting her have it."

"Like you did twelve years ago?"

He shoved another set of ACU pants into the bag. "Two months wasn't exactly enough time to know if I really loved her or not. Besides, we were young and had a lot of growing up to do."

Her sigh sounded more like a growl. "You're both so blind to what's sitting right in front of your noses." She stomped to the stairs, paused, and twisted around to jab the air with her finger again. "Don't you dare let her leave without knowing how you feel. Man up, Staff Sergeant." And with that, she marched up the steps.

Trace sank onto the edge of the bed and gaped at the empty spot where Julia had stood.

Lord, she's right. Danni is good for me. I can't let her go.

Chapter 10

At the heavy clomp down the hall, Danni peeked over her coffee mug. Trace entered the kitchen in uniform. The sight of him in his ACU's made her stomach jump. She averted her gaze and sipped some coffee, burning her tongue.

He poured a cup and leaned against the counter. "When do you want me to drop you off at the Broadmoor?"

"Whenever is fine." A funny tingling took control of her midsection. "What time do you have to report to Fort Carson?"

"Around noon."

"Eleven's fine then." Danni nearly choked on her words.

They were separating again. But she didn't know how to tell him she was willing to take him up on his offer. After talking longer with her mom last night, Danni realized a few days wouldn't cut it. They needed to mend their relationship. And her mom hoped to do the same with her remaining sisters. What Grams wanted in the first place.

Once she finished talking with her mom, Danni had called her volleyball partner. They both agreed she could give her knee a few more weeks of physical therapy. Her partner would take care of things for Danni in San Diego until she returned.

Now to let Trace know.

He brushed past her on his way to the breakfast bar, the musky scent of Stetson stirring her senses. He settled on a barstool and rotated the morning paper to face him.

Biting her lip, she stared at him. She could do this. She could tell him her plans.

He opened the paper, and the rattling unnerved her. Forget it. There was no way to tell him when her stomach was tied in knots and her brain ran rampant. Besides, this was a conversation best kept between them. Any moment now someone in his family could come barging in.

Maybe in the truck on the way to the Broadmoor.

Yeah. Danni took another sip of coffee. No one to interrupt. Just the two of them. She glanced at the clock. Seven thirty. About three hours until they headed into town. Three agonizing hours to kill before she dropped the bombshell. She winced at the analogy. Maybe using the word *bombshell* around someone with PTSD wasn't a good thing.

The paper rattled again, and her gaze darted to him. Trace held his mug near his mouth and sipped as he continued to read. His clean-shaven face looked odd after being scruffy for the past three days.

"Danni."

Their gazes clashed.

"Yeah."

"Could you stop tapping your foot? It kinda reminds me of gunfire."

"Oh, sorry. I didn't realize I was doing it."

He gave her a lazy smile. "It's okay."

Danni's heart turned to melted chocolate. When she'd left him in the barn, she sensed the frustration rolling off him in waves. Today he seemed different. Calmer, more reassured.

Oh no. What if he decided that he didn't love her, that it was a mere infatuation? What would she do then?

Good thing she wasn't staying in Colorado Springs for a bit just for him. After all, she and her mother needed the time together. And Danni wanted to meet the guy who'd claimed her mother's broken heart.

Did Trace claim Danni's? Did she love him or not?

"Danni, you're doing it again."

"I'm just. . ." She looked around and zeroed in on the sliding glass doors. "I'm going outside." She made her escape and slipped onto the deck.

Cool musk-laced air buffeted her heated face. She drew in a long breath and released it slowly. The tension drained from her body. Better. She peeked through the windows and saw a grin played out on Trace as he shook his head. Well, at least her mindless tapping amused him, instead of immobilizing him.

Danni drifted to a deck chair and eased onto the seat. Birds chirped in the nearby trees. Off in the distance a horse whinnied. She loved it here on the Bryant ranch. Hopefully the peacefulness of the ranch helped calm some of Trace's nerves. Once he was discharged, he'd return here.

The more she thought about it, the more she realized she could help him with his PTSD. A few calls and meetings with some people in the mental healthcare industry could help her know what to do to work with his recovery.

Lord, as long as You're in charge, we'll be all right.

The doors squeaked open. Danni looked up and flashed a weak smile.

Trace closed the door and joined her. "Didn't mean to scare you off."

She shrugged. "I'm not usually this jittery."

"Yeah." He gave her a peculiar look. "Got something on your mind?"

Too soon. Now wasn't the time. Her mom. She could tell him about their conversation last night.

"Actually, I do. I talked with my mom. She's getting married."

Trace rocked back in his chair and gaped at her. "Seriously?"

"Took me by surprise, too." Danni focused her attention on her coffee. "We had a good talk. Something that hasn't happened in a long time."

"That's a good thing."

"It is." She rubbed the side of the ceramic mug. "I think I finally realized why Grams wanted us cousins to get together. This meeting is the first step to get our mothers to reconcile."

"Do you think it'll work?"

She leaned into the chair backrest. "We'll have to wait and see. Mom sounded like she was willing."

"I hope you're right."

Silence fell between them. Danni finished her coffee, trying to quell the nerves that wanted to overtake her.

Trace braced his hands on his knees and pushed to his feet. "What do you want to do until we need to go?"

A thought hit her. "Are you packed and ready?"

"I am."

"Let's head into town. There's a place I want to visit."

He eyed her. "And where's that?"

"I'll let you know when we get into town."

"All right, we're in town." Trace stopped the truck for a red light and looked at Danni. "Where are we going?"

A gleam passed through her eyes, and she smiled. "The sand volleyball courts."

Gripping the brim of his field cap, he lifted it off his forehead and scratched. "Why there?"

"You'll see."

Cap settled back in place, Trace glanced at the light. Still red. He turned to study Danni. "What are you up to?"

"Trace, just go. It'll make sense when we get there."

"Yes, ma'am."

On green he turned left and headed for the city's recreational fields and courts. Occasionally he'd take a peek at Danni, but she kept her attention focused out her window. She'd been preoccupied by something this morning. Her constant foot tapping had reminded him of rapid gunfire from an M4.

The admission that her mom was getting married couldn't be the whole reason. Or was it?

"Are you okay with your mom remarrying?"

Danni looked at him. "Why wouldn't I be?"

"Before we went to the barn last night, you were really upset. Is that why she called you? To tell you?"

"She did." Danni let her head rest against the seat. "After I cooled off and thought it over, I called her back. Mom's happy, and that's a good sign."

The large grass fields peeked through the orange, red, and yellow foliage. Trace slowed the truck. "But are you fine with it?"

She sighed, a smile drawing up the corners of her mouth. "I am now."

He drove past the soccer fields and turned into the parking lot next to the sand courts. It was too early for any activities. The silence was nice. Choosing a spot, Trace parked the truck and killed the engine. He twisted in his seat to face Danni, one arm draped over the steering wheel. "Now what?"

"We get out." She popped the door handle and slid out of the cab.

Trace followed, joining her at the front of the truck. She grasped his hand. This was a first. Her taking the initiative. He allowed her to lead him through the maze of courts to the one he'd first seen her play on. Together, they sat in the grass on the edge of the court, letting the morning sun warm them.

"Remember those days you'd ask me to bring you out here and teach you a few volleyball fundamentals?" Danni braced her elbows on her thighs and bent forward. "And the nights after games when we'd sit here and talk?"

Trace let those good memories soak in. "Every night of every deployment."

A startled expression crossed Danni's face. "Every night?"

He took her hand and squeezed. "Most nights."

Danni closed her eyes and tilted her face to the sun. Trace chuckled.

One of her eyes opened and she looked at him. "What?"

"You act like you don't see the sun much."

She bumped her shoulder into his. "I just miss the mountains and the feel of autumn." She laid her head on his shoulder. "Along with a lot of other things."

Warmth spread like a wildfire through him at the contact. What was she doing to him? Setting him up for more heartbreak?

"Trace, I've been doing a lot of thinking." Her arm encircled his and she hugged it to her body. The cloth of his uniform jacket rasped against her skin. "A lot about your request last night. About me staying for a while."

His heart quickened. Was this it? Where she told him she was out of his life forever?

"Trace." She met his gaze. "I've worked it out with my partner. She's taking care of things back home in San Diego. I'll stay here in Colorado Springs until you've discharged."

Someone hit him with a mortar round. Stunned and speechless, he tried to latch onto what she said.

"Did you hear me?"

He cleared his throat. "Perfectly."

"But you're shocked."

The feeling wore off. "Wouldn't you be?"

She shrugged. "I guess so." She hugged herself. "I don't want to walk away, put miles between us and know I gave up a good thing. Again."

It was too good to be true. For years he'd hoped she'd come around. He'd kept her memory alive, and it kept him going when the world wanted to implode around him. And now she uttered the very words he thought he'd never hear her say.

"What changed your mind?"

"Mom." Danni reached out and caressed his cheek. "And you."

It was like she'd ripped his tongue out of his mouth and held it for ransom.

"Are you okay?"

His gaze jerked to her. "Uh, yeah."

Deep lines furrowed along her forehead, and she frowned. "Isn't this what you wanted?"

"Yes." He caught up her hands. "It's what I wanted."

"So why are you—"

Trace pressed his mouth to hers. No way would she get out

of this. She stiffened momentarily then her lips turned soft and yielding. He pulled her closer and kissed her thoroughly.

When they broke contact, she was breathing heavy and her face flushed pink. "So, you are happy."

"More than you know." He trailed a finger along her jawline. "Julia gave me the riot act last night."

"About what?"

"Losing you again. Seems Misty has her heart set on making you her aunt."

Danni smiled. "She does?"

Trace reached into his pocket and grasped the folded sheet of paper. "Do you want to be her aunt?"

A perplexed expression masked her face. "Maybe. What's that?"

Opening it, he held it out. Danni frowned and took the sheet. Her eyes scanned the document, widening as she finished. She gaped at him.

"When did this happen?"

Removing his field cap, he ran his fingers through his hair. "Yesterday. Before I took you to the VA I made some phone calls. The director there in turn made some phone calls and pulled some strings." Trace heaved a relieved sigh. "Once my enlistment is up, I'm headed for a special VA program in San Diego that works with guys like me who have PTSD. In return, I provide physical therapy for amputees and injured vets."

"You're moving to San Diego?"

Taking the paper back, he folded it up and returned it to his pocket. Then he grasped her hands and scooted around to face Danni. "Hopefully to be with my wife."

Danni's face paled. "Trace, I don't—"

"Whoa." He smiled and squeezed her fingers. "When I asked you to stay for the next six weeks, it was for you to get to know me better. I think deep inside you do love me. You weren't sure. 'Course last night you didn't give me the chance to say so."

"Oh." She blushed and dropped her gaze. "I was a bit hotheaded and stressed after getting Mom's call."

Tucking his knuckles under her chin, he tipped it up. "I do love you, Danni. And I'm still going to San Diego whether you want me to go with you or not."

"You'd do this for me?"

"For us."

Her eyes shimmered, and a weak smile appeared on her lips. "You make it hard not to love you, you know that?"

He wrapped her in a tight hug and soundly kissed her. Pulling away, he leaned his forehead against hers. "Are you saying you do love me?"

She brushed a kiss against his lips. "Yes, Trace, I can honestly say I do love you. Despite my stubborn independence and pride, God managed to stitch us together, after all these years."

Winter A. Peck is a storyteller at heart. Her first vivid memories are of summer family reunions spent listening to stories of the past. Winter leans heavily on her midwestern roots, her love of the Old West, and the rodeo, weaving each aspect into her books. When she's not writing, she's busy coaching junior high girls' volleyball, staying active in her church, and juggling the active life of a military wife. She's the mother of three boys and one cowgirl in training. Currently, Winter and her family live in north-central Illinois.

DESIGNED TO LOVE

by Marilyn Leach

"Be still, and know that I am God."

Psalm 46:10 NIV

Chapter 1

Eve Kirkwood scanned the magnificent five-star Broadmoor Hotel from the window of the idling cab. "Oh yes," she breathed. "The next fourteen days are going to be bliss."

She paid the driver a generous tip. The valet who opened the car door for her gathered her oversized luggage and escorted her through the grandiose portico painted with heavenly designs. He passed her bag to a bellman, who led her directly into the grand reception hall.

Eve's eyes widened as she gazed at her surroundings. She was suddenly glad she'd worn her fashionable wool sweater and black dress pants.

This early-twentieth-century hotel, with marbled floors, opulent ceilings, and fine sculpted stairway, swept Eve into the grand expectation of a relaxed and pampered holiday.

"The stuff dreams are made of," she whispered, adoring the carved angels fluttering above the concierge.

Brisk voices ricocheted their urgent-laden language all through the room. Two men wearing blue windbreakers with gray dress pants hurled their way through reception, ear pieces in place. They were hardly guests. A tall, handsome man was in the lead.

"Enforcement personnel at their best," Eve said to the bellman.

He grinned and nodded. "They keep the hotel safe and sound."

Eve smiled. "Safe and sound is acceptable. At the top of their game is best." She knew all about efficiency in law enforcement. In fact, in her job as a PA to an assistant police commissioner, she manufactured it. She decided that just now her greatest concern was to slip into a hot, swirling bath with fragrant bubbles and then wrap herself in a fresh hotel robe. Oh, yes. She knew this holiday would break the bank. But at this moment she had no affinity for glue.

After check-in, the bellman, a short jolly sort and almost elf-like, carried Eve's bag alongside her to her room.

Eve could feel the fellow stare at her as they walked the designed hallway. Her ivory skin and pale green eyes were not especially rare, but when topped by thick ashen-black hair, the uncommon combination often drew stares. She directed her eyes to the elf. He smiled and redirected his gaze.

A special bell tone sprung from Eve's pants pocket. "Sorry," she said to the bellman. "It's important."

"Hello Dad," she greeted.

"Hello kitten, you've arrived?"

"Yes, no fear." Her father had become overprotective when her mother, a successful negotiator for an international legal firm, began to travel with her work. Her career was demanding anyway, but the past three years she hadn't spent more than four months collectively at home. Though Eve could understand his doting, she didn't especially appreciate it. In fact, sometimes she could just barely deal with it.

"Now, Eve, get that box in the hotel vault as soon as possible."

"I'll get the box in the vault as soon as I get settled in."

Eve put her free hand on her hip.

"Don't wait too long. I want you to be safe. Get it locked up."

"I will, Dad. Stop worrying. Most people wouldn't even know that old thing is valuable. And besides, it's what's inside that's priceless."

A rather official-looking woman in black approached Eve and the elf.

"Gotta go. Bye, Dad, love you." Eve put the phone in her pocket.

The hotel woman politely tipped her head, her raven hair pulled back in a knot.

"George," she said to the bellman, "the gentleman in one-twenty is leaving, and he's requested you specifically."

She smiled at Eve. "I hope you don't mind. I can send another. . ." Her dark eyes flashed warmth and her facial features lit. "Eve? Eve Kirkwood?"

Eve stared at the woman. Then, like a sunrise, her childhood summers at Gran's house here in Colorado Springs came to light. "Isabel Cordova, is that you?"

"One pepper, two peppers, one big dish," Isabel said in a sing-song voice.

"How many pepper boys did you kiss?" Eve finished.

She laughed as Isabel gave her a heartfelt hug.

"You're working here?"

Isabel pointed to her employee badge and grinned. "Chief gopher in guest services. How long you staying?"

"Six days on my own. And I'll be with the cousins for a week after."

"Fun." Isabel's happy face glowed. "Listen, oodles to do at the moment, but we'll get together while you're here." She was already moving down the hall. "Phone the front desk.

Ask for Isabel Escobar." She disappeared around a corner.

"Will do," Eve said to the empty hallway.

George had departed without a word. "Oh well." She started gathering her bags.

"Here, miss," Eve heard a strong voice say behind her, "let me get that for you."

She turned to see a very tall, very muscular bellman with blond spiked hair and a well-trimmed goatee. *From elf to giant.*

The fellow came forward. "Your bag?"

"Yes, yes, please."

When they arrived at the room, Eve didn't wait for the giant. She expectantly flung the door open. From the large floral design of the long curtains to the gold lavatory fittings in the en suite bathroom, it felt like a palace.

The tall bellman stood next to Eve's luggage.

"Thank you." She smiled, tipped him, and he departed.

The moment the door closed, she stretched herself across the comfortable king-sized bed. "Oh, yes. Thank you indeed."

She popped up and went directly to the bathroom, where she started drawing her bath. She returned to her overstuffed suitcase, opened it, and pulled out a change of clothes.

And there it was, sitting atop her new cashmere sweater. She pulled the vintage box out and held it in her hands like a prize rose. The gold gild that plated the wooden box was regal. Tiny freshwater pearls encrusting the lid glistened a pink opalescence. But the real treasure, as far as Eve was concerned, was inside. She lifted the lid. The beautiful quilt squares Gran had painstakingly created so many years ago were placed, as it were, upon their throne. For Eve, they were of greater value than any gem.

"Oh, my bathwater."

She closed the lid and put the box on the night table. She made for the bathroom and a nice soak.

The world and all its frantic pace was shut out the moment Eve closed the bathroom door. Her high-pressured police administration job, including the unwanted advances from predatory detectives and the daily grind of urban life, all melted away as she slipped into the toasty, frothy water.

She wasn't sure how long she'd been in the relaxing whirlpool when she realized she'd drifted off.

Wrapping the hotel robe around her, Eve moved across the tile floor and chose a fluffy towel to envelop her hair. She stepped into the bedroom.

She would dress for dinner, take a quick stroll up to the lake, and then dine in the formal Penrose Room.

She picked up the sea-green cashmere sweater she had purchased for her trip. "You'll do quite well." She held it to her chest and glanced in the mirror. But in the reflection, she became aware that something didn't seem right. She looked past her sweater sleeve to the empty night table.

She spun around. It was gone. Her beautiful box was gone.

"Gran's quilt squares." The words burst from her mouth like the rush of an autumn wind spinning leaves into a whirlwind. "No." Eve shook her towel-wrapped head and dropped the sweater on the bed. "No." She took several deep breaths. *It could have simply fallen.* Frantically, she searched the floor around the table. No, it was definitely gone.

She unwrapped the towel from her head, allowing the masses of waves to drop past her shoulders. She went to the room's phone, lifted the receiver, and dialed.

"Front desk," a pleasant voice answered.

"I want to report a theft," Eve all but yelled into the phone. She could hear her voice become ragged. "It just occurred."

"We'll have a security team there right away."

"Good." She banged the receiver down and lowered her head. "Lord, help."

Chapter 2

Eve sat on the bed and opened the night table drawer. "God bless the Gideons." Her frenzied shock was soothed by the presence of a Bible. When she picked it up, it dropped from her hands and fell open on the floor. As she retrieved it, she noticed pen-noted lines and a star with the words *for you* written next to them. The red underlining drew her like a magnet to true north. *"Be still, and know that I am God."* Eve blinked. "I know I asked for help, but what's that got to do with Gran's quilt squares being pinched?"

A loud bang sounded on her door. She put the Bible on the night table and moved to answer it. "Yes?"

"Security," a male voice called.

Eve opened the door to find the tall man she'd seen in reception, his short, blond colleague just behind him.

The square of the man's jaw, just above the blue windbreaker, drew her eyes up past his tantalizing lips, past his aquiline nose, to dark eyes that burned with an autumn fire. His dark brown hair was well groomed.

"Security," he said again.

"Credentials?" Eve put on her no-nonsense attitude.

He smiled broadly and flashed his employee badge.

She scanned the credential. Detective Jason Gregory. Even his employee ID picture couldn't hide his pleasing features.

"There's been a theft?" Detective Gregory eyed the robe.

Suddenly aware of her appearance, Eve pushed a dripping strand of hair away from her eye. Heat rose to her face as she realized the enormous robe she wore was more akin to a puffy pink pillow. In defense, she stood as tall as her slender five-foot-seven frame would allow.

"Yes, something priceless has gone missing." She put her shoulders back. "My grandmother's hand-sewn quilt squares."

"Your *what*?"

"My deceased grandmother left them to me. They've been stolen."

The detective knit his brow. "Costly fabric? Historical value? Insured art work?"

Eve lifted her chin. "None of those things. Precious, nevertheless."

Detective Gregory placed his hand against the doorframe. "You called because your grandmother's stitchery's gone missing?" His tone was stiff, and she could hear a smothered laugh from the fellow behind.

Eve pursed her lips. "I work in law administration. I am aware of police procedure, and at this moment, I don't see you applying it."

"Police procedure?" he snorted. "Just now, ma'am, I've got a real theft I'm investigating over in the cottages."

Eve could feel the pink of her former blush go red. "A *real* theft? Mine is a made-up crime?"

"Inform guest services about your dilemma. They'll get a housekeeper to help you look."

"Oh, I'll inform them, all right." Eve put her hands on her hips. "I'll inform them that you don't know how to do your job."

The detective's jaw tightened. "Right, well, fun as this has been, I've got to go." He turned and strode down the hallway, his comrade in tow.

Eve leaned out into the hall, looking after the departing detective. "Don't let the door hit you on your way out," she trumpeted.

Jason's brisk pace nearly set the hall carpet ablaze. "Bingham, how is it that someone with such intoxicating eyes can be so obnoxious?"

"Search me," Bingham fired back, trying to keep pace.

"A twenty thousand-dollar necklace stolen, and she wants me to find her granny's needlework," Jason huffed.

Bingham smiled. "I know her kind. Very high maintenance."

"We've got much more to do than coddle an impetuous female guest."

"Yes sir, we do."

Then why can't I get her out of my head? Jason's pace picked up even more speed.

Like a spitfire, Eve once again dialed the front desk. "Manager." She paced.

"Guest services," a courteous male voice said. "How may I assist you?"

Eve took a deep breath. "I would like to lodge a complaint against Jason Gregory."

"Complaint? Concerning Mr. Gregory?" The gentleman sounded surprised. "What complaint?"

"He was rude." Eve fingered the phone. "He was arrogant, incompetent, and"—she stumbled—"and he was rude."

She hung up and felt a bit foolish. She wasn't even making any sense. And she had let the detective's rudeness make her rude, too. How dare this handsome stranger at her door unnerve her so?

What now? She'd just have to carry out her own investigation. She sat on the edge of the bed. Her job, though just an administrative position, had made her privy to more than a few criminal investigations. One method used to solve a crime was to retrace your steps. She had come up the hallway with the elf. Her father called. She felt her stomach do a flip-flop. Dad. How on earth would she tell him what happened? She shook her head, as if to dismiss such a thought. No, she wouldn't tell him. Focus. Hallway, elf, Isabel, the giant.

Eve examined the door's automatic lock. There was no forced entry at the door or at the window. Someone with a professional lock, pick, a pass key? She added the thought to her process. "Giant and I entered, he left, bathwater, box on table, in the bath." She took a deep inhale. "I was in the bathtub when someone entered my room." She put her hands to her cheeks. A sense of violation turned her stomach inside out.

Like the sound of thunder in a dark October storm, the ringing of the telephone wrenched her from her fresh illumination.

She picked up the receiver. "Yes?"

"Miss Kirkwood?" The gentle voice of the manager was on the other end of the line.

"Yes?"

"If you please, will you come to my office in fifteen

minutes? I do hope it's not a huge imposition."

"No, it's not a problem. Yes, I'll come."

"Grand, see you then."

Eve did a passing glance with the blow-dryer on her long, thick hair. A little blush; some light, sandy-colored eye shadow; a flit of mascara; and a touch of warming pink lip gloss was her slapdash attempt to dress her fair skin a bit.

She put on a light tank top and buttoned her blue cotton sweater over it. Her most comfortable jeans were close at hand and she popped them on in a scurry to exit. A quick spritz of her favorite botanical scent as she eyed the clock, a slip into her black leather flats, and she was out the door. "Four minutes left," she said as she moved down the hallway. "I can do that."

When Eve entered the supervisor's office, a middle-aged man with graying temples and smart glasses extended his hand to her.

"Miss Kirkwood, I'm Peter Hill. Please sit down," he invited.

Eve sat in a large Queen Anne chair covered in floral brocade.

The manager looked toward Eve as she took a good look around. The office wall was littered with framed recognitions and service awards. And Mr. Hill's desk was littered with files and folders. He took a seat behind the cluttered desk. "Our guests' satisfaction is our highest objective."

"Thank you. I look forward to things being made right." Eve relaxed against the back of the chair, placing her hands on the arms.

At that moment she heard a familiar voice outside the office and the half-closed door flew open.

"You wanted to see me, Pete?" Jason's voice was buoyant. When he stepped inside he caught sight of Eve.

Mr. Hill inhaled deeply. "Now, calmly, tell me what has happened, and what has created such animosity?"

Chapter 3

"Pete, I'm currently investigating another situation. Can this wait?" Detective Gregory remained on his feet, ready to launch into his former task.

"Please sit down, Jason." Mr. Hill pointed to a chair near Eve. "Bingham can proceed momentarily without you." He came around to the front of the desk. "This situation needs attention." He took off his glasses and fiddled with them. "Let's try to get things in order here."

Eve felt a flush rise again to her face.

"Facts first." Mr. Hill spoke with wonderful calm. "Now, what's missing?"

"My grandmother's quilt squares and a valuable antique box." Eve worked at keeping her anxiety at a polite level.

"Box?" The detective knit his brow. "This is the first I've heard of a valuable box."

Eve raised her chin. "Yes, well, perhaps I neglected to inform you about the box."

The manager leaned against the desk. "How valuable is this box? Can you describe it?"

"It's antique, gold gilded, and the lid is encrusted with freshwater pearls."

"O-kay," the detective said. He looked at the manager, then at Eve.

She caught his warm brown eyes with her own and rubbed

her hand on the chair arm. "But what means the most to me is my grandmother's handiwork inside the box."

"I was told one thing was missing." Detective Gregory raised his index finger. "The handiwork."

"You would say, then, Miss Kirkwood"—Mr. Hill elevated his brow—"that the contents of the box are of great *sentimental* value."

"Yes. I informed Mr. Gregory that the quilt squares were priceless to me."

"Ah." Mr. Hill put his glasses on.

Eve pulled her shoulders back. "I think a hotel employee is the thief."

Mr. Hill reared his head. "That is a serious allegation, Miss Kirkwood."

"I wouldn't make it if I didn't think it were true."

The phone on Mr. Hill's desk rang. He moved a file and grabbed the phone. "Guest services," he said into the receiver. He paused, glanced at his watch, and frowned. "Yes, yes, I'll be right there." He hung up and stood military straight. "Jason, why don't you look through employee files with Miss Kirkwood and get more information from her."

"Right." The detective inhaled deeply and let the air escape slowly.

"Miss Kirkwood." The manager smiled. "Jason Gregory is an incredibly capable agent and"—he turned his gaze to Jason—"this is a noteworthy crime. Do you think we can call your initial contact a misunderstanding and move on?"

Eve balked. She turned her gaze to the detective, whose jaw was tightly clenched. Still, she nodded.

He hesitated and then gave a quick nod as well.

"Good." Mr. Hill tipped his head to Eve. "Miss Kirkwood."

He reached the door. "Jason, use my computer." He departed.

Mr. Gregory came to his feet. He eyed Eve, who tried to smile warmly while sitting on her urge to tackle the computer herself. She returned the eye contact.

"Shall we get to work then?"

Eve rubbed her hands on her knees. "I feel like a twelve-year-old in the principal's office."

"Just like," he confirmed. "Heaven knows I was there often enough." He raised a hand to his chest and unzipped his windbreaker. "Well, water under the bridge."

Eve stood, and the detective pulled another chair up to the computer at the desk for her. She sat down, and as he loosened his tie, he dropped into Mr. Hill's chair.

Eve sensed how close the two chairs were and became aware of the detective's long, masculine frame. He clipped his sizeable fingers across the keyboard.

"Here we are," he said. "Employee photos."

He sat back in the chair. "Miss Kirkwood, why suspect a hotel employee?"

"There was no forced entry, which suggests a professional pick or passkey."

His face gave a note of restrained professional regard toward Eve.

"I had contact with three people before I entered my room, all hotel employees."

"Did you talk to them or anyone here at the hotel about your possessions?"

"No one. I had a quick phone call from my dad in the hallway, that's it."

"I'm sure you had a bellman. Would you recognize his photo?"

"*Their* photos," Eve corrected. "There were two."

"Two." Detective Gregory leaned toward the computer. "Really?" He maneuvered the mouse. "Here are the bellmen. Take a look."

Eve bent forward to see the screen. As she did, her shoulder touched the detective's arm.

He clicked the mouse and unfamiliar faces popped up.

Eve shook her head after each one until the elf appeared, with his whimsical grin and rounded cheeks. "Yes, he carried my bag from the front desk, until he was asked by a guest services worker to see to another guest."

"George Spiros?" The detective ogled the photo. "Not a likely suspect. Been here for years, a father of six, good work ethic."

He continued through the pictures.

Eve tried to move her shoulder away from the detective's arm, but she found herself sensing a certain amount of comfort being close to him, almost a kind of ragged shelter in a whirlwind storm.

"That's it," he announced.

Eve shook her head. "No, the giant wasn't there."

"Who?"

"The giant. The tall, athletic fellow, with blond, spiked hair, a goatee, in a bellman's uniform. He carried my bag and put it in my room." She paused and put her hand to her lips. "He's not there."

"I'll check with HR on new hires—maybe he's not in the system yet," Detective Gregory said. "When did you notice the box was missing?"

"I was running my bath—I pulled the box out, went into the bathroom, and when I came out, it was gone."

He looked into Eve's eyes. "You were in your room when it was stolen?" She could see a twinge of genuine concern register in his eyes.

"Yes," she said.

"So it's robbery, not burglary."

Eve bit her lip as a chill ran across her neck.

The detective pressed his arm kindly against Eve's shoulder and leaned toward her. "This kind of thief is only after the money, nothing else. You're safe, we'll see to that."

"Yes, safe." The strength of his presence reassured her.

"Am I interrupting?" a smoky female voice asked.

Eve raised her eyes to see a tall woman with cropped blond hair and voluminous satin lips. The deep blue sheath dress she wore accentuated the best of her slim figure.

"Priscilla," Detective Gregory spouted as he stood to his feet. "No, we're—I'm—just working a case."

The woman smiled and dipped her chin. "You won't be too long, I hope."

He glanced at his watch. "No, not long."

As Eve leaned back in her chair, Priscilla moved to the detective's side.

"My client will be gone in another hour," the lovely woman said. She placed her well-manicured hands on the detective's tie and scooted the knot upward to its proper position. "Remember, my sister's joining us for dinner tonight."

"Right." He cleared his throat. "Priscilla, this is Eve Kirkwood, a guest of the hotel." He swung his gaze to Eve. "Priscilla is the Broadmoor's wedding planner."

I'd say she's a bit more than that.

The beautiful blond twined her fingers into the detective's.

"Well I won't keep you from your work." Her smile was coy. "Don't be late."

He nodded. "See you then."

Priscilla gave a parting glance toward Eve that was less than warm and left the room.

Detective Gregory turned back to Eve and ran his hand down his tie. "I think it best if we relocate you to a different room. Just as an extra precaution." He smiled.

"Yes, I agree." Eve returned the smile.

"Well, we've found something we both agree on. Good. I'll see to your move personally. We'll have you resettled in less than an hour's time."

"Thank you." Eve came to her feet. "I want my squares, and I want the thief."

"We'll begin the investigation right away." He zipped his windbreaker back up, his eyes soft. "Don't worry."

True to his word, in an hour's time, Eve was settled in her new room just up the hall from her old one.

Jason made a call. "Hey Jimmy, you're on overnights, right?"

"I'm your man." Jimmy's voice always sounded like gravel in a cement mixer.

"Keep an eye on 144 East. Single woman, a robbery victim."

"Expecting a repeat?"

"No, but keep an eye."

"Extra protective. Attractive, is she?"

"Hey, I'm meeting Priscilla's sister at dinner tonight, actually in twenty minutes."

"The sister. Good luck. Sounds tedious."

"Thanks, Mr. Sunshine. You have a great night, too."

Unpacked and her room service meal eaten, Eve pondered her day as she snuggled into bed. It had gone much differently than planned. *Know that I am God,* she recalled. She felt a surge of confidence. "Don't worry, Gran, I'm going to get the squares back. The question is, will Jason Gregory be up to the challenge of helping me?"

Chapter 4

The autumn sun announced the dawn with a beautiful pink and lavender sunrise. Eve thanked God for its beauty. After a restful night, the hope of finding Gran's squares blazed in her. Despite the difficulties so far, and the arrogance of Jason Gregory, she had a sense of good winning out over the bad.

And then it struck her. She had worked on her own square on the plane yesterday. She had put one of Gran's squares in as a sample to inspire her own pattern. She'd jammed it all in her purse when landing. She grabbed her handbag. There were the squares, stuffed in a corner.

"Yes." She pulled out a baggie that held her almost completed square, Gran's square, a needle, and thread. Her shoulders relaxed. She held the treasure bag to her chest. "One down, and the rest to go."

A few laps at one of the specialized single-lane pools would be the perfect way to celebrate her find and energize her thoughts.

Eve donned her emerald-blue swimsuit. Some might call it retro, but the sweetheart neckline and the tie at the nape of her neck made her feel glamorous.

Five minutes later, she was gliding on her back, lifting her arms to push her body along, the coolness of the wet splashes vitalizing. Her flutter kick gurgled. Water caressed her head, and she closed her eyes.

Who took Gran's squares? Eve's thoughts moved with her body. *The thief: dressed in a hotel uniform, comfortable as a bellman, knew the lay of the land, impeccable timing.* In her relaxed glide through the water, she put it together. *He's a former employee.*

Jason exited the weight room, moist with heavy lifting, and endorphins dancing. He cut through the pool area to head for the employee showers and spied Eve in the swim lane. The confident movement of her hands and her silhouette framed in blue drew him to her. *Lord, she's beautiful.* He took a deep inhale. *Hands off,* he reminded himself. *This is purely professional.* The security regime was very strict about fraternization with clients.

"Good morning, Miss Kirkwood."

The words pulled Eve from her thoughts and broke her rhythm. She opened her eyes and went into a stationary dog paddle, her brows elevated and breathing quickened.

"I didn't mean to startle you." Detective Gregory stood at the edge of the lane, almost over her head.

"You didn't," Eve lied, continuing to tread water.

He crouched down. His workout gear clung to him.

"I was in the weight room." He nodded to the area just past the dive pool. "I'm glad to have seen you—I need more input on the case. Can you meet me at reception in an hour?"

"What if I told you I have plans at that time?" Eve asked,

even though she didn't. Did this guy think she was at his command?

"I'm afraid I'd have to advise you to change them. It's important."

"Oh." Eve blew a light breath out. "Well, if it's that important, then."

"Thanks." He smiled, stretched to his full height, and took steps away while Eve continued to paddle.

"You're welcome." She watched him go, and her obstinacy turned to an eagerness rising inside. What had he discovered that so urgently needed her attention?

Jason grinned and shook his head as he walked away. He was amazed at how apparently stubborn this otherwise attractive woman appeared to be. He thought she wanted his help, but at the same time it seemed she didn't. She was a puzzle. And wasn't it amazing that his job was to put puzzle pieces together to solve crimes. Perhaps, just like the crime, she would become a puzzle to solve. A very lovely puzzle.

Eve was at the front desk just before the hour passed—dry, casually dressed, but in her best colors and ready to get on with the job.

"I'm meeting Jason Gregory." She smiled and looked at the employee badge on the young man at the desk. "Binjani."

"Yes, miss. Your name?" He lifted the phone receiver.

"Eve Kirkwood."

"Ah, Eve Kirkwood." Binjani pulled a sealed envelope out from under the counter. "Someone left this for you."

Eve took the letter and smiled. "Isabel."

As the young man spoke Eve's name into the phone, she opened the envelope. The note inside was obviously computer printed.

If you want valuable information concerning your recent theft, meet me on the back terrace of the piano lounge on the mezzanine, midnight tonight.

Eve stuffed the note back into the envelope. This was *not* from Isabel. "Who left this for me?" She clenched the envelope in her fist.

"It was here when I came on duty this morning." Binjani returned the phone to the cradle. "Mr. Gregory is coming."

"I need the night desk manager," Eve demanded, ferocity elevating her voice.

"He's gone home."

Eve thrust the envelope forward. "I need to know who wrote this."

"Is there a problem?"

"What problem?" Jason Gregory's voice boomed across the marble floors.

Eve crammed the envelope into her jeans pocket.

Binjani spoke up. "This lady received. . ."

"No, no problem," Eve interrupted.

The detective eyed her pants pocket where a corner of the envelope peeked out.

"Thank you, Binjani." He nodded. "This way, Miss Kirkwood."

In the guest services office, Detective Gregory directed Eve to a chair then seated himself across from her.

"Enjoy your swim?" he asked.

Eve nodded.

"Now, I know you believe your thief is a hotel employee."

Eve elevated her brows. She could sense a *but* coming.

"But we'd really like you to take a look at some local police mug shots. They are of known thieves believed to be active in the area." He gave her a coaxing look. "It won't take long."

Eve crossed her arms. "My thief's not going to be there."

"Don't be hasty. Study the photos." He turned the monitor so she could see.

Eve pursed her lips then leaned toward the screen.

One by one, she looked at the photos and, one by one, rejected them with a shake of her head.

"Are you sure he's not there?" The detective tapped the desk with a pen.

"No, he's not there."

"Absolutely no possibility?"

Eve rose and glared across the desk. "Listen, Mr. Gregory, not to put too fine a point on it, but this has been a complete waste of time."

The detective took to his feet as well and leaned across the desk into Eve's space. "I'm really sorry you think so, Miss Kirkwood, because if indeed he's not here, we've just eliminated the known criminal element of Colorado Springs. That's hardly a waste of time."

Eve dropped her chin. "All right, not a waste."

"Now." His eyes were intense, and he straightened. "That envelope in your pocket. It's related to the theft, isn't it?"

Eve ran her hand across the top of her hip. She felt the offending corner of paper and pushed it deeper.

"Miss Kirkwood, I'll go to the desk and speak with Binjani to get as much information from him as possible." His voice became stern. "And then I will track you down. So you can tell me now, or you can tell me later about that *problem*."

Eve acquiesced. "I was trying to find out who had left the note when you came."

"Anonymous is it?" He tipped his head and stuck his hand out toward Eve, palm up. "Please." He nodded toward her pocket.

Eve reluctantly pulled the crumpled envelope out of its hiding place and smacked it into his waiting palm.

He took the note from the envelope and read it. His brows knit, which only built Eve's resolve. "I don't like this; it's not safe."

"I'm going to meet them, whoever they are."

"I highly advise against it."

"Thank you for the advice. I want my property back, and I've only got five days to get it."

"There's nothing I can do to dissuade you?"

"Nothing."

"Fine." He crossed his arms. "I'll meet you at eleven thirty tonight on the back terrace."

"What? No. They asked for me. They certainly didn't invite you."

"Dress warmly, Miss Kirkwood. It's supposed to be quite cool tonight."

Chapter 5

The night sky was littered with sparkling stars that danced above the rugged mountain horizon. Cool air pricked at Eve's cheeks, and the smell of wood smoke drifted across the tiled terrace. Several couples occupied the hardy outdoor furniture sprinkled across the area. Eve sat in front of the twenty-foot stone fireplace, where the rustic chairs snuggled together to catch the heat of the blaze.

She dug her hands into the pockets of her down-filled jacket. It, as well as her wool scarf, provided much-appreciated warmth.

And yet, despite the chill, the beauty was almost palpable. How could anyone not take joy in this place where everything but God's splendor was stripped away?

If Eve were true to herself, in her heart of hearts, she had to admit she looked forward to Detective Gregory's company, not just for the sake of the case, but to share all this beauty with him.

"Oh dear," she said aloud. She knew the signs of that *Mars-Venus* attraction, which wasn't bad in itself, but she also knew she had to be careful. She recognized that starlit nights could so easily lure her away from business and into a moment's fancy. How could she be attracted to someone who didn't take her seriously and already had a girlfriend? "And inefficient"—Eve turned to look at the clock through the window of the piano lounge—"and unprofessional. He's ten minutes late."

"Miss Kirkwood." Detective Gregory suddenly stood next to her. "I apologize for being late. It couldn't be helped. I just dropped Priscilla at her apartment and looked in on Lucy."

Lucy? How many women does he have in his life?

He seated himself in the chair next to Eve and leaned back.

She noticed the black turtleneck under his washed-out jean jacket, and the well-fitted relaxed Levi's. *Not in his security gear.*

"Are you undercover?" she joked.

He grinned. "I'm off work, technically."

"Well, no sign of the grass yet."

"Grass?"

"Informant," Eve clarified.

"Yes, I know what a grass is." He smiled. "You've been watching too many crime shows."

Eve stared hard at him. "I don't watch much TV. I work in a large metropolitan police department."

"You never said that." He returned the stare.

"Oh, but I did." Eve held her eyes steady.

"What do you do there?"

"I'm the assistant police commissioner's personal assistant."

"Oh, a PA. You keep the big boys playing fair and on time."

"Well, I keep them playing anyway," Eve corrected.

He laughed and she joined him.

She pulled her hands out of her pockets and rubbed them vigorously together. Then lifted them to her mouth and blew on them.

"Forget your gloves?" he asked. He pulled one of his own off and wrapped warm masculine fingers around Eve's frosty hand. "Your fingers are frozen."

The warmth of his hand brought momentary relief and comfort.

He took off the other glove. "Here." He handed the large suede gloves to her. "Not a fashion statement, but they're warm."

"I'm fine," Eve claimed between chattering teeth.

"Take them, Miss Kirkwood."

Eve relented. She flashed a smile in his direction. "Since we're sharing outerwear, you can call me Eve."

"Only if you call me Jason."

Eve put the gloves on, and the heat left from Jason's hands felt like a campfire. She gave a little shiver, but it wasn't from the cold.

Jason stood and stepped to the massive fireplace, grabbed a log, and added it to the blaze. His back was to Eve, and she took in the full length of him: his broad shoulders, long legs, and a stirring confidence. Then she spotted them and smiled. He wore cowboy boots.

Jason turned to face her. "Do you like working in criminal justice?"

"Quite frankly, it's not this." She waved her gloved hand across the sky. "Completely the opposite," she confessed. "Work's a pressure cooker, always with a lid about to blow."

"Been there," Jason said as he looked into the fire. "I used to be on an urban SWAT team."

"Really?" Eve tried not to sound startled. She looked at Jason, so calm, so forthright, his features soft in the light. "How did you end up here?"

"Life's too short to live in a pressure cooker. Enforcement

is my career, but I needed to reset my compass, slow down, listen."

"Listen to what?"

Jason pushed a pebble aside with his boot. "Little things. Rain hitting dried soil, a hawk's cry across the pines, snow falling in the darkness. And in here"—he pointed to his chest—"to the One who created it all."

Eve cocked her head and blinked. Who would have thought this was the same man who had no interest in her—in her case that is—yesterday afternoon?

"I try to go riding after work as often as possible," he added.

"Riding?"

"Horseback."

"I use to ride when I was a girl, here in the Springs, when I came to visit my grandmother." Eve grinned. "Sounds wonderful."

"Does it?" A look of surprise played across Jason's face. "Some of us are riding tomorrow afternoon. Interested?"

His enthusiastic smile caught her in its disarming warmth.

"Why not?" She grinned in return.

"Eve Kirkwood?" A soft female voice interrupted.

Eve was ripped from her unguarded attitude and she jumped up. "You're early," she said tersely to the petite young woman in housekeeping gear.

The young lady looked puzzled. "I have an envelope for you."

"Jenny?" Jason eyed the young girl.

"Jason." She smiled. "Hi. Good to see you. Is Priscilla around?"

"No Priscilla. What's going on?" Jason's expression intensified as he fired the words at Jenny.

"I'm delivering this. That's all." Eyes wide, she extended

the envelope to Eve, who grabbed it and tore it open.

"Who gave you that?" Jason asked the hotel worker.

"I don't know," Jenny said. "I found it in my employee mailbox. There were directions to deliver it here to Eve Kirkwood after I finished my shift. Is something wrong?"

Jason's voice softened. "You've no idea who left this for you?"

"Another employee?" She shrugged. "I thought maybe it was a love note or something."

Eve opened he note.

Look in the former employee files.

Eve's eyes caught Jason's. She handed the note to him. "I thought so," she said.

Jason took a handkerchief from his pocket and took the paper. His eyes scanned it.

"Jenny, I want you to go inside." Jason's gentle tone softened the command. "Jimmy, from security, will be at the door of the piano lounge. Tell him every move you've made for the past three days."

"Something *is* wrong." Jenny's eyes grew large.

"Don't worry, Jenny, just follow my directions." With that, Jason sent the housekeeper along. He folded the paper still in his hands, taking care to not imprint it. "Jimmy has been keeping an eye on us," he said, nodding toward the large windows of the piano lounge.

"Spying on us, you mean," Eve rephrased.

"Backup," he retorted.

"I'm trained in self-defense."

"Nonetheless." He nodded toward the door. "Come on, let's go run those files."

"Now we're getting somewhere." Eve raised an eyebrow. "Didn't I say employee?"

"It's *former* employee," he corrected with a chuckle.

Twenty minutes later, Eve fingered the giant. "That's him. He's dyed his hair blond and grown a goatee, but that's him, no doubt about it."

"Gotcha," Jason said enthusiastically. "Logan Briggs, we're going to get you."

We're. Eve felt a broad grin well up from inside. *Good. Let's see if you can keep up with me, Mr. Jason Gregory.*

Chapter 6

Eve held the hot tea and Danish she had just purchased from the Espresso News patisserie in one hand and dug into her pocket for the room key with the other. She could hear the phone ringing inside. "Hold on, I'm almost in."

"Yes?" she said when she finally answered.

"But I haven't asked yet."

She recognized Jason's voice. "What's that supposed to mean?"

"Still interested in riding today? There, *now* I've asked."

Eve grinned. "It is a great day for a ride." She admired the October sun outside her window. She genuinely wanted to go, but hesitated. Was it the horse ride or the person who invited her that interested her the most? "It's been a while."

"You know what they say, it's like riding a bike," Jason urged. "I have more information on the case, too. I'll tell you what. We're gathering at the alpine stables around noon. Come if you like."

"Fair enough," Eve responded.

Jason inhaled deeply. Some people were repelled by the odor of the stables, but he was drawn by it. Mingled with the scent of fall leaves and pine, it was the aroma of respite.

He patted his mount. He considered Diamond Jack his horse, even though the stable owner might have something to say about that. The three-year-old male was the friskiest in the lot. Only accomplished riders were allowed on him.

"He's ready to run," Jason said to his friend Dale. Candy, Dale's wife, nodded. Young Bingham, the short blond who was Jason's security partner, grinned. They, too, were on their mounts. "I guess our other rider is a no-show." Jason hid his disappointment. *And just why should I feel let down? She's only a client.*

"Who's the no-show?" Candy asked.

"Just a client." Jason took a deep breath and exhaled.

"An obnoxious, gorgeous-eyed client," Bingham added.

"She's not so bad," Jason protested.

Bingham's eyes popped as he shot a look of disbelief at him.

Jason let go a long whistle. "Lucy, come on, girl," he called.

A black Labrador retriever bounded out of the trees to join the crowd. "Good girl," Jason said. He loved to bring his dog out on the rides, and she relished it.

The foursome, and Lucy, left the stables. Candy and Bingham's nags didn't really want to go, but with a little urging, they all made their way into an open tree-lined meadow.

Eve galloped into the meadow on Cheyenne, an impish and snappy mare. She spotted Jason and his friends.

Jason grinned as she approached the group. "I'd say you're not just on the bike, you've made the Tour du France," he called to Eve. "Cheyenne can be a handful."

"She's wonderful," Eve called back.

"Eve," Jason introduced when she joined the group, "you know Bingham."

The fellow tipped his head with a wary look.

"And this is Dale and Candy. They're youth sponsors at the church I attend."

"Hats off to you both." Eve nodded to them. "I taught Vacation Bible School for a week, first and last time. I think it was the dripping popsicles that got to me."

The couple chuckled, and Jason looked pleasantly surprised.

"Well, shall we hit the trail?" Dale coaxed.

Jason scanned the horizon. "Lucy!" he summoned. Eve saw a dog pop her head up from behind a low-lying bush and come running.

Lucy. Eve smiled. "No Priscilla?" she asked.

Everyone but Jason laughed.

"Priscilla has made it clear that she loves horses in paintings and on calendars," Jason explained.

"More than clear," Candy added. "Personally, I think horses are cuddly."

"Don't let Jack hear you say that," Jason teased, patting his horse's neck. "Anyone for the pines?"

Eve had Cheyenne in motion before Jason finished his question.

"Last one there rubs down the horses," she called over her shoulder.

Eve rode with wild abandon across the rusted colors that graced the high meadow, and Jason rode toe-to-toe with her. The flowing wind urged her on, and she inhaled the energy of God's creation. She sensed that Jason shared that energy as he flew past her. Eve reached the meadow's edge and entered the pine woods only seconds after Jason had reigned in his mount there. Lucy, panting, had joined the race.

Eve looked over her shoulder to see the other three riders sauntering in the direction she and Jason had ridden.

She heard Bingham's sharp voice. "Oh, please, don't wait for us."

Eve and Jason laughed. Their eyes locked. Autumn fires burned in Jason's eyes. Eve wondered if he had spotted those same flames in her own.

"I'm glad you came, Eve," he said in a low tone.

Oh, yes, he's spotted them. "I'm glad, too," she breathed.

At that moment, it was Eve, Jason, and the skyward thrusting pines. The sweet whisper of the trees caressed Eve, and by the look on his face, it captured Jason as well. The gentle whisper became a passionate serenade.

"Your mounts are far more fiery than mine," Dale announced, arriving ahead of the others. He patted his horse and looked at Jason, then Eve. Eve felt her face go pink. "Am I interrupting something?" he asked.

Jason grinned. "We're just waiting here for the rest of you." He shot a glance toward Eve, who steadied herself in the saddle.

Candy and Bingham rode up and joined them.

Eve, aware once again that she was in a group, turned her eyes to the spreading woods, where she spotted movement. She sat high in her saddle and strained to see. "What's that?" she mumbled. She squinted. It was a man—but not just any man. She gasped when she realized just who it was. "It's the giant."

"What?" Jason's voice had surprise in it. "Where?"

Eve pointed into the woods where the large man with

spiky blond hair was now running away from them.

"A giant?" Dale asked.

Jason nudged Diamond Jack. Like a quarter horse out of the starting gate, he was off in the direction of the thief. The giant, on foot, had a huge lead on him.

Eve and Cheyenne joined in rapid pursuit behind Jason. It was a precarious chase, because Logan Briggs, though large, was swift and moved into thicker cover.

Eve guided Cheyenne with instant reflexes through the trees. But she was no match for Jason's acute skill. She could just make him out ahead. He had already passed through the clearing she now entered.

Laying her head low to Cheyenne's neck, Eve's heart beat like a native drum, adrenaline coursing through her body. She could feel Cheyenne's strength beneath her. "Get him," she coaxed.

Suddenly, Cheyenne balked. She neighed wildly and raised her head as if in terror. The skittish horse came to a sudden halt just in front of a hefty decomposing log.

Unable to keep her equilibrium, Eve blasted over the horse's neck like a bullet. She flew over the splintered wood. She screamed as she tumbled to the rough forest floor with a thud, landing hard on her leg. Pain shot from her heel to her thigh, and she rolled over on her back. Her gaze went skyward, and the towering evergreens melted into the swirling blue of the sky. She closed her eyes.

"Eve?" She could hear a voice that sounded like distant water. She struggled to open her eyes and saw Bingham kneeling over her, Dale at his side. "Tell me what hurts," Bingham said matter-of-factly.

Eve winced. "Cheyenne."

"That horse is in better shape than you are," Bingham said flatly. "What hurts?"

"All of me." She groaned and touched her left leg. "My ankle."

"Candy's gone back to the stables for help," Dale consoled her.

"Did Jason get him?" Eve closed her eyes again and caught her breath as pain screamed up her shin.

"Jason always gets the bad guy," Bingham said as he pulled her tennis shoe off with a gentle tug. He poked the bottom of her foot. "Can you feel that?" he asked.

"Yes," Eve responded as a tear rolled down her cheek. No, she wasn't going to cry, no matter how much it hurt. "I want my grandmother's quilt squares back."

Bingham shook his head. "You and those quilt squares. If anyone doubted your resolve before, they don't now. Let's get you back to the hotel."

Chapter 7

Eve winced while trying to fluff and rearrange the pillows piled against the headboard of her hotel bed. She pulled herself up to a sitting position, which was not an easy task. Her pink pajama tank bunched around her middle.

Everyone on the ride had been very gracious and helpful. After trained stable personnel got her back to the hotel, Dale scurried her to the hospital.

"No broken bones," the ER doctor had assured Eve. "A nasty sprain that needs a few days bed rest," was his prescription.

After the hospital visit, Candy established Eve in her hotel room, making sure all the procedures and needed items were in place according to the doctor's specifications.

Even Bingham showed concern, by arranging for fresh ice packs to be delivered to the room every four hours. The only person who was nowhere to be seen was Jason.

"Taking care of business, I'm sure," Bingham had assured Eve.

And why should she expect that he would be doing anything else but taking care of business?

Eve eyed the clock and downed a pain pill.

"A couple of heated glances don't mean anything more than natural attraction, nothing to do with a real relationship," she said to the pillow she wrestled. "He's involved with another woman. He has a certain assurance that can border on arrogance." Now she punched the pillow into a favorable position. "It's a necessary, purely professional relationship."

She lifted her quilt square from the nightstand where Candy had placed it after retrieving it from Eve's purse. With tender attention, Eve took tiny embroidery stitches to recreate the design of Gran's quilt square. "Just like me," she said to the square, "you have cousins to meet. Only yours will be delivered to you by a very handsome man." She stitched in a steady rhythm until her eyes became heavy and she fell into sweet slumber.

Jason entered the open meadow. Diamond Jack was fatigued. Lucy crept behind. The late afternoon sun created long shadows across the ground. Jason glanced around, feeling a sense of frustration. "Come on, Jack, Lucy, back to the stables."

When he arrived at the corral, Shelly, the stable manager, had a face like thunder. She approached Jason with determined steps. "I have a bone to pick with you, John Wayne," she said with fire in her voice. "Galloping like mad after the bad guy doesn't sit well in my stables, and leaving someone injured behind makes it worse."

"Injured?" Jason asked. "Who? How?"

Eve was awakened by a gentle knock on her door.

"Yes," she called. Her eyes were heavy. "Is it my ice? Come in." She knew the maid had a passkey.

Eve kept her eyes closed as the person entered the room. "Put it here on the nightstand, please," she mumbled.

"Eve?"

Her eyes became slits. She was able to just make out the figure. "Jason?"

He wore a light blue shirt under a black sport coat that made his shoulders seem even broader. She smiled. "You've rescued my quilt squares."

"Eve. . ." Jason's voice was flat.

She blinked and roused herself. "Look." She displayed her quilt square to Jason. "This yellow fabric is from my gran's kitchen curtains." She ran her finger across the design and grinned. "Gran and I would sit and stitch in that little kitchen, talk about everything from how the pea vines were growing to the hope of eternal life. Some of my sweetest memories. Every stitch I take keeps those memories alive."

Jason dropped his head then raised it. "Eve, I don't have the squares."

"Oh." Eve tried to pull herself forward and grimaced.

"I have these, though." He held out a small vase of orange and yellow asters.

Eve brightened. "How sweet." She took the flowers and sniffed them. *He was thinking of me.*

She caressed the petals with her fingertips as she set them on her nightstand. Jason moved the large chair across the room close to the bed. "How are you feeling?"

"I'm managing." Eve nodded. "Thanks."

A heavy silence draped itself across the luxurious room until Jason stirred.

"I could sit here and lecture you about how you shouldn't have gone off riding at breakneck speed onto dangerous ground like that." He gripped the arm of the chair. "Even in the case of going after a thief."

"Could you?" Eve tilted her head. "Wouldn't that be a bit like the pot calling the kettle black?"

Jason's jaw set. He sat forward in the chair, concern registered across his face. "Eve, I ride almost every day, and I know my horse. *I'm* the law enforcement agent."

Eve swallowed and smoothed the floral comforter. "Point taken."

Jason leaned back again. "This shouldn't have happened."

"This?"

"This." Jason waved his hand toward the bed. "You, getting hurt. As a professional, I'm supposed to protect the client."

Eve stared at Jason. "The client."

He turned his eyes away from Eve. "And Briggs got away."

Eve felt an arrow of pain and panic zip to her heart, and she knew her face wore it. "He was so close. How? I thought you had him."

Jason steadied his gaze back to Eve. He twisted forward in the chair again and ran his hand through his hair in frustration. "He went into the woods. Lucy and I tried to track him, but. . ."

Eve took a deep breath. Suddenly everything caught up to her. The thief, so close, had gotten away. This meant her precious quilt pieces were still missing. Confined to bed, how would she get them back? Her blissful holiday was now completely sideways. And if that weren't enough, the emotional confusion that raged at being Jason's *client* caught in her throat. A nasty pain radiated up her leg. Deep disappointment made a salty mist well up in her eyes. She couldn't contain it. A single tear hit her cheek. She wiped it quickly, but Jason was gazing straight at her.

He squeezed his lips. Like a wild hare from its burrow,

he sprang up from the chair.

Eve looked downward, avoiding eye contact. "These pain pills make me a bit soppy." She tried to cover her disappointment.

Jason grabbed a Kleenex box sitting on the desk and laid it by her on the bed.

She wanted to grab his hand and ask him if the shared moment earlier today in the pines meant anything at all to him. But she couldn't risk the answer.

"I'm sorry, Eve. I'm really sorry." Jason fumbled for words. "I–I've got to go. I'm picking up Priscilla in ten minutes."

Eve kept her eyes down, nodded, and grabbed a tissue. *Priscilla.*

Jason opened the door. "You work on getting better, Eve," he encouraged. "And don't worry. Briggs is mine."

He left, but the words hung in the room like a mountain mist. A mist that came rolling down Eve's face.

Jason fumbled the dessert menu.

The waiter stood patiently as Priscilla purred the order. "We'll take two Death by Chocolates, please."

"None for me," Jason corrected, and handed the menu off.

"You aren't acting like someone whose birthday is in a few days." Priscilla smiled. "Two forks, please," she instructed the waiter.

Jason pulled his thumb through the condensation that collected on the outside of his water glass.

"You've been quiet all evening, Jason." Priscilla leaned across the table. "You're sulking."

"It's just that I let a client down today." He took a deep

inhale. "They got hurt on my watch."

"On your day off?" Priscilla took Jason's hand. "We've all let people down. The question is, have you let yourself down?" Her brow lifted. "We all have disappointments. It's a part of life." She relaxed and released Jason's hand. With a well-manicured finger, she fiddled with her glistening earring. "We're resilient beings. We get back in the saddle."

"What makes you say that?" Jason asked. "Back in the saddle."

"We move forward, Jason."

He looked into Priscilla's beautiful face. Her words sounded so warm. So why did they feel so cold?

The waiter arrived with the decadent tower of rich chocolate cake and two forks. "Here you are."

"The bill please," Jason requested.

Priscilla handed Jason a fork. "I won't be here for your birthday. So let's enjoy our time together now. And you do remember you're taking me to the airport tomorrow?"

"Right." Jason's reply was brisk.

"Now, soon-to-be-birthday boy, indulge. Tomorrow you'll do well, and your clients will adore you."

"Right," Jason repeated, laying his fork aside.

Chapter 8

Jason stared at himself in the bathroom mirror. His face half shaved, he realized his eyes told the story of a sleepless night.

"Pleasant, with heavy afternoon showers expected in the foothills," the morning weatherman blared from the alarm radio in the adjoining bedroom.

Lucy lay on the fuzzy bathroom rug near his feet.

"What do I do?" He pushed shaving cream from the corner of his lip. "It's not fair to either one." He continued the automated movement of shaving. "Even when I'm with Priscilla, all I can think about is Eve." He rinsed the razor. Clenching it in his hand, he shook his head and looked at Lucy. "I've known her for three minutes, and I'm letting things get personal, very personal. I can't keep a professional distance."

Lucy lifted her head.

"Priscilla and I have dated for close to a year. I can't just give up on that, even if her sister appears to eat nails for breakfast." He turned to the mirror and finished up the last few strokes. "This is crazy." He splashed water across his face and slapped aftershave over his chin and cheeks, permeating the room with a spicy aroma. "Maybe I can clear my head while I take you for your walk."

With the word *walk*, Lucy was up on her feet, tail wagging vigorously.

"I'm glad someone's happy," Jason said as he scratched Lucy behind the ear.

Eve finished brushing her hair. It was only part of her morning routine complicated by crutches. But she was ready to attempt hobbling her way to breakfast. This large, luxurious room had become quite small in the past twenty bedridden hours. And there were only four days left to find Gran's squares.

As she moved to the door, the telephone rang.

"Oh no." Her tightened grip on the crutches made her knuckles white. "If I don't get out of here soon, I'll go mad."

Resigned to the interruption, she grabbed the phone. "Yes?"

"Eve, it's Jason."

She swallowed hard. "Jason."

"Listen, I've sent Bingham to your room with a wheelchair."

"Wheelchair?" Her brow furrowed.

"I'm treating you to coffee in the Express News."

"I drink tea."

"Eve, please, don't fight me. He should be just arriving."

The words no sooner hit Eve's ear than there was a knock at the door.

"Honestly, Jason."

"I need to see you."

"Oh, all right." His admission tamed her indignation. "I'll be there." She hung up and sighed.

"Coming," she called and hobbled to the door.

Bingham maneuvered Eve to a table where Jason stood waiting, just inside the coffee shop. His security gear, the blue windbreaker and gray dress pants, did nothing to obscure his muscular physique. Still, it was his tense jaw that struck Eve.

Jason's nod sent Bingham just outside the entry, and he sat down across the table from Eve.

"I'll come straight to the point, Eve." Jason zipped the words out then paused. He looked into her eyes and leaned back in the chair as if distancing himself from her.

Eve's stomach tensed.

"I'm handing over the investigation of your case to Bingham."

"What?" Eve blinked. "But. . ."

"I've contacted local Colorado Springs authorities. They're aware of the developments. Frankly, petty theft doesn't rate high on their to-do list. However, Bingham's a good man. He'll get the job done."

" 'Logan Briggs is mine,' you said."

"Eve." The word sounded forced. "I've betrayed my professional standards. I've gotten too close to the case."

His words swirled around Eve's head and sank straight into her understanding.

"You mean you've gotten too close to *me*." Her grip tightened on the wheelchair arms. "Is that so bad?"

"Eve, don't make this any harder than it already is." Pain salted the determination in Jason's voice.

"You may give up, *on the case*, but I'm not. I'll get the giant myself."

"Eve, look at you. You can barely walk. You're just angry."

"I'm determined." She pushed herself from the table. "Stuff breakfast, this conversation is over."

"Eve." Jason tried to take her hand, but she wrenched it away.

She placed her hands on the wheels and turned the chair

to the door. With awkward stops and starts, she guided herself to the exit, just missing a young man and bumping into a chair. *Too close to the case.* Jason's attempt to comfort her became nothing more than an empty gesture as she departed.

Jason ran his hand through his hair. He tried to rise from the chair, but he felt like he was just stomach-punched. *Lord, if I'm doing what's right, why does it feel so wrong?* He took a deep breath, struggled to his feet, and made his way out to the hallway.

"I can see that went well." Bingham nodded toward the empty wheelchair by the wall.

"You let her walk?"

"Limp, more like. Her call." Bingham grabbed Jason's arm. "Listen, Jason, you've got Priscilla. This one"—he nodded down the hall—"is a wildcat. You'd have your hands full with her."

"Wouldn't I love to have that problem?" Jason exhaled.

Bingham shook his head. "You got it bad, dude. Forget her, it's not worth it. She's a client. Go take your girlfriend to the airport."

Jason looked at Bingham skeptically. "You'll work on getting Briggs."

"Hey, Jason, I got your back."

"Thanks, Bingham, I owe you one." Jason took several steps then turned toward his pal. "Would you go help her?" He nodded toward the wheelchair. "She's got to be in pain."

Bingham blew a large puff of air. "She's really gotten to you." He shook his head and gripped the wheelchair handles.

Jason moved down the hall toward Priscilla's office. "I'm

afraid you're right, Bing," Jason muttered. "Eve's really gotten to me. And if I'm not careful, I could fall in love with her."

By the time Bingham reached Eve, she was reproaching herself for being so inane. Her leg ached. She settled into the wheelchair without argument. All the while he rolled her along she berated herself. What had made her think she could possibly walk all the way to her room? She hadn't thought. That was the problem. She was reeling from her sense of abandonment and the fear of never getting her treasure back.

Be still and know... The words tumbled through her mind.

"I'm doing security sweeps all afternoon," Bingham told her. "I'll continue the employee probe when I've finished. Now listen to me, Eve, sit tight and don't move."

After Bingham's strong directive, Eve settled herself back on her bed and watched him go. She was right back where she'd started twenty minutes earlier. She slapped her hands down hard on the bed.

"Lord, what do I do?"

Her cell phone caught her eye. She needed to talk to someone. Someone who could help get her head sorted. "I just hope my heart listens." Talking to her father was out of the question. He was still unaware of the whole situation. She put a pillow under her leg. Her cousin Zoe may have arrived, but unless something had changed, Zoe had plenty of her own messes to work out. Eve sighed. *I need someone who's near.* She brightened. "Isabel." What was it she had said? Call the front desk and ask for Isabel Escobar.

Within five minutes Eve had called her childhood friend in guest services to discover she was only working a half day.

They were going to lunch at Good Times. Eve wanted to cheer. Not only was she getting out of the room, but off the grounds as well.

Eve waved as Isabel pulled her SUV to the curb.

Isabel leaned across to open the passenger door. "Hey, Tiny Tim, jump in," she teased.

Eve tossed the crutches in the back and clipped her seat belt on in the blink of an eye. "I'm starving." She grinned as a fresh surge of energy coursed through her.

"I can smell those hamburgers grilling," Isabel joked. She started her SUV forward, but a black pickup pulled right in front of her. She hit her brakes, sending Eve into a lurch toward the windshield.

Eve laughed. "Hey, Isabel, I've been banged up enough, don't you think?"

Bills and change flew across the floor from a tipped-over paper bucket at Eve's feet.

"When did you take up panhandling?" she asked.

Isabel chuckled. "Actually, I'm collecting for one of our employees. His youngest daughter is having a kidney transplant."

"Oh, tough go." Eve tried to scoot the money into the fallen bucket with her good foot.

"Insurance doesn't cover all of it, and he's got five other kids to feed," Isabel explained. "George Spiros."

"The elf." Eve smiled.

"That's him. Sometimes we call him Santa's helper." Isabel looked out the windshield. "Hey, what's this guy in front of me doing?"

Eve watched the driver exit his truck and put something in the back.

"By the size of him, he must be a football player," Isabel observed.

Eve's eyes widened. "Isabel, it's him. Oh, my dear Lord, for a second time, it's him." She watched the spike-haired blond put a red baseball cap on and jump back in his truck. He pulled the vehicle into the street and peeled off without a glance back at the women.

"Isabel, follow that truck!"

"What?" Isabel scrunched her nose.

"Seriously, follow that truck. Go."

Isabel launched the SUV forward. "This is crazy. What are we doing?"

"A good thing, a Godsend." Eve leaned forward. "Don't be obvious, but don't let more than two cars come between him and us. Just stay with him, Isabel."

"Eve Kirkwood," Isabel wailed, "what have you gotten us into?"

Chapter 9

The gravel crackled beneath the tires as the SUV crept up the constricted mountain road.

"There." Eve pointed. "Park there in that grove of trees."

The black pickup had pulled to a stop ahead of them, and the giant leaped out. He ducked into what looked like a deserted miner's shack.

"Okay Eve, I'm starting to get scared." Isabel pulled into the protected spot, the vehicle well hidden. "So this guy is a thief, and you're going to get him." Eve had filled her in on the gist of the situation. "How? You'll knock him out with a crutch?"

Eve knit her brow, paused, then pulled out her cell phone. She dialed and held it to her ear.

"Bingham, I've got him."

"You've got who? This is Eve, right? I'm in the middle of a security sweep."

"I've got Briggs. Well, I don't actually have him *yet*."

"This isn't happening. Where are you?" Bingham's words sounded like hisses through clenched teeth.

Eve looked around. "Where are we, Isabel?"

"I don't know." Isabel shrugged. "In the middle of a mountainous nowhere."

"Some dirt mountain road," Eve offered. "We left pavement

probably twenty-five minutes ago. And I think"—Eve looked at a nearby mountaintop—"we could possibly be a couple miles from the backside of the meadow where I fell off my horse."

"We? Someone's with you?"

"Isabel Escobar," Eve told him.

"From guest services?" There was a pause. "Eve, I want you to turn the vehicle around, wherever you are, and quietly leave the area."

"You must be mad."

"Me? I'm not a one-legged female, stuck in a remote area, with an oversized robber at my door."

"He's not at my door. He's in a barely standing excuse for a cabin. Are you going to help or not?"

Bingham's exasperated sigh sizzled in Eve's ear. "Eve, I *said* I'm on a security sweep."

Eve could hear a rough voice tell Bingham to hang up.

"Go back down the road, call 911, and let the police handle this, now."

"Thanks for all your help, Bingham." Eve hung up.

"What's happening?" Isabel rubbed her palms on her thighs.

"Looks like the cavalry won't be arriving. They're busy sweeping." Eve's disappointment fired into resolve.

"Oh great," Isabel moaned. "Just great."

Jason turned on the blinker and maneuvered his classic Jeep Wrangler to the lane marked for airport traffic.

Priscilla looked stunning in her silk top and body-hugging skirt. There she sat, chic and fashionable, on the stained seats of his dated Jeep. Though she always suggested they take her Audi, she'd never once complained about the Jeep. At least he had left Lucy at home, which he knew suited Priscilla.

"You're quiet this afternoon."

Priscilla looked out the window, hands in her lap. "It's a big conference."

"It's not like you to worry about that." Jason took her hand. "You'll have a great time. You love New York."

Priscilla gave him a weak smile and nodded. "I do. Very much."

They soon arrived at the airport. Jason held Priscilla's hand as he pulled her large bag through the crowds. At the ticket kiosk, Priscilla scanned her e-ticket.

"You've got everything?" Jason asked.

"My bag." She released Jason's hand and took the handle from his grip. "Shoulder bag, carry-on, purse, ticket. Everything."

The crowd hummed around them.

"You're taking a lot of gear for a three-day conference."

"Um, that's the thing, Jason. I'm staying in New York for a few days after the conference." Priscilla ran her finger across her luggage tag. "You needn't see me to the gate."

"I took the time off so I could do just that. How many days, exactly?" Jason took her elbow. "Why didn't you tell me?"

She pulled away. "Jason, we need to talk."

"Right here in the middle of the airport?"

"Well it's now or in a text message later." She lowered her chin.

"Priscilla?" A foreboding sense raised its ugly head and Jason braced himself. "What's going on?"

Jason's cell dinged its text message notice from inside his

pants pocket. *Could the timing be any worse?* He pulled the phone out and eyed it. "It's work. Bingham."

Priscilla bit her lip, and then a look of relief stole across her face. "Go on, read it."

Jason brought up the message. *Wildcat up to neck in hot water. Call me ASAP.*

Eve tapped her fingers on her knee. "We can use your vehicle to block the road."

"We? Have you got a mouse in your pocket?" Isabel's dark eyes sparked. "I have a husband and a two-year-old son at home who think I'm lunching with my old friend at Good Times."

"Isabel, I'm desperate." Eve cringed as the words stabbed at her self-reliance, but there it was.

"And I'm a mom," Isabel retorted. "I can't go around playing Russian roulette with cars and thieves."

Eve lowered her head. She hadn't seen this venture from Isabel's perspective until now. "You're right, I didn't think it through. I saw the culprit and spun into action."

"Eve, look. This is for the police to handle, not an anxious mom and an invalid."

Eve nodded. As much as she hated to admit it, she and Isabel were not in the best position to go after the giant. *Be still and know.* The words danced through her mind.

A quiet fell upon them until Eve's cell phone pierced the air. She grabbed it and had it to her ear before it could ring a second time.

"Bingham?" she whispered into the phone.

"Eve, what on God's green earth do you think you're

doing?" Jason's words fell on Eve's ears like a resounding trumpet.

"Jason, he's so close I can see his earwax," Eve breathed.

"Eve, please. Listen to me. I'm in the middle of a situation here."

Eve watched as Briggs stepped out of the shack and walked toward his truck.

"Oh no," Eve whispered.

"What?"

"He's leaving." She trembled. "He's going to get away, *again*."

"Is he carrying a suitcase or a backpack or anything like that?"

"No, nothing."

"He plans to return," Jason said with confidence. "Has he seen you?"

Eve glanced around. "We're pretty well concealed."

The giant started his truck.

"Jason, I've got to stop him."

"Eve, he will be stopped, but not this minute. I'll do a stakeout as soon as I can get to it. Can you remember how you got to where you are?"

"I couldn't give directions, but I think I could direct someone, if I were in the car."

"Could you direct me?"

Eve felt a tingle dance across her stomach. "Yes."

The pickup started moving.

"He's heading this way."

"Get low," Jason yelled.

Eve sunk down, pulling Isabel with her. She could just make out Logan Briggs driving past. He left only clouds of dust behind him.

"He didn't see us."

Jason blew out an extended breath.

Eve sat back up. "You'll follow through?"

Jason's voice quieted. "Yes, Eve. Listen, I do care about you."

The words engraved themselves into her heart.

"Go straight back to the hotel and stay there. I'll see if I can get any help from the CSPD, but I'll need you to get me to the scene."

"Okay." Eve surrendered.

"Be in reception in two hours." Jason sounded pressed. "I've got to go."

"Two hours."

He hung up.

Eve slumped against the seat. "What a roller coaster ride of a day."

"At least we're still on the track." Isabel sounded relieved.

"I'm afraid there's a bumpy ride ahead. Jason and I are doing a stakeout here later."

"Really?" Isabel raised her eyebrows. "Together? You and Jason Gregory?" She turned the key in the SUV. Tiny splatters of rain fell on the windshield.

"Pray we get this guy, Isabel."

"Oh, I'll pray you get your guy all right." Isabel managed to sound both resolute and amused at the same time. "The one in the cabin and the one next to you in the car."

Chapter 10

Eve sat on her bed with her leg elevated and aimlessly surfed the channels of the wide-screen TV. She learned about Broadmoor amenities and how to fillet skate fish, and a weatherman informed her that the rain would intensify in mountain areas and eventually turn to snow. But all Eve could think about was the stakeout.

She turned the TV off and threw the remote on the bed. *Lord, what will I say when I see Jason?* She rubbed her leg. *Will he be angry with me? Is he doing this purely out of duty? Did my spin with Isabel today push him back onto the case? And then there's Priscilla.* She sighed and drew a pillow to her chest. *He said he cared.* She placed her chin on the pillow. Remembering his words brought a touch of fuel to her emotional gas tank, which was hovering near empty.

Eve glanced at the clock. Twenty-five minutes until she would meet Jason. *I know You said be still, but to do nothing when so much is at stake makes me crazy.* She discarded the pillow and limped to her crutches. *I'll be still down in reception. Whatever's going to happen will happen.* She put on her thick wool sweater and wobbled to the door.

With all the energy she could muster, Eve pulled the door open, caught it with a crutch, and used her hip to widen the opening. Once she pulled half her body through, she somehow managed to wiggle the rest of her into the hall.

"Oh, yes," she panted, "I'm a fine companion for a stakeout."

Jason pulled his Jeep up to valet parking in front of the hotel. He watched the back-and-forth motion of his wipers clearing rain from the windshield.

"I needed someone to love me, and there you were." The words of the Michael Buble CD that Priscilla had put in the player on the way to the airport filled the Jeep. She loved this rendition. Jason wrapped his arms around the steering wheel and leaned his forehead on it. "I just want to stop and thank you, baby. How sweet it is to be loved by you."

Jason pulled his head up. He snapped the CD player off, his jaw set. He took a deep breath then rubbed his tired eyes. He needed time to think.

The soft jingle of Lucy's dog tags made the music now. He turned and stretched his arm to the backseat as she stood up. He patted her. "Lucy, I can always count on my good girl."

There was a rap at Jason's window. He rolled it down. "Tim," Jason greeted the valet. "I need to go pick up a client. I'll be right back."

The young man nodded.

Jason jumped from the Jeep and walked through the portico. He wanted to take Eve into his arms and hold her, but that was the most dangerous thing he could do right now. He forced a puff of air out his lips. He had to get a grip and focus on the case, not the client.

Eve leaned heavily on her crutches and watched Jason through the glass of the entrance door. She caught her breath.

His hair was moist and the North Face form-fitting rain gear announced his rugged build.

But as he came closer, she could see that he didn't seem his usual self. His eyes looked worn, his brow was knit, and he didn't walk as tall as he usually did. Her eyes caught his. She smiled, but he didn't respond.

"Are you all right?" she asked him when he entered.

"Let's go," was all he said as he wrapped his strong arm around her back and nearly carried her. She didn't try to resist. The mellowed scent of exotic spice invited her to lean against his chest. She surrendered herself to the strength of his firm support.

When they arrived at the Jeep, the valet opened the door for Eve.

"Thanks, Tim," Jason said.

"Anything for our security guys," the young man answered as he settled Eve inside and put her crutches in the rear of the vehicle.

A clatter of dog tags greeted Eve from the backseat. "Lucy." Eve smiled. As Jason entered the driver's side, she reached out and stroked Lucy's head. The dog's tail spun into motion.

Jason closed his door. "She likes you."

"What's not to like?" Eve chuckled.

"Eve." Jason paused. "It's been a difficult day."

"Yes, it has."

"I really don't want to talk about it, any of it." He gripped the steering wheel. "You get me to Briggs, I'll do the rest. That's what we're here for. Agreed?"

Eve wanted to tell him how sorry she was for all the grief she had caused him, how much she appreciated that he was here. She wanted to ask if she could do anything to make him feel better, to tell him that she cared about him, too. Incredibly so. But all that came out was a quiet, "Okay."

Apart from Eve giving directions to Jason as they went, few words were spoken.

Despite the cool downpour that was taking place outside, the atmosphere inside the vehicle was heat-laden. Eve only dared look at Jason when he kept his eyes ahead on the road. Alone with him in the Jeep, she heard distant notes in her mind from the serenade of the pines she and Jason had shared on the horseback ride. Warmth rose to her cheeks.

Lucy snoozed in the backseat until they left pavement and hit the dirt road. The jostled ride awakened her.

Although sheets of rain and little washed-out gullies made the trek a rough go, bounces across ruts, sharp turns, and inches of mud were no match for the sturdy Jeep. A couple of rough bumps made Eve grimace as pain shot up her leg.

Jason gave her a glance. "Sorry."

Eve just nodded.

They arrived at the grove of trees where Eve and Isabel had parked. Jason skillfully maneuvered the Jeep into the cover of the evergreens.

Just visible through the downpour, the black pickup sat idle in front of the shack.

"He's in." Jason sized up the lean-to. "That roof looks like a sieve. He must be getting wet in there."

Jason removed his rain jacket. His black T-shirt bared his muscular arms and clung to his chest.

"What are you doing?"

"I can't maneuver well with my jacket on." Jason checked

his rearview mirror. "In case of a confrontation."

"Right." Eve swallowed.

"He could be making a move soon."

Eve redirected her eyes to look straight ahead and ran her fingers across her leg. "I'm afraid I'm not much help."

"Eve." Jason's voice was firm. "I've asked Bingham to follow us. He should be arriving any minute now. He's going to take you back to the hotel."

Eve watched the rivulets stream down the windshield. "I see."

"Eve, look at me."

She worked at keeping her composure and directed her gaze to him.

"I don't want you to get hurt. This could get dangerous."

Eve was not in any shape, physically or emotionally, to argue. She nodded and turned her eyes back to the windshield. "Please, don't take any unnecessary chances."

"Let me see." Jason chuckled. "This is where I say, 'Isn't that the pot calling the kettle black?'"

Eve gave him a weak smile. "Point taken." She sighed. "Chances that involve me are one thing, but today I jeopardized the well-being of a good friend."

"I know how that feels." Jason adjusted the rearview mirror and stared into it.

"I saw Briggs, right there in that truck in front of us. A second time. My instinctive need to get him kicked in." She ran a finger across her brow. "I didn't even think about Isabel; I had no plan. I just barreled after him. And you know what makes it so ironic?"

"I've a feeling you're going to tell me."

"All my training, my whole career, is organizing other

people's lives. Thinking ahead, creating schedules, sticking to the plan." She tapped a finger on her chest. "I'm a professional organizer. And yet, right now, my own life is out of control."

Jason smiled. "Eve, will you listen to me if I give you a word of advice?"

She swallowed hard. *Here it comes.* She nodded.

"You're a beautiful, capable woman, eager to take the bull by the horns, head on."

She stared at him.

"That's good, and"—he took a deep breath—"deadly attractive."

Eve felt her face flush. "But—"

"Sometimes the best thing we can do is just be still."

Eve blinked. Weren't those the very words, *be still*, that had been in the verse she read? The one that had been coursing through her brain the past few days? And now Jason was saying the very same thing. She looked down and poked her sore leg. "I'm learning a lot about that right now."

"It's not always an easy lesson."

"I'd say it's a very difficult lesson, at least for me."

"It will get better, Eve," Jason breathed.

His tender words pulled Eve toward him. "Will it?"

His eyes caught hers. She tried to turn away, but his warmth wouldn't let her. It seemed stoked by the rhythm of steady rain dancing across the Jeep's roof. A glisten of perspiration formed above his lips. Leaning toward her, he lifted his hand and moved it near her cheek. The expectation of his touch made her stomach flutter. Suddenly, Jason pulled his hand back. He turned away and sat back.

"Where's Bingham?" He gripped the steering wheel, his knuckles going white.

Eve looked out her window. She felt the suppressed heat ricochet throughout the jeep.

Keep looking out the window. She heard the rapid movement of Jason rolling his window down. The cold, moist air rushed in and she inhaled, letting it cool her yearning.

"Come on, Bing." Jason's words sounded like a desperate plea.

Chapter 11

Splashes of icy rain hit Jason's face. It was the next best thing to a cold shower, and right now he needed it. This was a stakeout in the woods, not a necking session on Lover's Peak.

His text alert sounded and he grabbed his phone.

Lucy, lounging on the backseat, raised her head, and Eve gave her a couple comforting pats.

Jason's shoulders tightened. "Oh no."

"What?"

"Bingham's stuck in the mud." Jason slammed the cell phone down. *Icing on the cake of a rotten day.*

"Jason, if it helps any, I really can take care of myself."

Jason could hear the sincerity in Eve's voice. Her light green eyes set against her ivory skin held tender earnestness. The luscious black hair that cascaded down her well-shaped shoulders made her seem so vulnerable. He wanted to protect her.

He nodded toward her hurt leg. "Right."

He had to reestablish focus. He took a deep breath. "We're"—he cleared his throat—"*I'm* here to take care of Briggs. Bingham or no Bingham."

Eve shifted her sore leg into a different position. "You're going to get the giant and the goods, Jason."

Jason rubbed his hand on his thigh and stared through

the windshield. The bitter cold rain from the open window ran down his neck and soaked into his T-shirt. A quick shiver, and his mind was razor sharp. *Keep Eve safe, and still get Briggs.* "How?"

"How?"

"Think like the criminal. Briggs is in the shack, getting doused."

"His possessions as well." Eve's eyes grew large. "I hope my squares are okay."

"He wants to get his stuff where it's dry. He's going to make a move soon." Jason ran his finger over the steering wheel as he focused on the older-model black pickup. *Snap.* "Disable his vehicle."

"Yes. Brilliant." Eve squinted. "How?"

"Not an issue."

He pulled his trusty tool from under the driver's seat and handed his phone to Eve. "Press two. Tell Bingham I'm going in. If Briggs shows, call 911. We're on the logging access to Gold Strike Hill."

"Logging access, Gold Strike Hill." Eve nodded.

Jason opened his door. Rain pelted the floor as he spun out into the deluge. The tiny stings of frozen liquid that assaulted him were no match for his energized body. Adrenaline pumped.

"Eve, whatever you do, stay in the car. Don't leave the Jeep," he yelled above the downpour. He reached in and put his hand on the gear box. "If for some reason something should go horribly wrong, even with a sore leg, this vehicle becomes your weapon."

Eve grabbed his hand and squeezed it.

A zip raced through Jason's already keyed-up body. He

could go toe-to-toe with Briggs right now and win. He flashed Eve a confident smile, pulled back out into the rain, and slammed the door.

"I care about you, too," Eve called, but Jason was already racing forward. She closed the window. "Oh, God," she prayed, "give him strength."

Lucy gave a low whine then jumped forward into the driver's seat. She put her nose to the window and followed Jason's movements.

Eve pressed two on Jason's phone.

She watched as he opened the unlocked door of the pickup.

"Come on, Bingham, pick up."

Jason popped the hood and wasted no time getting into the engine area, hunching over to do his work.

Eve pressed END then two again. "Okay, Bingham, listen to your phone. Pick up."

She watched the cabin through the rain. Suddenly, the door flew open.

"No, oh please, no."

Lucy barked and whined. Eve realized the urgency in her voice had aroused the Labrador.

The giant stepped out. A rain poncho, draped across his large body, magnified his proportions.

Eve dropped the phone. "Lord."

Jason was still bent over, working on the engine.

Briggs stopped in his tracks. Then he bent low and began to creep toward Jason.

"Jason," Eve yelled. As quickly as her leg allowed, she

scooted closer to the gear shift, leaned over to the steering wheel, and hit the horn. She made a fist and pounded it, over and over.

Jason straightened up just as the giant attacked him. Briggs threw a punch toward Jason's head. Jason blocked him and jabbed a fist into the giant's ribs.

Lucy launched onto the window, her front paws pressed on the glass. She bounced with every aggressive bark.

Briggs's fist caught Jason across the forehead, leaving a gash. Jason tumbled to the ground.

"God, what can I do?" Eve screamed. She took a deep breath. "Be still. Stay in the Jeep." She calmed herself as Lucy continued her tirade.

Briggs opened the pickup's door.

"Show yourself strong, Lord. Please, for Jason."

Jason regained his feet and struck a blow to Briggs's back before he could enter the vehicle. Briggs staggered and turned. He punched Jason in the stomach.

"No," Eve shrieked.

Lucy pushed so hard on the window, Eve thought it would break.

Lucy. With all the strength she could gather, Eve lifted and inched herself over the gear box. She pressed the dog against the back of the seat. "Lucy," Eve commanded, "help Jason." She leaned past Lucy and opened the door.

Lucy bounded from the vehicle and flew several feet before her paws touched the moist earth, her barks full of fury. Undaunted by the icy sleet, she rocketed toward the fisticuffs.

The giant pulled his arm back with force, a fist ready to pound Jason's face. Then he caught sight of the enraged black animal. Stunned, he watched it race toward him.

Jason seized the moment and swung hard. He planted a terrific blow to the large man's shoulder. It sent Briggs sprawling against the cabin with a crash, Lucy at his throat.

"Lord, please," Eve shouted as she leaned out the open door of the jeep.

The large eave that hung in a haphazard slant from the roof broke loose and came crashing down. It hit Briggs and smacked him flat against the ground.

Splashes of light cut through the pines. Eve scrunched her wet eyes and then opened them. Red and blue danced across the cabin as a white SUV marked SHERIFF pulled up to the scene. Three law officers and Bingham jumped from the vehicle, guns drawn.

Briggs was out cold, but they took every precaution.

Eve couldn't hold back any longer. Forgoing the crutches, she scooted from the Jeep and hobbled through the rain that was turning to snow.

"Eve." Bingham bounded toward her. "You need to stay clear."

She looked around. "Where's Jason?" Panic stirred her voice higher. "He was right there."

"Jason can take care of himself."

"But he's hurt."

Jason emerged from the cabin. "Almost every valuable thing reported missing at the hotel in the last three weeks is in there," he informed the sheriff.

"Well done," the man told him. Then he called to the other men, "Gather it up, boys."

"Jason." Eve began to totter to him, but Bingham caught her by the shoulder.

"He's got work to do."

Eve pulled herself away from Bingham's grip and limped forward. "Jason." Cold and wet seeped into her every pore. Pain shot up her leg. But nothing could keep her away from Jason.

He turned to see her. "It's okay, Bing. She's a part of this operation."

With every bit of energy she possessed, Eve impulsively threw her arms around Jason's shoulders. He embraced her, and passionate warmth rushed through her chilled body. The strength of his shoulders and chest, his arms, made her want to stay forever. She felt him shiver.

"Jason, we're going to take you to the ER," the sheriff announced. "That's a nasty gash."

Eve pulled back to look into Jason's bloodstained face. She placed a finger near the cut.

He flinched.

"You did that for me?"

Jason smiled, his brown eyes warm, despite the injury. "And I'd do it again." He wrapped his long fingers around Eve's hand and squeezed it. "You look like the night I first saw you." He ran a finger through her wet, wavy hair.

Eve felt a spark and laughed. "Yeah, well you look pretty rough, not at all like the first time I saw you."

Jason leaned in toward Eve's face, his moist breath inviting her to kiss him. She lifted her lips to him.

"Let's mop up," Bingham yelled.

Jason pulled back.

If Eve had the energy, she would have thrown a very large stone at Bingham.

"Let's get the thief collared." The sheriff raised Logan Briggs, cuffed and still woozy, to his feet.

"Gotcha," Bingham whooped and shot a fist high into the frigid air.

As a calmed Lucy ambled to Jason's side, one of the lawmen exited the shack. He held several items in his arms, one of which was Eve's box.

"My box," Eve shouted. "Thank God. I'll take it now."

"Sorry, miss. You'll have to wait. This is evidence." The man continued his stride.

"No." Eve stepped away from Jason to go after the lawman.

"Eve, it's okay." Jason drew her back.

"It is not. I've got two days until my cousins gather. I've got to have that box."

"Eve." Jason nodded toward his waist. He pulled up his T-shirt to reveal Gran's quilt squares rolled up and pushed into the waistline of his jeans. "Shh," he cautioned in a low tone.

Eve grinned. "How can I ever thank you?"

"Jason." The sheriff approached.

Jason quickly smoothed his shirt down.

"We'll need you to fill out some paperwork."

"Yes, sir," Jason replied. "Bingham, can you take Eve and Lucy home?"

"In the Jeep?" He grinned. "My pleasure."

"And don't get stuck," Jason teased.

Bingham made his way to the Jeep.

Jason grabbed the quilt squares and discreetly handed them off to Eve. Just as discreetly, she jammed them inside her sweater.

His eyes lingered on her. "Got to go." He turned and took steps toward the sheriff's SUV.

"You know what this means?" Eve called after him.

Jason turned toward her. "What?"

"I'm not your client anymore."

A huge grin spread across Jason's face, and he climbed into the vehicle.

Eve watched the SUV pull away. "My real-life hero," she whispered. "And the emphasis is on *my*."

Chapter 12

Jason felt a gentle shake to the shoulder. He had fallen asleep. The odor of germicide collided with the harsh fluorescent lights of the waiting room. Distant sirens and an intense headache reminded him he was still at the hospital.

Bingham was at his side. "Jason, I'm here to take you home." The young man stared at Jason's bandaged head. "Aren't you supposed to stay awake for the next four to five hours?"

Jason nodded. "I'm tired, Bing. It's just a precaution. They don't think I'm concussed."

"Maybe you should stay with Dale and Candy tonight. I'll take you there."

"What about Lucy?"

"I'll take care of her. Come on; let's get out of this place. Hospitals and I are not fond of each other."

In the parking lot, Bingham helped Jason into the passenger side of the Jeep.

"CSPD said you filled out the paperwork in the ER while you waited to be treated." Bingham raised a brow. "How many stitches?"

"Ten." Jason put a finger on the protective bandage and looked at his reflection in the rearview mirror. "Yep, here they come. Two black eyes, just like the doc said."

"Cool. Scars of combat."

Jason blew out a long breath. "Scare the clients more like." He shivered. "I could do with a strong cup of blazing hot coffee."

"Eve said you'd probably need some." Bingham held up a thermos. "She ordered it at the hotel and sent it along."

Jason smiled and took the thermos. "You got her to her room okay?"

"Yeah. You know what she did? After you left the crime scene and we were ready to go, she stood by the Jeep. She just stood there. Finally, I rolled down the window and asked her what she was doing. You know what she said?" Bingham scrunched his nose. "Listening. Now what's that about?"

Jason's smile broadened. The action pulled on his stitches and it hurt. He put his finger on the bandage again. "The silence of snowfall can speak to you, Bing. You should try it sometime."

Bingham just shook his head.

Jason opened the thermos and poured some coffee into the cup. Steam rose in the evening coolness of the Jeep's interior. The harsh blue light of the neon hospital logo flooded the inside of the vehicle.

Bingham gripped the steering wheel and watched as Jason took a sip of the coffee. "I know your head's bashed up, but this is a great moment. You got the bad guy."

"I did. With Eve's help." Jason took another long sip.

"You should be celebrating."

How could he tell Bingham that for all he gained today, he had lost something, too? Despite the excitement of capturing the thief in the presence of a desirable woman, there was also disappointment.

Bingham started the Jeep. "Is Priscilla going to be

displeased that you went on a stakeout with a female client?"

"No." An ache flashed through Jason's chest. "Priscilla gave me the push today."

"What?" Bingham killed the engine. "She found out about Eve."

"She found out about Harry."

"Harry?"

"Her old flame. Climbing the ladder of the East Coast financial sector. Has a posh Manhattan apartment. And he's back on the market."

"They're reconnecting?"

"They're reconnected."

"When did she tell you this?"

"At the airport."

"Ouch, that's cold."

"She said it was either that or a text message."

"Gruesome." Then Bingham's eyes sparked. "But that makes the way clear for you and Eve."

"It does." Jason ran his finger up and down the thermos cup. "Right now, I'm pretty banged up, and not just my head."

"Do you want to tell Eve to get out of your life?"

"No!" Jason took another long sip of coffee. "I dated Priscilla for almost a year, Bing. You don't just walk away and pretend it never happened."

"Why not? Priscilla did."

"You're a great comfort, Bingham." Jason pursed his lips. "And to add to it, I've known Eve less than a week. In a few days, she leaves. Despite all that, I think I'm falling in love with her. Nothing makes sense."

"Since when did love make sense?" Bingham started the Jeep again. "Anyway, Eve's full of surprises." He smiled at

Jason. "She really is full of surprises."

Jason noted Bingham's silly grin but was too exhausted to ask questions. "That's great, Bing. Now can we get a move on?"

Candy and Dale's home was a warm welcome. Candy had some chili and hot corn bread ready for him, and a hot shower relaxed his muscular pain from the fight with Briggs. But Dale's words were the real medicine.

"Priscilla was an important part of your life, Jason, but don't let that hurt steal away a relationship with Eve." Dale always had such keen insight. "To be honest, Candy and I think Eve is far better suited for you. We really like her."

Their endorsement meant a lot to Jason.

"I don't want to bounce to Eve on the rebound. That wouldn't be fair."

"Rebound? You were drawn to her before Priscilla left."

"You knew?"

"I have eyes, Jason."

"That obvious?"

"For someone who knows you well, yes. Don't cheat yourself here. You've got an opportunity ahead of you. If you think about it, could the timing be more divine?"

What Dale said made a lot of sense. Jason knew he couldn't let Eve leave his life, even though she would leave Colorado Springs. He pulled out his phone and called her.

"Eve, hi, just wanted to say thanks for the coffee."

"I knew you'd be ready for some hot java."

Her voice was a sweet melody to his ears. "How's your leg?"

"Sore, but much better since I've warmed up. How are you feeling?"

He gulped. "Feeling?"

"How's the head?"

"Oh." He felt warmth on his face. "Apart from the sensation that a herd of wild horses just galloped across my skull and kicked me in the eyes, I'm fine."

"I wish there was something I could do to make you feel better."

"As a matter of fact there is." Jason took a deep breath. "Meet me tomorrow after work."

"I've got something going on then."

Jason gripped the phone tighter. "Oh."

"Could we meet later in the evening?"

Jason relaxed his grip. "Yeah, that would be great. I'll call you after work."

"Jason, thanks for all you've done. I'm going through Gran's squares right now."

"I'm glad we got them back." He paused. "See you tomorrow evening."

Jason rang off. He sent an arrow prayer of thanks. A sense of solace made him relax, and yet he couldn't wait for tomorrow night.

A busy work day has no respect for aches and pains, and it was busy. There was news that explained some details around the theft of Eve's box. Logan Briggs fingered George Spiros as an accomplice in three of the hotel thefts. Eve's was one of those three. George said he hated stealing from the guests, but the cash Briggs offered him was too much to turn down. George admitted he was struggling to get money to pay for his child's operation. He overheard Eve's phone conversation with her father that concerned something valuable to go in the vault and told Briggs. He had great remorse about all of it, though, and was the one who put the tell-tale note that broke the case in Jenny's employee mailbox. That would buy him some clemency, but it was yet to be seen what would happen to him. Jason decided not to tell Eve all this. In time, it would become public information.

On his way home after work, Jason wondered how Eve would react when she found out Priscilla was out of his life. He took a quick breath when he thought about how to tell Eve that he was falling for her. How would she respond? In a few hours, all his questions would be answered.

Chapter 13

Jason was relieved to be home. But as he got to the front door of his townhouse and turned the key, something didn't seem right. He didn't hear Lucy's jingle of dog tags that usually greeted him at the door. He steeled himself for the unexpected and swung the door open.

"Surprise!" His friends, wearing pointed birthday hats, were scattered all across his living room. Colorful streamers decked the walls, and big bunches of balloons waved above the backs of chairs.

"Happy birthday, Jason," Candy called, and Dale held up a glass.

Jason laughed as he surveyed the crowd in his living room. He wondered if his bandaged knot and two black eyes would put anyone off, even though they were friends.

"Here's to the conquering hero," Bing cheered, and Jimmy smiled.

"You really are John Wayne," hooted Shelly, the owner of the stables.

"We had to celebrate your birthday," Jenny, the sweet employee who helped with the case, added. Binjani, the desk receptionist who had also helped, nodded in agreement.

Even Lucy had a party hat. She pawed at the plastic band under her chin.

When Jason regained his equilibrium, he had to ask.

"Who did this?"

Everyone pointed to the figure emerging from the kitchen with a Superman birthday cake in hand.

"Eve." Jason's pulse quickened. In her pointed, pink polka-dot hat, her presence was like a candle that lit the room. She stood without the aid of crutches.

"Happy birthday to my hero," she said.

Jason stepped to her side. The scent of meadow flowers overwhelmed him as she placed her lovely, warm lips on his cheek and gave him a sweet kiss.

A flame sprang up in his stomach. Forget the cake. He wanted to hold Eve and tell her how she had stolen his heart. He couldn't see anyone else in the room.

"You've got to cut the cake before we can eat any, Jason," Isabel coaxed.

"I told you Eve's full of surprises," Bingham said.

Jason regained his awareness of the people around him. "And I thought all I was going to get for my birthday was a slurp from Lucy."

Everybody laughed.

"So this is what you were 'too busy' doing after," Jason said to Eve in a low tone. "How did you know it was my birthday?"

Eve nodded toward Bingham.

Jason smiled. "No crutches?"

"My leg is much better."

He leaned close to her, inhaling her scent. "We'll talk when everyone's gone," he whispered.

Eve was stacking cake plates in the dishwasher when Isabel entered with more soiled dishes.

"Here you are, Eve."

"Isabel, thanks. Set them here." Eve pointed to the counter near the dishwasher.

"Hey, when do you get together with the cousins?"

"Tomorrow afternoon. I can't wait to see everyone."

"Tell them hi from me," Isabel chirped.

"Of course," Eve chirped back.

"This party has been so much fun, Eve."

"It has been. I'm so glad it worked out that Bingham could lend me Jason's key."

"Jason was so surprised." Isabel lowered her voice as she stacked the dishes with Eve. "And now it's your turn for a surprise. You'll never guess what Mr. Hill told me today." She grinned.

"He's sending you and Raul to Hawaii for a week?" Eve chuckled and placed a couple of plates in the rack.

"I wish. No, his assistant who's out on maternity leave has decided to stay home with her baby."

"Oh, that's nice for her."

"Eve, don't you see? That means there will be a job opening, right away. Mr. Hill needs a new administrative assistant."

"Oh." Eve widened her eyes. "Do you think I could—"

"I've got you signed up for an interview tomorrow," Isabel interrupted. "Ten o'clock in Mr. Hill's office."

Eve yelped.

"It may shrink your wallet, but, from the looks of things, it could be a gold strike for love." Isabel giggled.

"You okay in here?" Jason asked as he and Raul, Isabel's husband, entered the kitchen carrying dirty glasses and cups.

Isabel laughed. "We're fine."

Eve's stomach flip-flopped. An interview. Could God be opening a door for her and Jason to be near one another? Things seemed to be galloping along at high speed.

"That's it. All cleaned up. Everyone else has gone home," Raul said. He set the glassware on the counter.

"We need to go get Mateo," Isabel said. "My mom's probably ready to give him back." She wiped her hands with a towel and gave Eve a wink. "Behave," she whispered as she and Raul left. Jason saw them to the door.

Eve removed her party hat and stacked the glasses in the dishwasher. She took several deep breaths when she heard Jason's steps return to the kitchen. She was alone with him now, and his nearness made heat rise within her.

"I loved my party."

Her back was to him as she loaded more glasses. "Yes, I think everyone really enjoyed themselves."

"Leave those." Jason took her hand. He turned her to face him. "Come with me."

Eve enjoyed the clasp of his hand around hers. He took her to the sliding glass doors that led out to his redwood deck.

Eve observed the bright stars that danced across the now dark sky.

Jason opened the door and pulled her out with him.

"It's cold," she objected. Even though she had on a warm sweater, she could feel the chill of the mid-October night.

"Don't worry about staying warm," he said with a tease in his voice.

A small fire pit danced with orange flames. Jason brought her close to it, and she let the warmth fill her as he squeezed her hand.

"What are we doing out here?" she asked, looking into

his face. His warm eyes sparkled, despite the blue circles. His bumps and bruises were badges of bravery to her.

Jason took a deep breath. "Something has happened I think you should know about."

"Priscilla's a fool for leaving you." The words tumbled out of Eve's mouth before she could stop them.

"You know then."

"Candy told me." She put her hand on Jason's chest. "I also know it must hurt."

"But I can't let that hurt stop me from what you and I might have together." He ran a finger through a wave of her hair.

Eve swallowed hard. "What you and I might have?"

"You know exactly what I'm talking about," Jason said with a faint smile. He placed his palm on Eve's hand, still resting on his chest.

Yes, Eve did know. But she wanted to hear it from Jason's lips. "What are you saying?"

"Eve, we've known each other less than a week, and you leave Colorado soon. But I don't want you to go. I want you in my life."

Eve felt fire rise to her cheeks.

Jason looked down and took a deep breath. He raised his head and stared straight into her eyes. "I know Priscilla just left. But I had feelings for you before that. It sounds insane, but I'm falling in love with you."

Eve felt a swirl start in her stomach that raced to her head. "Then we're both crazy."

He leaned his bandaged forehead against hers. "Eve," he whispered.

He pulled back. His eyes danced with those autumn fires

she recognized the first time she met him. But the blaze was more intense now. He pulled her to him and wrapped his massive arms around her. The considerable heat of his sturdy body warmed her against the chill. She let her arms find their way around his strong back and lifted her lips to him. He softly placed his mouth on hers and kissed her.

His kiss was all that she had imagined, and more. Fireworks coursed through her, and she kissed him back. He squeezed her with the warmth of a hundred fires then drew back and wrapped his fingers around her hands.

"I can't stand the thought that you'll be a thousand miles away. How are we going to do this?"

"Jason, God brought us together, and He'll make a way. I believe that." She grinned and raised a brow. "It seems just yesterday, someone I respect and admire told me, 'Sometimes the best thing you can do is be still.'"

Jason smiled, "Let's see, who was that?"

Eve squeezed his hands. "Pray. Who knows what God may do?"

Chapter 14

Eve reeled with the sense that her interview with Mr. Hill this morning had gone well. He had all but promised her the job. And Jason's declaration of love still made her pulse race.

But now, she was headed to the cottage on the eighteenth hole where she would meet her cousins. She had to focus all her energy on this gathering.

Posey Winston, her grandmother's legal representative, had telephoned this morning and said the thousands-a-night cottage was reserved and paid for long ago. Posey informed Eve that she would meet with her and her cousins at three this afternoon.

Eve pondered as she walked. It had been years since the cousins spent time together, apart from a two-hour funeral a year ago. Would they enjoy each other like they had as children? Who would get the finished quilt? Would they end up in a savage split like their mothers? Only a few minutes stood between her and the answers.

Her arrival at the cottage was uneventful. She was greeted by Zoe, Carla, and Danni.

The silver-haired Posey Winston had already arrived and was seated in an ample upholstered chair. She officiated as if holding court.

"Eve, I was just telling your cousins that I met your

grandmother at a quilting club years ago, Stitches in Time. Thursday afternoons we'd quilt and chat. I miss Lizzie and those lovely times. I don't suppose any of you are in a quilting club."

The cousins shook their heads no.

"It's a shame. Not much of that kind of thing today. Quilting machines have nearly erased the old community quilting bees."

Posey wore a tooled leather jacket, wool pants, and large boots. She looked more like a ranch wife than a lawyer.

"My primary work is in water rights, but Lizzie insisted I do her personal legal affairs. So, down to business." Posey opened a black briefcase and removed some papers. "Let's begin with the issue of the quilt." She put on a pair of black-framed reading glasses and scanned a document. "It has caused considerable trouble in the past."

"Our mothers fell out over who would get money, not the quilt. After all, they only had a few squares stitched together," Zoe spurted. "Why all the fuss?"

"When your grandfather's will left everything to his wife and nothing to his daughters, it brought out the worst in your mothers and the quilt became an impossibility. But your grandmother saw it differently."

Danni uncoiled her legs from the chair she sat in and leaned forward. "What was the real reason Gramps cut our moms out of his will?"

Posey shrugged. "It was no secret he wanted boys. And I'm here to tell you that it broke your grandmother's heart. But there were issues going on with your mothers long before the problem of no paternal inheritance."

"Like what?" Zoe asked.

"Your mother, Zoe, always felt Danni's mom, the firstborn, was the favorite. It was a never-ending competition. And, I understand, Danni's mom didn't try to dissuade her sisters of the notion."

Zoe shot a glance at Danni.

"Carla, your mom, the baby, felt smothered by her sisters. She had to leave to breathe her own air."

"What about Eve's mom?" Carla questioned.

"Lizzie always said Eve's mother ate ambition for breakfast and determination for lunch. Not endearing traits for sisterly relations."

"No," Eve agreed.

"All that to say your mothers never could work it all out. Lizzie tried to get your mothers together to work on the quilt with the promise of money when she departed this earth. Even then there were too many unforgiven hurts, I suppose. They couldn't sit in the same room long enough together to do it. So, your grandmother's dying hope was that her granddaughters would find common ground and complete the quilt together in peace. I just suspect she thought if you all came together, perhaps you might influence your mothers to do the same someday."

Danni crossed her arms. "And that's why we're here?"

"Yes. Indeed." Posey adjusted her glasses. "But there is one small hitch."

"Hitch?" Eve raised a brow.

"The quilt needs to be completed in seventy-two hours or you don't get the financial inheritance of fifty thousand dollars each."

"Lord have mercy." Zoe collapsed back in her chair. "That's not much time to lose a bucket of money."

"Lizzie made this stipulation as an extra incentive to make sure every effort was made to work together and complete the project. Think of this cottage as your home for the next seventy-two hours."

"An entire quilt in three days." Carla's eyes were the size of teacups.

"Well, I must be going now," Posey said as she rose from her throne. She placed a business card on the coffee table and a sewing bag on the dining table. "Ring me if there's anything I can do to help. I'll return"—she glanced at her watch—"at three thirty sharp, in seventy-two hours."

And with that, she was out the door.

"Let's get to it." Danni's words cut through the shock that gripped them all.

Eve's organizational skills kicked in. "First, let's gather all our resources. Bring whatever squares you have to the dining room table, and we'll dump out everything in that sewing bag. Now."

Four minutes later, the table held embroidered squares plus surplus embroidery floss and cloth. There were Gran's squares from Eve's trove, squares from the sewing bag, squares their moms had stitched years ago, and the cousins' work. All were splayed across the table.

Danni picked up a square Gran had sewn. "Wasn't this from one of Gramps's favorite shirts?" Her eyes danced as she fingered it. "I remember him wearing it when he took me fishing."

"Grandpa took you fishing?" Zoe ran a finger across a design.

"Of course." Carla grinned. "Grandpa always doted on you, Danni."

Danni looked up from the square she was holding. She parted her lips as if to speak and then closed them tightly.

Eve sensed some discomfort. "And that's Grandpa's issue, isn't it? Not ours."

Carla picked up another square. "Grams made me a sundress out of this cloth." She smiled. "I loved that dress."

Eve's face lit up. "She made one for me out of that fabric, too."

Zoe eyed the fabric. "I remember it, Eve. You looked so cute in that dress."

Danni watched Carla scrunch the fabric. "Carla, you looked like a little lamb in yours."

Carla's eyes glistened. "Grams used to call me her little lamb."

"She called me pumpkin," Zoe said.

Danni grinned. "And I was chipmunk."

Eve searched her memory. "I don't think I had a nickname."

Danni picked up another square to examine. Her eyes brightened. "Firecracker. That's what Grams called you, Eve."

Eve chuckled. "I'd forgotten."

" 'My cute little firecracker,' Grams said. You had an explosive temper, Eve. . . But we loved you anyway," Carla said with a slight tremor in her voice.

Eve felt heat rise to her face.

Zoe put down her needlework. "You okay, Carla?"

"I'm fine," she said half-heartedly.

"Really?" Zoe eyed her carefully.

An awkward silence spoke volumes.

Carla's shoulders drooped. "Look." She slipped her hand under several of Gran's squares and pulled one folded piece of fabric out from under them. "This is all I have to bring to the table that's all my own." She laid it in plain sight.

It was easy to see that Carla would not take a prize in handcrafts at the state fair. "And it took me four months." Carla's eyes grew moist and her lips trembled. "I have so little to offer in getting this quilt done. We'll all lose our inheritance and it will be my fault. I should just go back to Kansas."

"No you shouldn't." Danni wrapped her arm around the youngest cousin's shoulder. "You're here. That's what counts."

"I'm just not very good at this needle stuff," Carla said.

Zoe shrugged. "It's okay."

"Gran just wants us to be together, work together," Eve reminded them. "We are not our mothers. We're free to do the right thing."

Danni beckoned Zoe and Eve to join her and Carla in a circle. She extended her arm and put her hand out to the center in a gesture she'd made hundreds of times with teammates before a volleyball game. "We're going to do this."

Eve put her hand on top of Danni's. "Right."

Zoe put hers on Eve's. "And we'll do it together and on time."

Everyone looked at Carla. A sheepish grin stole across her face, and she added her hand to the stack. "By God's grace."

A sense of great expectation glowed as warmly as the fire in the hearth.

Eve made some calls and rummaged up a quilting frame from a member of Stitches in Time. She sent Jason to fetch it. When he arrived, Eve and Danni helped him get it from the Jeep.

"This is huge," Danni huffed.

"But at least it's collapsible," Jason said. "You ladies have fun." He kissed Eve lightly and left.

Danni smiled. "More than an errand boy?"

Eve grinned. "Much more."

Once back inside, Eve set about putting the frame together. Carla sorted all the embroidery floss by colors while Danni and Zoe sorted squares.

"We still haven't said who will get the finished quilt," Zoe reminded them.

"I've been thinking about that," Carla said as she grabbed another red skein to add to the pile. "We could give it to a quilt museum. Then we could see it whenever we visited."

"But it's a family heirloom," Danni countered. "It's meant to go from generation to generation."

Eve and Zoe agreed.

"What about rotating it?" Danni asked. "It stays with each of us for one year and then we rotate to the next cousin."

Carla paused. "So each of us would have the quilt one year, then not have it for three years, then have it again."

Eve tightened a screw on the frame. "As a family heirloom, the bigger question is whose child then gets it when we all die?"

"That's right," Danni said. "The more kids there are, the longer in between times to have the quilt."

"There's a solution out there somewhere. We just need to think outside the box," Zoe reasoned.

Danni's face lit up. "Collapsible. Jason said it. Collapsible. Make it smaller."

Eve looked at Danni and widened her eyes. "Are you saying what I think?"

"Four blankets." Danni smiled. "Divide the quilt into four smaller ones."

"Can we?" Carla asked.

Eve was already dialing Posey's number.

"Perfect. We still accomplish what Nana wanted and each of us gets a quilt." Zoe inhaled. "I can smell my floral shop now."

"Yes, Posey, that's what we want to do. Take all the squares for the one quilt but make four small ones." Eve paced. "Will that still comply with the will?"

Danni, Carla, and Zoe's eyes were glued on Eve.

"Still have to work together to do it, of course. Yes, we are already helping each other. We'll make them together, one at a time. Have to keep the same deadline, yes." Eve smiled at her cousins. "Posey wants to drop in and check our progress."

"Come on over anytime, Posey," Danni called out.

"Did you hear that?" Eve asked and laughed. She gave her cousins a thumbs-up.

Carla yipped, Zoe cheered, Danni let go a deep sigh.

Eve rang off. "Four blankets it is."

"Thank God. Well, we've got our work cut out for us," Zoe quipped.

The others laughed.

"Pun not intended," she added.

The cousins worked well into the night. Early the next morning, everyone took just long enough to gobble some ordered sweet rolls and then began the quilting work, assembling one blanket at a time.

Eve noticed that each of her cousins wore engagement rings. "We seem to have an abundance of sparklers," she said. One by one, each woman told the story of her way to love.

Zoe, and her disastrous trip that turned to utter joy with Dewayne, had proved all things work together for good.

Danni's resolution to a new commitment, engagement to Trace, and Olympic training on the horizon, had truly led her into love, mercy, and forgiveness.

Carla had realized that committing one's way to the Lord brings love and life at its best. And for her, that included Todd.

Eve shared her discovery about being still and the heroic love Jason had demonstrated.

"It's all happened in the last two weeks. Do you think Grams knew something?" Carla speculated.

"We know she wanted us to overcome the hurts of our mothers," Zoe said.

"And reunite us," Danni added with confidence.

"Finding love along the way was God's plan. He just used Gran's plans for us to get us there," Eve said.

For hours the cousins quilted and chatted. As one day turned into the next, they shared their hearts together, sleep being the only thing that separated them. A true bond was developing among them. It was clear that as Zoe, Danni, Carla, and Eve stitched square to square, their lives were knitted together as well.

Just as she said, Posey showed up at the cottage a couple times to see how the girls progressed. Then, seventy-two hours to the moment they started, she arrived to reward their work together. Along with a checkbook, she had a bottle of sparkling apple cider. After viewing the beautiful quilts, she wrote the checks and left the four exhausted but energized women to bask in their accomplishment.

Eve went to the kitchen, found four glasses, and returned to the living room, where she filled the glasses.

"A toast," she ordered.

All four lifted their glasses.

"To Nana," Zoe proposed.

"To family bonds regained," Carla said.

"And love along the way," Danni added.

"To threads of love that bind us together," Eve concluded.

The four cousins clinked their glasses and drank from cups that overflowed.

Marilyn Leach has enjoyed writing for the stage as well as for publication. She became a "dyed in the wool" British enthusiast after visiting England, where she discovered her roots. She currently teaches art at an inner-city school near Denver, Colorado, and lives lakeside near the foothills.

Instructions for a MEMORY QUILT by Cynthia Hickey

Supplies:
fabric squares*
embroidery needle
thread
fabric for border and binding
sheet (for back of quilt)
quilt batting

*Fabric squares can be any size, depending on whether you are sewing a quilt for a bed or a quilt for a wall hanging. I prefer using squares that measure 10 inches by 10 inches for a bed.

For the memory blocks, plain white squares work best with either photos transferred (you can buy special paper for this) or embroidery. If you choose to alternate your memory blocks with plain squares, you can use white or colored fabric.

Cut as many squares as you need for the size of quilt you are making. Embellish squares with embroidery, special fabric, or photos. When your squares are finished, you are ready to sew them together. I sew my squares together on the sewing machine. Once your squares are connected, sew on a border in the width and design you prefer to complement the rest of the quilt. After the quilt top is finished, you are ready to put the front and back together.

Layer the back, the batting, and then your quilt top on a quilting frame. Quilt a design of your choice on the blank squares and along the border. If your sewing machine can handle quilting, this doesn't have to be done by hand, but it's more fun! Once all your decorative quilting (through all layers of the quilt) is complete, you are ready to sew a thin strip of border (or binding) to finish off your edges.

My memory quilt is one my grandmother and great aunts started and passed down to me to finish. It has plain white blocks with their names embroidered in the squares. I will quilt a rose in the blank squares as I complete the quilt. My grandmother and great aunts have all passed since the quilt was handed down to me, making it even more special.

If you enjoyed

THREADS OF LOVE

be sure to read

STITCHED WITH *Love* COLLECTION

A true treasure of historical romance, this keepsake collection features nine stories of courageous women hoping for a life stitched with love.

Available wherever great books are sold!